MAN UNDER

Brian Shaughnessy

Shannon Road Press
Los Gatos, CA
www.shannonroadpress.com

To my wife and best friend, JoAnne, who believes in me
more than I ever would.

Forward

Subways have been a part of New York City for over a hundred years. The first trains were elevated stations and tracks. Underground trains were added on October 27, 1904 when, after taking four and a half years to build, the **Interborough Rapid Transit (IRT)** opened to the public. The IRT and the **BMT (Brooklyn-Manhattan Transit)** lines were privately owned and had no police. The new **IND (Independent)** lines, however, which began in 1932, were owned by New York City and run by the Board of Transportation. These lines originally had "station supervisors" employed to police them, their names having been taken from the NYC Police Department's hiring list.

On November 17, 1933, six men were sworn as New York State Railway Police. They were unarmed but were still responsible for the safety of the passengers on the IND line, as well as guarding the system's property. Two years later, 20 more men were added for police duty. The 26 men were soon given powers of arrest, but only on the IND line. And thus the **New York City Transit Police Department** was born.

Over the years additional men were added. Beginning in 1949, the question as to who should supervise the Transit Police Department was one continually brought up by city administrators. In 1955, the decision was made that the Transit Police Department would become a separate and distinctly different Department, ending almost two decades of rule by the NYPD. With crime on the rise, the number of Transit officers increased so that by 1966, the Department had grown to 2,272 officers. By early 1975, the department comprised nearly 3,600 members and by 1994, there were almost 4,500 uniformed and civilian members of the Department, making it the sixth largest police force in the United States.

Over time, however, the separation between the NYPD and the NYC Transit Police Department created many problems. Redundancy of units, difficulty in communications, and differences in procedures all created frustration and inefficiency. As part of his mayoral campaign, Rudolph Giuliani pledged to end the long unresolved discussion and merge all three of New York City's police departments (the NYPD, the Transit Police, and the NYC Housing Authority Police Department) into a single, coordinated force. Mayor Giuliani took office on January 1, 1994, and immediately undertook to fulfill his promise and end a problem that had defied final solution for almost half a century. Discussions between the City and the New York City Transit Authority produced a memorandum of understanding, and on April 2, 1995, the NYC Transit Police was consolidated with the New York City Police Department to become a new Bureau within the NYPD.

Preceding information gathered at www.nyc.gov.

Aids to the Reader

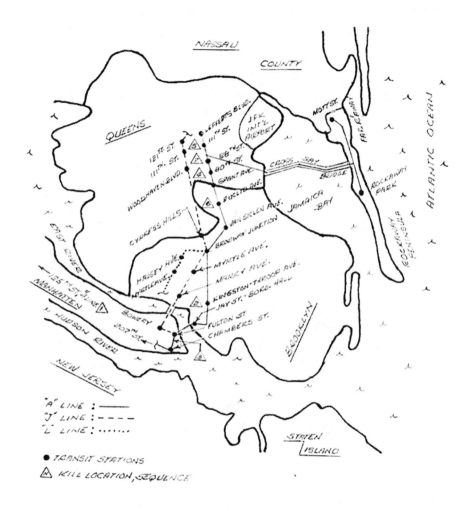

NYC Subway (partial)

MAN UNDER is the story of an elite investigative unit within the New York City Police Department's Transit Bureau. The squad's most recent assignment involves the suspicious deaths of three homeless people killed in increasingly more bizarre circumstances within the New York City subway system.

The Unit

Kevin McCaffrey, a twelve year veteran of the police department, catapulted into the unit years ago by record-breaking felony collars and a heroic act that finally got him the recognition he deserved. Kevin is well-grounded and even-tempered, essential traits necessary to balance out the rest of the colorful unit.

Tony Malaro, a nineteen-year officer who was tossed back to uniform patrol from the ranks of the Detective Squad for a questionable shooting incident in his past. He might have something to prove in order to get back into "The Squad."

Sam Jones is a loner among black officers who decides to care a little too late in his career. After years of mediocre detective work and lackluster performance, something (or someone) gets him back to his old form.

Vincent Venera, whose ethnic personality and brashness are only eclipsed by his actual size. Vinnie is a top-notch detective with a history of poor marksmanship and trashed Radio Motor Patrol cars.

Erica Wheeler is the abrasive new-comer who needs an attitude adjustment. When touched by tragedy, Erica begins to look within herself and to Vinnie Venera to become a better cop.

Sergeant Mike O'Shea, the consummate Irish politician who runs the squad like a well-oiled machine. Mike uses his skills to keep the squad fresh with talented people. His contacts are useful and rise high within the ranks of the NYPD.

Captain Alan Reitman, the District 23 command supervisor, is a leader in rank only, spending nearly all his time in his office trying to keep a low profile. He is not happy his command is the location of multiple homicides.

Prologue

February 4, 2006,
Chambers Street on the 'A' line, NY, NY

"Watch the closing doors."

"Watch the closing doors."

He could barely hear the conductor because he was daydreaming again when he heard the voice over the intercom. It sounded like the train man was frustrated. His mind was somewhere else though. He didn't take notice that the conductor was directing his comments to him as he was poking his head out of the doors of the downtown #2 train at Chambers Street. He was in the rear car and was beginning to snap out of it.

Stupid.

It was 11:15 at night and he had been riding the trains for three hours now, looking for the right moment, the perfect time, place and person. It wasn't difficult for him to achieve those conditions. It just took time.

"Watch the closing doors before I come down there and make you!" the conductor bellowed over the intercom.

"Shit!" He muttered under his breath as he retreated back into the subway car. The last thing he wanted was for someone to notice him.

Nice going, jack-off.

He knew that the chances of running into the same conductor sometime in the future were minimal, but he was *that* careful. He hated when he went away like that, not paying attention to the world around him. It was usually only for a few seconds.

Perfectly normal.

It happens to everyone. It isn't really blacking out.

He considered it daydreaming, as he let his mind drift again and the details flowed in and out of his head—how he would take down Number Three.

He got off the train at the next stop. He always admired the intricate mosaic tile on the subway wall that contained only the letter 'P' for the station at Park Place. He began walking through the myriad tunnels towards the 'J' line. The subterranean tubes were ten degrees colder than the already chilly Manhattan air. He zipped up his leather bomber and walked up the long staircase to the 'J' subway platform and waited for the next train headed to Brooklyn. He thought about this latest misstep. Above all things, he never wanted to bring the slightest attention to himself. If he did, he would abort his plans, wait a week or so, and try again. He was *too* careful the first two times. Nobody even noticed. It aggravated him that all his plotting and time amounted to absolutely nothing. He took great pains to kill the first two victims and the events were largely ignored by the media.

Number Three will be different.

It was not his intention to kill too many, just enough to be noticed, enough to meet that objective and only those who wouldn't be able to care for their own.

Seven skells should do it.

But things weren't coming together as he'd originally planned.

The police had cleaned up Number One three months ago on the northbound subway platform at 125th Street in Manhattan, on the #4 line. At 4:00 a.m., the detectives at the scene categorized Number One as a normal DOA because they failed to notice that the pregnant, forty year old former mental patient was bludgeoned to death with a couple of heavy blows to the head. The responding investigative team mistakenly decided that the victim fell and cracked her skull; a simple determination that did not lead to a more comprehensive exam at the morgue. That fact, coupled with the conviction that the victim was a homeless "nobody." He'd recently read that the New York City Administrative code in 2005 estimated there were 35,000 such homeless persons living in New York. Five thousand of those lived in the streets, parks and subways. Number One was one of the unobserved, or rather unacknowledged, people who lived and traveled the subways every day. She had no funeral and no one would ever visit her grave in Potter's Field, marked only by a small metal stone with the number 198-154.

Number Two had been a little trickier, but also involved the killing of another dispossessed soul. A young black woman was hanged by her neck, with her hands tied behind her back, in an abandoned subway room over a month ago. The killer would know immediately from the news when they found her. He also knew there would be no way to classify it as an accidental death or miss that she was near-term as well. The problem was that no one ever found Number Two. She was *still* in that room, forty feet from an abandoned control tower, one hundred feet into the tunnel at Myrtle and Wyckoff, on the 'L' line in Brooklyn.

Hard to believe no one ever went in there; it was a great place to hide.

Unfortunately, there would certainly be no one who would report Number Two missing. The killer considered making an anonymous call, but dismissed the idea as too risky. He could get another victim easily. It would be a little tricky to find another pregnant one though. It didn't matter. A homeless man would be almost as good. They were vermin and there was a seemingly endless supply. He also believed that once he got what he wanted, once he received the recognition he deserved, he'd stop.

No one can do things like this forever and not get caught.

He found it interesting to think about it though.

If I didn't stop, who would catch me?

MAN UNDER

As he boarded the next inbound 'J' train and departed Broadway and Nassau, he observed another homeless person lying on the train bench seats in the last car. The putrid smell of urine and months without bathing hung in the air. He walked into the next car forward, sickened. As the train went over the Williamsburg Bridge, he looked down in the street as it approached the first stop in Brooklyn. Marcy Avenue was an elevated station, as were half of the subway stations in Brooklyn and Queens. From the tracks high above the streets, he could see more homeless in pockets, hovering over fifty-five gallon drums containing roaring fires fueled by discarded wood from abandoned buildings. He remembered a commercial from 20 years ago, during a political campaign. It was an advertisement for some local politician running for a councilman seat. The commercial showed a recently terminated executive looking over the East River at his former office building in Manhattan. The executive was now homeless and huddled over a fifty-five gallon drum of fire to warm himself.

Who believed that shit?

He thought back to the 1980's, when there was an unprecedented cutback at the state level of government in New York. The resulting fiscal crisis focused on saving money for the state by closing most of the major psychiatric hospitals. The mentally ill were deemed releasable to halfway houses or alternatives to state-sponsored care. Most were then systematically ejected from the system. However, the newly classified out-patients didn't stay in any home or halfway house. They made it to the city and the subways in droves. Anyone who rode trains knew their fellow passengers with unbearable odors weren't former executives from Manhattan. Cops called them *skells*. They were more like zombies, moving from one train to the next. Some of those people seeking to survive and obtain shelter from the elements were also found burrowing in hidden rooms underground, near the tracks. Back in the 80's, nobody knew what to do with them. The Mayor of New York

City knew what to do when they were cold. He had them scooped up by the Transit Police and put in shelters. Grand plans were made when the temperature went below 15 degrees, because street people really did drop dead when it got that cold. Twenty years later, the situation had not changed too much. Some homeless were still scooped up in the winter. Throughout the rest of the season, the papers occasionally contained headline news about the most recent tragedy involving those perpetually ignored and living on the streets for years. Three years ago, a front page article featured a homeless person who crowned some Wall-streeter in the head with a brick in downtown Manhattan. Two years ago, a construction worker was killed when he asked a person to move from his makeshift home under the Van Wyck expressway. The squatter had a gun. The worker didn't. Last year a baby was stabbed near SoHo. Cries from politicians would ring out about what should be done to combat the epidemic of thousands roaming the street, more and more with children. The fervor would die down and a year later another tragedy would hit the papers involving a homeless child who died, or another mentally ill person who hurt someone. It was a disturbing cycle that he knew no one really addressed adequately.

"Myrtle Avenue, next stop," the conductor announced over the PA system.

He got off at the above ground station, contemplating the future.

Number Three would be different. Even a moron would notice this one couldn't be natural causes. An investigation would take place, not a very lengthy one because the victim would be nameless, and not many resources would be allocated to it.

He was a little disappointed though. Now he had to wait another week.

MAN UNDER

February 12, 2006, 11:00 PM
'A' line, NY, NY

Eight days later he was on the 'A' train, after switching trains only three times. He'd been riding for two hours this time before he noticed Number Three. She was a young girl. He had seen her before. He'd observed her being ejected from a train near where he worked about two weeks ago. A police officer had kicked her off and filled out a report.

Might have been pretty once.

He had been riding in the car alone with her, only ten feet away, for three stops. They were in the second to last car. He didn't have to worry about the motorman. He was driving in the front of the train. The conductor never left his area in the middle of the eight-cars; that's where he turned the key to open and close the doors for the entire train. The killer just had to watch for cops.

Simple enough, don't be near anyone.

Many times when he was riding, he recognized the Anti-Crime or decoy cops. He'd been fooled once or twice in the past. They were good at what they did. He thought he was good, too, and believed he could see most things others wouldn't observe. However, one night he saw an "unconscious drunk" along with another disconnected passenger in a business suit, jump from their seats and pounce on some poor kid who was stupid enough to reach for a ten dollar bill that was sticking halfway out of the pocket of an apparently unconscious, drunken passenger. Both "passengers" arrested that lad for larceny.

No.

He'd make sure he wouldn't underestimate those cops. The plan was to make sure no one was within two cars of him and Number Three.

Don't have to worry about passengers being cops or civilians if no one was around at all.

It just took a long time to get those conditions and plenty of switches between train lines and boroughs. He knew that almost no police assignments would involve patrol between two separate counties. Easy enough, there were over 400 miles of track in New York City.

His plan was to be completed at the last stop before the underground tunnel that connected Manhattan and Brooklyn. Chamber Street was coming soon and Fulton Street was next, the last stop in the borough before the train went under ground for four minutes towards Brooklyn. He heard the conductor call out "Chambers Street, next stop." He got up from his seat and looked through the cars. The train approached the station, came to a stop, and the doors opened. There were no passengers getting in his car and he had a clear view of three cars ahead of him and the last car behind. The doors closed. He moved closer to the girl.

"Next stop, Fulton Street." came over the speaker system.

Let's see if I can do it right with this one.

The train jolted forward and he nearly lost his balance. He walked up to the girl quickly. The smell was overwhelming, but it didn't bother him. He observed that she was wearing a dirty Mets cap along with a bulky sweater and soiled jeans.

Boy, she sure deserves this now!

He shoved her shoulder to get her attention. He could feel the layers of clothes underneath. She was out cold.

Probably high, drunk, or both.

"Wake up bitch, I got something for you."

She started to stir, but he didn't have time to get her fully awake. There was no need to see the terror in her eyes.

MAN UNDER

I'm not a psycho...doing this bitch a favor, keeping her from rotting to death on these trains.

The Fulton Street station would be coming up in two minutes. He grabbed her by the lumpy hair with his gloved, left hand. His right hand was straight at his side. He pulled her head down to her knees. She barely resisted as she slowly became conscious, but she would not be conscious for long. With her head pulled down, he used his right hand and plunged an ice pick into her neck, at the notch where the back stops and the neck begins. He drove it in, and the pick only stopped where the full 5-inch steel shaft ended at the wooden handle. A sharp spasm from his victim almost knocked him down, as her last conscious thoughts might finally have grasped what was happening, but she was helpless to do anything about it. She stopped struggling and slumped back in the seat, the pick still protruding from her neck.

Okay...would this be natural causes?

He looked down at the body. She was wearing a leather thong necklace that looked old. It had a broach at the end with an ivory face of a woman. It probably was a fake, but might be an antique. He tried to take it quickly, but it was a struggle and it finally had to be yanked off. He pulled off his gloves and calmly placed them back in his coat, He then reached in his breast pocket for a long, black, jewelry case. The black box looked like it might have contained a necklace at one time. He placed the broach in it and snapped it shut, and then put the necklace box back in his coat. He sat her back up in the position she had been in and folded her hands. The Mets cap wound up on the ground and he picked it up and carefully placed it on her head, covering her eyes.

"Fulton Street." came over the intercom.

He quickly walked up two cars before the doors opened and then exited the train. He casually rode up the escalator and stepped onto Broadway in Manhattan. Number Three remained on the train when it pulled slowly out of the station, headed towards Brooklyn.

19

Chapter One

The Next Day
February 13th, 2006, 8:00 AM
Mott Avenue, Far Rockaway, Queens, N.Y.

      The County of Queens is near the western tip of Long Island and is coincident with the Borough of Queens. Queens is bounded on the east by Nassau County, and on the west by Kings County, which is coincident with the Borough of Brooklyn. On the north, Queens County faces the East River and Long Island Sound. The Rockaway peninsula is on the southernmost side of Queens County and fronts on the Atlantic Ocean. The peninsula area was a popular beach locale years ago. Part of its former allure was also the large amusement park called Playland, which closed in 1985. Some of the buildings and developments in the remaining neighborhoods sported more of a seedy look now than that of a resort area. However, crime was relatively low and developers were starting to take a renewed interest After all, Rockaway beaches were among the most beautiful on the East Coast.

      Number Three was in the second to last car, number 4576 on the Southbound 'A'. There were no witnesses who remembered seeing her get on the train at any station, but Mott Avenue, in Far Rockaway, was the last station and the farthest east passengers could ride on the 'A' line. Just a short few miles away, the City of New York ended at the Nassau County border. The Transit Authority calls the end of a line "Terminal Stations." At terminal stations, the conductor of the train is required to make inspections of each car on the departing train, to ensure that sleeping passengers don't ride the trains all night. Nobody really knows how long *she* rode that train. Later interviews indicated that earlier train conductors and motormen swore they swept the train for people and debris after each run in the Rockaways and at the top of the run at 207th Street in Manhattan. In addition to the body, there were also some discarded, folded newspapers and a couple of empty coffee cups and beer bottles that had rolled around throughout the trip. But for the most part, car 4576 was fairly clean for a subway car.

Malcolm Sturbridge had been a conductor on the 'A' line for ten years. He was just beginning one round trip shift on the 'A' train and was explaining routes and procedures to a new conductor trainee, William Tyrell, as they walked from the front of the train, car to car, performing a quick inspection.

"One of the 'A' trains is the Lefferts Blvd. 'A', the other is the Rockaway 'A'." Sturbridge lectured.

"Now you need to get this shit straight because this is where people don't pay attention and start yelling and screaming during a run. Doesn't matter if you make the announcement a hundred times, at Rockaway Blvd, the Lefferts 'A' goes to Lefferts Blvd and the Rockaway 'A' goes to Far Rockaway. If they stay on the wrong train, they'll be screwed up for over an hour going back and forth. They can't screw it up too much if they head into Manhattan because all the northbound 'A's wind up at 207th Street. The ride from here to Harlem and back is just over four hours."

Malcolm looked at the confused rookie.

"Got it?"

It was more of a statement than a question.

Earlier, Malcolm and Tyrell had come down from the Mott Avenue control tower and walked the open-air, island platform. There was no wind and it hadn't rained or snowed in a week. It was just a cool, crisp evening. The signal lights to release the train were red and the two conductors had four minutes before their train was scheduled to depart.

There was always time to kill on subways and everyone who rides, waits. On paper, the trains were all on time. Malcolm explained to Tyrell as they continued their stroll.

"If a run is eighteen minutes behind schedule, they cancel the last four stops, discharge all the passengers with a bullshit 'failure with equipment' excuse and arrive at the terminal station on time. Simple. The Long Island Railroad does it, and so do the New Jersey PATH trains and Metro North."

Tyrell looked at Malcolm. "Why?"

Malcolm answered, a little frustrated that the rookie wasn't getting the point.

"All the train companies have a 95-98% 'on-time' record. The timekeepin' is a little different for passengers who actually ride the trains. The records are accurate. The trains *are* on-time. Only sometimes when they arrive at the terminal stations, there are no passengers on them. But even with those dead-head trains that are empty, most runs throughout the system are pretty reliable and run about every 20-25 minutes."

Prior to the walk on the platform with Tyrell, Malcolm had spent forty-five minutes playing checkers in the Mott Avenue tower at the end of the 'A' line in Far Rockaway. The tower was the nerve center for most of the trains and tracks in the vicinity. There were several towers and terminal stations where shift changes occurred and employees changed from their civilian attire into uniforms. Most of the towers on the train lines were similar, and the Transit Authority in general was a reserved club; New York City's best-kept secret for African-American domination of a civil service job. It was not an exclusive club, per se. There were several cultures and nationalities found in the Transit Authority system, but the line workers were predominately black. For the most part, Caucasians just didn't apply for those positions. From time to time, one might observe some white cops who would eat their lunches in the Mott

Avenue tower. NYPD cops assigned to the Transit Bureau didn't have many choices on where to eat when the subway was their post. However, Malcolm noticed there were no cops in the tower that night. There hadn't been one since the second shift police officer went home at 3:30 PM.

Malcolm had already changed from his street clothes into his neatly pressed blue uniform. He took pride in his dress. He was a tall man with a clean-shaven face and shaved head. He also sported a Fu-Manchu mustache. While he ironed his own blue pants, his gleaming white shirts were sent out to the dry cleaners. He wore polished shoes and a gold pocket watch. One of the other things of which he was proud was that he ran a tight train. When Malcolm had the older subway train models, he'd call out all of the stations over the intercom on the way up to 207th Street. He'd call them all the way back to Queens, too. He inspected every car before leaving each terminal station. He was breaking the rookie in right.

Malcolm and the trainee had started in the first car and walked back slowly, picking up large garbage items and throwing them into an outside platform pail. There was a porter who was to clean each train as it arrived, but Malcom knew he was often a no-show and sporadic at best. As he walked, he continued to talk to Tyrell. The second car from the front had two teenagers on board, a boy and a girl. One was smoking a cigarette. Malcolm walked through and said nothing until he left the car heading toward the next. He then called over his shoulder in a stern voice, loud enough for the teenagers to hear.

"No smoking."

That would be the extent of his confrontation. He tried to avoid any negative interaction with rule-breakers.

"Tyrell, we're not paid enough to wrestle with passengers over bullshit."

He kept on walking and continued to give the rookie pointers.

"If they put the cigarette out great, if not, there are plenty of Transit Cops to take care of that nonsense."

He paused and looked in the next car.

"Most of the cops do the right thing, but there are a few posted out here that don't do shit. They spend most of their tour in the Tower watching some sort of ball game, depending on what season it is...you'll know who they are right away, they stay in there for hours at a time."

Who was on tonight?

He thought about it briefly.

He'd remember later on. Malcolm always made mental notes of important details and who was working in case he needed help sometime during the night. By the time they reached the second to last car, they had passed a total of four people including the porter who was making a quick run between cars, picking up large items. Car 4576 was clean of large debris but not up to Malcolm's standards. Malcolm sighed heavily as he walked down the car slowly. He had looked up and noticed her in the back right corner as soon as he entered. He heard the double buzzer from the motorman which was the signal to go. Malcolm was a stickler and he was thorough, but as he told Tyrell,

"When the tower chief says go, you go."

He mumbled "Fuck it" and was about to leave her to take the long ride back to Manhattan, but then decided to get a response from the still woman before he left. He'd ask her to take the next train. Malcolm and his rookie partner walked up to her. She stank. They all did, but he didn't toss *all* of those homeless people out. Malcolm was particular. He had to be. Some got nasty. Some were violent. Malcolm approached her and the stench was more pervasive than usual. The buzzer from the motorman to close the doors rang again from the closed cab in the back of the car. Malcolm could tell by the menacing reverberation the motorman was annoyed. Something was wrong though. He looked at her again. Number Three had blonde, matted, almost Rastafarian-type

24

hair and was wearing a Mets cap. She was carrying the mandatory inventory of the homeless; a shopping bag full of junk, and she smelled like they all smelled; a mixture of months-old urine, feces and eight to twelve-month old body funk. It was unreal to the newcomer. Most would gag their first time inhaling that mixture, which is exactly what the trainee did.

"Phew, this one's ripe." Tyrell whispered as he covered his mouth and nose.

She was wearing green sweatpants under the blue jeans. They were the top two of countless layers of clothing. The homeless had to stay warm somehow. The girl also had a blue sweat jacket at her side and a dirty sweater top. It looked like it could have been white at one time. She was slumped with her hands folded as if at the beginning of an evening meal at which she was about to say 'Grace'. Her head was bowed down, the cap covering her eyes.

"Hey!" Malcolm shouted.

He had no time for amenities. The Motorman hit the buzzer again. Malcolm heard it from the cab at the back of the car. The buzz was long and sporadic. The motorman was ready to leave.

"Last Stop, Sugar!" Malcolm shouted.

No response.

"I got no time for this shit." Malcolm muttered to the rookie.

He put on his leather gloves. The rookie did the same. Everyone who worked in the subways had a set of gloves. The subway's a dirty place. Some of the people were even dirtier. Malcolm began to shake her like he had done to other homeless people a thousand times before. They were usually stoned, drunk, or both. Malcolm verified his awful feeling that something was wrong. Her shoulder was stiff like a mannequin.

This ain't good. Malcolm thought to himself.

He was about to drag her off and put her on the bench. Conductors did that from time to time.

Shit, cops did that from time to time.

"Fuck this" Malcolm said to the rookie.

He gave her one more shove. Her shoulder and the rest of her body continued moving. Number Three slumped down on the floor. The legs buckled and her head tilted up. Malcolm could see her gleaming face now, no longer a *skell* or a mannequin. One eye was open, one eye half-closed. Her hair and clothes were filthy, but Malcolm noticed a trace of beauty had once been there, sometime, when she was younger. She finally stopped moving and lay on her side, collapsed on the floor, hands still firmly clasped together. Malcolm had been working ten years and had seen three *man under* train accidents. He had witnessed chain snatches, assaults, even two stabbings. Something stirred within him. Maybe because like everyone else who came into contact with the homeless, in the recesses of his mind, he too had felt they were sub-human. Or maybe it was the ice-pick sticking out of the back of her neck. He swallowed hard. He was more likely moved because when she fell, it exposed her plump belly. It appeared that she was about five months along. His eyes welled up. The exact times would be determined later. She'd been riding like that for over nine hours.

Chapter Two

Twelve years earlier
July 10, 1994
Gramercy Park, NY, NY

Sticky. Uncomfortable. He ran down Second Avenue in Manhattan, barely seeing through a blurry haze which stretched for blocks, curling over into the buildings in waves. He looked at his watch.

30 minutes.

Not today. He prayed to himself.

Please not today.

It was 7:00 AM. The humidity that hung in the air already made it feel like it was 2:00 PM. There weren't any clouds, but a blue sky wasn't visible either. Thirty minutes ago he had stepped off the Long Island Railroad underground into New York City and changed for the subway at 34th Street and Penn Station. The next hurdle was when he boarded the wrong train at 34th Street, the one headed to the Bronx. When he realized his mistake, he jumped off the train as the doors were closing and crossed over to the opposite platform and waited for the next train. He looked at his watch.

18 minutes.

He boarded the next train and was back on track, in Manhattan, headed in the right direction. Union Square and 14th Street was just ahead. The rest of the morning's trek would be above ground. He scurried up the subway stairs at 14th Street and looked for a cab.

Ten minutes.

After frantically scanning the street he found one, only to be stuck in traffic three blocks away from the 20th Street Police Academy.

He'd have to run the last of the journey, carrying the thirty-pound black bag of books and equipment he'd received yesterday from Equipment and Supply. He looked like an out-of-place Boy Scout running down Second Avenue. He was five-feet, nine inches, and one hundred seventy-five pounds. He had dirty blonde hair and blue eyes. Anyone could guess that his ancestors were Irish. He looked like he'd fallen off a Lucky Charms box. Not classically handsome. But sky-blue eyes, a dimpled chin and high cheekbones made him good-looking in a clean-cut way. He was wearing neatly pressed, new blue nylon pants. The creases were sharp. His light blue shirt had long sleeves, and his shoes, made of imitation black patent-leather, were shiny. Topping off the uniform was the Navy-type, rectangular blue cap. Completing the outfit was the dead give-away, clip-on tie with an NYPD tie clasp.

He was "On the job." It was the title that everyone in New York recognized as being a police officer in the NYPD, Housing, or what he was, A New York City Transit cop. His heart was thumping. He and every other new recruit had caught a lot of yelling and screaming yesterday when they had been sworn in. The screaming was a primitive, yet effective way to straighten out those rookies with a quick temper or short fuse. He made it to the 20th Street entrance. He glanced down at his wrist.

Four minutes.

He was going to make it. He entered through the glass doors and passed a recessed desk area.

"Hold it, Rookie," someone shouted from behind him while he was waiting for the elevator.

Shit!... Yeah, Yeah. He thought to himself, but didn't dare to mutter it out loud.

He did a military, heel-to-toe about-face, and saw the crew cut and a worn face chiseled out of granite, sitting behind a desk.

"Rookies take the stairs." He yelled without looking up as he continued with some paper work.

"Yes sir," he replied.

He saw that Chisel Chin had some sort of stripes on his sleeves.

What did the three stripes mean again? Fuck it, but I better make sure I figure out who's who, quick.

He took to the stairs.

Only eight floors and four minutes to get to the roof. I can handle it.

By the time he got to the top of the building, his shirt was wet from the creases under his arms down to his belt. But, more importantly and to his relief, he wasn't late. He found his company, 89-94, and lined up on the tarred, black roof of the NYPD Police Academy. The rooftop had a moderate view of 20th Street and the Gramercy Park area. The sun was eclipsed by the surrounding structures, but it didn't lessen the impact of the heat.

"*I can do this*," he said to himself. *I can do this... and for God's sakes, keep your wise-ass mouth shut...Well, I should be able to keep my mouth shut for six months in the academy anyway.*

Kevin McCaffrey knew there would be some other eager volunteer who would gladly pick-up that "wise-ass flag" and run with it.

This time it wasn't going to be him.

There were twenty companies with about thirty-five recruits in each. All recruits wore the same dark blue trousers, light blue shirt, clip-on tie and the rectangular cap. Each officer had a regulation black leather carry-all to hold material and books. Every woman had her hair cut short or tied in a tight bun. Nearly every man had a crew or semi-crew cut. There were some men who tried to come close with the hair length.

Idiots. Kevin thought. *Any guy who wanted to stand out, for any reason, was asking to get his balls busted.*

Those who were singled out were squared away and had shorter cuts than anyone else by the second day in the academy. Initially, the training was a serious matter. During the first two to three days, there was a lot of yelling and chewing rookies out. The former military guys had it easier. The academy was a joke compared to the military. By day four the yelling stopped. They didn't really want recruits to quit, no matter how unfit some of them actually were. New York City invested a lot of money in the process of hiring new officers. The testing and subsequent investigation of each prospective officer for six months prior to entering the academy was a lengthy and costly process. Once they made it into the academy, almost all of the recruits graduated.

"Company, *ten-hut*!" A voice commanded.

Recruits were to stand at attention and keep their eyes straight. The Police Officer in charge of Company 89-94 inspected each recruit every tour. His name was P.O. Brown. Brown was a tall black man with eleven years on the job. He had some medals on his chest and was somewhat tough at first, but eventually he mellowed out. Six months was a long time. Occasionally he did enjoy his work, though, and day one in the Police Academy was one of them.

"DeSantis?" Brown yelled.

"Yes sir," Danny DeSantis answered, staring straight ahead.

Kevin glanced over with his eyes. His head never moved.

Danny was the one. He was going to be a target today and right through the next six months. He was just begging for it. Not a bad guy, but he looked soft.

DeSantis was older than most. He had a furry mustache and a flat top haircut that spiked a full three inches above his head. His belly slightly lingered over his tight belt. He looked like a Greek Lou Costello.

P.O. Brown got right in his face.

"Officer did you comb your hair with firecrackers this morning?"

Muttered snickers were heard from the rest of the company.

"No sir," he answered back loudly.

Brown yelled again.

"I want that bush high and tight by tomorrow! Is that clear DeSantis?"

"Yes sir."

It was like that the first day, a lot of yelling and screaming. A couple of women were crying. Kevin believed he saw a couple of men's lips quivering too. A man in the next company was told, "No *Madonna* haircuts, sweet boy."

That got a chuckle too. Kevin glanced over and recognized a guy who lived in his hometown of Central Islip, Long Island.

The treatment lightened up on the second day and the rest of the time throughout the training. There were plenty of rules though. Recruits were to address all superiors as "sir" and "ma'am." There was to be no talking in the hallways, no smoking in uniform, no derogatory comments, or alcohol, either. One guy did quit as soon as a training P.O. got in his face. He just handed over his equipment and said "Fuck this." That was a bad choice, considering that every day after the first one or two was a piece of cake.

When all the background checks, records checks, and personal interviews were completed, the goal of the department was to pass everyone. There were a few recruits who were unavoidably weeded out. They were caught with drugs off duty or were arrested for DWI during their academy training and were let go. The academic portion was even easier then the physical fitness training. But the fitness training was tough on many of the recruits simply because they were in poor shape. There were plenty of men and women who just made the weight limit to get in the academy. They lost twenty to thirty pounds to get the job, and gained it all back within two months after the training period.

Six months flew by and Kevin was standing in Madison Square Garden with fifteen hundred recruits. The Mayor and the Police Commissioner spoke. Kevin thought to himself how he wanted to make his mark as a police officer. How, above all else, he would be a better cop than his father was. Kevin remembered the stories the old man told and how his father laughed about the beatings he inflicted on "niggers and spics." Kevin promised himself he wouldn't be that way. He promised himself he wouldn't break the law to uphold it. He wouldn't steal or shoot anyone unless it was necessary. Kevin snapped from his thoughts as he heard the Commissioner's closing remarks.

"People will be caught smoking pot...don't do it."

Inspirational.

Chapter Three

January 10, 1994
East New York, Brooklyn

The first two weeks on patrol were the most nerve-wracking. Growing up on Long Island hadn't prepared Kevin for East New York, Brooklyn. It was also the only time Kevin was actually scared. He was working with a different training officer every night. It was a flip of a coin whether the night would fly by with someone who was quality, or drag on with someone a little edgier, whose only contribution to the evening might be to coax an emotionally disturbed person into a wrestling match. The field training the department had for rookies when they left the academy was poor. Field Training Officers were paid a minor stipend by the department to train rookies. The most experienced or more serious cops did not want to be saddled with rookies, not for minimum pay anyway. Many old-timers felt they didn't want to get hurt by dumb remarks uttered by the inexperienced which occasionally set people off. Officer John Pulaski was one of the better training officers. He was taller than Kevin and wore his uniform like a bag of dirty laundry. He also needed to cut his almost shoulder-length blonde hair. He sported a long mustache and chewed gum constantly. Pulaski explained to Kevin during one tour as he chomped his gum.

"There are usually a handful of Transit rookies that make more felony arrests in six months than most of the five to ten year *pails* in the NYPD make in their whole career. Transit cops interact with more people in their first year than most other cops in the country see in their lifetime."

Pulaski went on. He liked to talk...and chew.

"That's not a bragging right, just look at the numbers...eight million people in the city, seven million a day use the subways. The sheer number of people on the trains exposes Transit Cops to quite an array of shit. The fact that virtually all of the foot posts are single-man patrols down here means that the cops deal with more things on their own. That's why most of you vegetables learn quick; you have no choice."

"Hey, why 'Vegetables'? Kevin asked. "And why do most of the older cops hate rookies so much?"

Pulaski didn't answer right away. He wanted to be truthful, but not insulting.   He began.

"Mostly because the radios never work, cops are stuck with, well...whoever."

He paused.

"...Look, working with cops you don't know is a gamble, especially if you can't call for help on the radio if you need it. You can't really blame anybody for not wanting to work with rookies. The older *pails* don't want new people fucking up jobs, escalating situations and getting them hurt."

"All right, I get ya'. It makes sense when you think about it."

Kevin paused, then went on,

"I learn fast though."

"That's good, Veggy. I noticed, and so have some others; just don't get too cocky, and always think of ways not to get hurt. It's better to use your mouth than your fists any day."

Kevin learned a lot from Pulaski. He learned where to eat in the worst neighborhoods, and there were plenty of those. He learned where to keep warm in the winter, where the heated rooms and the clean toilets were located. He even learned how to use subway maps as sanitary toilet seat covers. Kevin learned how to peep through a hole and catch people who jumped over the turnstiles to beat the fare.

"Cops could catch three or four summonses if they just waited in the room rather than running out and just getting one..."

He also learned about *free searches*. Pulaski explained.

"If you have some turkey jumping the turnstile and he pulls the 'I don't have any ID' bullshit, according to the law, he can be arrested. If somebody doesn't have ID, no matter how small the infraction is, you can collar him on a misdemeanor. Think about it. Everybody would just tell cops they didn't have any identification. So remember, a summons is in lieu of arrest...No ID... free search, subsequent to arrest for all the mutts who pull that shit..."

"Most people come up with some sort of ID though. They don't want to go to jail for a petty summons."

Kevin liked the nights when he worked with Pulaski. Kevin had heard in the locker room that Pulaski liked his beers, but he didn't notice anything like that, nor did John coax him into any drinking on or off duty.

Last night Kevin had worked with Johnny McCardle. McCardle's bottom button on his uniform shirt was missing and his large belly, covered by a short tee-shirt, was always exposed. He was a *born again* Christian who wouldn't stop talking the entire eight-hour tour. He started right after roll call, walking up to the 'J' line. McCardle, a 12-year veteran, also affectionately referred to all rookies as *Vegetables*. He had some valuable tips about other Field Training Officers though.

"Mostly *pails* are the ones who train new cops, Kevin. All those shiny, soon-to-be new *pails* learn a lot from shitty cops." Johnny said.

"What are *pails*?" Kevin asked.

McCardle answered.

"Pails of shit. Don't be one of those cops, Kevin. Some of your buddies will learn where to sleep, what rooms to hide in and how to get off the train when they're supposed to be riding train patrol runs. The mediocre rookies will struggle and learn on their own through trial and error and eventually adapt and take care of business. Just try not to be one of those cops who need a throw-away knife or gun to put on a mutt to justify their actions."

Kevin was exhausted after the night with Johnny, but he did pick up some useful information. Throughout his training period, which only lasted two weeks, Kevin made it a point to absorb what was necessary for survival from some of the Field Training Officers, and disregard most of the bad advice.

This night, Kevin was paired off with Vin Black, a black cop with a shaved head and long mustache who had two years on the job. He was a good cop but had no use for rookies, never mind a white rookie from Long Island. Kevin's first summons of the night was an awkward one at Nostrand Avenue. A black male jumped the turnstile and Vin grabbed him. Kevin asked the man for his identification and a story began. Kevin was getting a little frustrated and told the fare-beat he didn't want to play any games. Vin escorted the man away quickly and whispered something in his ear. It was a "brother-to-brother" conversation; Kevin wouldn't understand. The man came back with Vin and then complied with all of Kevin's requests, albeit grudgingly, but without incident. The fare-beat and Vin acted as if they were related after that. Kevin wrote the summons. The man accepted the summons, gave Vin a handshake and hug, and off he went with a free ride. Kevin didn't like working with Vin.

He didn't even know that guy!

Vin probably thought he was doing Kevin a favor by making it easier, but it only embarrassed him. Vin was very quiet the rest of the evening. It was a long eight hours. Kevin would've taken Johnny McCardle back for a tour of religious preaching in a heartbeat. It was obvious that Vin didn't want to be partnered with a cracker and Kevin knew that was exactly what he said to the fare-beat. Kevin thought that

Vin was warmer to the mope he just gave a summons to then he'd ever be to him.

All in all, a shitty evening.

As Kevin drove home later in the evening, he was going over the incident with Vin and the summons in his mind. The more he thought about it, the angrier he got about the whole situation. Then it dawned on him. He was getting angry with the fare-beat when Vin had intervened. Vin had de-escalated the situation. He still didn't like the way Vin did it. Kevin thought it was overboard, a respect issue; he had heard this before and it made sense.

"You want respect, you give respect." Who was that?...Brown *from the academy?*

He thought it over some more and realized he had learned something from Vin, too. Kevin was a white cop in the heart of East New York. He needed to figure out what worked and what didn't or he'd be wrestling on the ground with somebody everyday.

Chapter Four

February 21, 2006
80th St. and Hudson on the 'A' line
Ozone Park, Queens

District 23 in the Transit Bureau of the NYPD was historically a pretty slow house. Lately, it had been picking up. There had been some booth robberies in the vicinity and some chain snatches on the local 'C' line in Rockaway. The District ran three shifts of approximately two hundred police officers consisting of a plainclothes Task Force, Anti-Crime units, Auxiliary Police Units, the works. The Crime Scene Unit and other support services were in regular NYPD precinct houses. The District was located in the Rockaways at 116th Street at the Rockaway Park Station, and shared jurisdiction with a number of police precincts that followed the 'A' line. In Ozone Park, both District 23 and the NYPD 103rd Precinct shared jurisdiction for the crime scene at elevated 80th Street station, where Number Four was discovered by a passenger. Nobody had any reason to believe that the dead girl who rode the train for nine hours last week had anything to do with this death. The bodies were found under different circumstances, and different detectives caught the cases. One of the newspapers indicated the last victim, the one with an ice pick in her neck found in Rockaway, might have been "Hunted Down" – or so the headline read.

Detectives Feuss and Jones were the first team to arrive after the station cop from the post radioed for assistance. Billy Feuss had twelve years on the job, was of average height, had red hair with thick side-burns almost down to his jaws, and was always impeccably dressed. He was an experienced cop, but like many officers, infamous for avoiding *heavy* capers when he was a uniformed police officer. There had been a few times when he worked in uniform on the City Wide Patrol Force, that he was seen by-passing stations when calls for a cop were transmitted. He was especially known to keep right on going past incidents or calls if it was near the end of his tour. He would respond with everyone else when a crowd of cops were around, but nobody looked for him to spearhead any incident by himself.

No one really spoke at length about it. He was just one of a few that cops didn't count on. Other cops couldn't figure out if he was a wimp or just didn't want to get involved. It was probably a combination of both. One scene that he had shown up at about five years ago had resulted in him being named in a two million-dollar lawsuit because he used his nightstick on the head of a stoned black kid who's father was a local minister. The kid was violent and deserved the whack on the skull, but he was sued anyway. Cops were sued all the time; mostly nothing came of it. But Feuss was nervous about the lawsuit and it nearly consumed him. He never stopped talking about it. He was always asking fellow officers "Do you think I did anything wrong?" It had been a house joke in District 20, when he worked there as a Transit cop prior to the merger of all three police departments.

He wound up in the Detective Bureau by a fluke. He was peeking through a bathroom hole, trying to catch turnstile jumpers. One perpetrator went through and Feuss grabbed him. The mope had no identification, which led to an automatic "free search." A gun turned up that had been used to rob some Alderman's daughter from Queens. The career criminal gave up his friend who had pulled the job, and the Alderman returned his gratitude by making a couple of calls which resulted in Feuss becoming a Detective in the Major Case Squad.

Feuss's partner, Samuel Jones, was a nineteen-year veteran going through the motions before retirement. Jonesy wore a full length overcoat and a fedora when he was working in the Detective Bureau. He had mutton chops that turned into a well-trimmed beard, littered with gray. He was a little shorter than Feuss at an even five-eleven. Jonesy had seen it all and slept through half of it. He'd been a good cop when he first came out of the academy, making collars and writing summonses. After the first two years, a couple of officers approached him about making them look bad. Their argument was that the average rotating, uniformed police officer wrote about five to ten summonses a month and rarely made any arrests. If someone started writing fifty tags a month and making two felony arrests a week, it made the rest of the shift look suspect. The bosses would want to know what the rest of the squad was doing. So Jonesy, at the behest of his friends, slowed down, found out where the best rooms were to sleep and how to avoid Internal Affairs. Eventually, he began to drink with his buddies, sometimes on duty, sometimes off. He gave his five summonses a month and met girls in uniform. Over a twelve-year period, he progressed into a *pail,* with two daughters and a failed marriage. Seven years ago, members of the "Guardians," a fraternal organization that represented African-American police officers, persuaded him to go for a position in the Major Case Detective Bureau. The Detective Bureau needed some color and Jonesy knew he had more potential than most of the crackers who made it for a variety of reasons other than merit or ability. He knew there were a handful of good cops who busted their butts and didn't have any *hooks* to get into the Bureau, but there weren't many.

When Feuss and Jonesy arrived at the station, the platform was full of civilians trying to get a look at what was going on. The assigned, uniformed, post cop was Tony Malaro.

Like Jonesy, he also had nineteen years on the job, but didn't look a day over thirty-five. He wore the same size uniform as he had when he first got on the job almost two decades earlier. Tony walked with a slight swagger and never hurried into anything. He not only had the look, but the knack of always knowing how to run a job. Occasionally, he would wait for direction when bosses arrived at the

40

scene. He got a big kick out of watching inept Sergeants bark out a slew of orders and screw it up.

Tony was a former Transit Police Detective who'd had the highest clearance rate in the Major Case Squad in the now-defunct Transit Police Department. He was in an NYPD uniform now. After the Transit Police merged with NYPD in 1995, Tony got involved in an incident where an alleged bad shooting took place, and was busted back to uniform patrol. He still wore the medals he had earned as a detective. They were piled high over his badge. He wore them because he knew it aggravated some of the bosses, especially Sergeant Quinn. Two of the medals were the highest you could earn in the NYPD.

Malaro had a reputation as a no-nonsense cop. There were a few guys who would show up at any job and always take care of business— quickly, cleanly and professionally. Tony was one of those guys. If someone was to be locked up, there was no conversation, just a quick speed-cuff technique and off to the command, usually without a scuffle and more importantly, without injury. If he wanted to diffuse situations, which most bosses preferred, it would be over within five minutes and formerly disgruntled parties would be on their way. "10-90z" was the code for the job being classified as "gone on arrival." Tony was a desk officer's dream cop; squash as much as possible. Don't bring anything back to the house unless absolutely necessary. The only jobs handled inappropriately on Tony Malaro's posts were those where certain bosses arrived at the scene and "took charge." This was soon to be one of those times.

Jonesy and Feuss approached Tony on the northbound 'A' platform. Tony was bouncing up and down trying to keep his hands warm. He looked up at the two detectives, jotted something down on paper with his pen and then squatted back down, examining the victim. It was warmer than the previous day, but still chilly outside.

"Whatcha' got, Tony?" Jonesy asked.

Tony stood straight up, looked at the slightly taller Jonesy, and smiled.

"Hey Jonesy, long time no see. Still sucking up that overtime?"

Jonesy smiled.

"Can't let you crackers make all that money by yourselves now, can I?"

Jonesy knew Tony was hitting the overtime for the same reason he was. Getting out. Retiring. They were attempting to kick up that base salary where calculations on pensions were made.

Tony got back to the business at hand and squatted down again.

"Fuckin' shame. This guy shouda' been shacked up somewhere in a shelter."

Tony continued as if he'd never left the Detective Division.

"...male/black 25 years old, 145 lbs...Looks like a .38, close range; one shot from the front, bullet exited back of left ear and went over the platform."

"Yeah?" Feuss said with a grin.

Feuss liked Tony. He just hoped he wouldn't break his balls too much like he sometimes did. Pruess went on.

"Do you know what he had for lunch, too?"

Tony looked at him with a wide smile.

"What's the matter *Feussy*, didn't you learn about close range entrance and exit wounds of a .38, or didn't they cover that under the Alderman's desk?"

Jonesy let out a howl.

Feuss laughed.

"Fuck you, ya' prick."

"You see Feussy..." Tony said, continuing to mock him.

"...when a gun goes off close range, the bullet leaving the barrel exits with debris, most of it still hot, some of it on fire if the gun is not that clean. When that debris exits, it leaves pit marks or burns on the skin and clothes if you're too close, not to mention the damage the bullet can do to you when you're hit right in the face."

Tony crouched over and pointed with his pen to the hole in the victim's face, careful not to touch anything.

"If you take a close look, you can see the miniscule burn marks next to his eye. The further away the shot, the fewer the pit marks. I'd say our mutt was no more than twelve inches away, or maybe closer. A forty five that close would leave a larger hole and a twenty-two would be a lot smaller."

Tony was having fun now.

"Oh and by the way," Tony continued. "He was eating a tuna sandwich."

Feuss's eyebrows rose and he smiled.

"Yeah right...How'd you guess that one, Sherlock?" Feuss thought Tony might have been the best—way back when—but not anymore.

Tony answered.

"It's from the garbage pail, moron. It's still all over his fingers and beard."

Tony pointed to the garbage receptacle on the platform.

"The rest of the sandwich is sitting on top of the dumpster."

Malaro looked over Feuss' shoulder. Sergeant Quinn was walking up the platform now.

"Fun's over," Tony whispered. "Here comes the asshole."

Billy Quinn had the face of a cherry-nosed Irishman. His neck was obscured by a roll of fat and the last button on his shirt was about to launch into space. Quinn was a well-known Fire Island homosexual, but pretended he wasn't. He always had something to say or a comment to make, no matter what the circumstance—like he needed to show what a tough bastard he was. Billy was the original *know-it-all*. He never realized the reason people avoided him like the plague had nothing to do with being gay. He was just designated throughout the department as a verified asshole.

He approached the group without any amenities, his white hair peeking out the sides of his cap like wings..

"Did you call for the crime scene unit, Malaro?"

"Yes sir!" Tony answered in his best "yes-man" voice, and ran the rest of it down for Quinn.

"I also called for an ambulance, the Duty Captain, separated witnesses and got down initial info in case they disappeared while we were waiting for our elite squad here."

He pointed to Feuss and Jonesy.

"Good," said Quinn, thinking quickly for something to add.

"Did you do that booth relief at Rockaway Boulevard, Malaro?"

Tony would put no more effort into this conversation.

Let him fuck it up now, like he always did.

"Thanks for reminding me, Sarge, I was heading over right now."

Quinn smirked like he'd just squared away an eleven-year-old for spilling milk on the kitchen floor.

"Okay then, we'll take over now; don't forget to call operations and fill them in... Oh, and I want that complaint report turned in by the end of the tour."

"Okay Sarge, I'll get right on it."

Malaro smiled and waved goodbye to the two detectives.

"I'll make sure I do it right after the booth relief."

Tony walked away, the complaint report already filled out impeccably before the detectives had arrived. He'd filled in the last information earlier, when he'd observed Jonesy and Feuss make it to the top of the stairs and knew what team was going to take the job. Malaro slowly walked to the other side and caught the next southbound train to Rockaway Blvd.

After Malaro left, Quinn started spouting off what little knowledge he had about police procedures and crime scenes. He was a mediocre cop with one felony arrest as an officer, a bunch of worthless misdemeanors, and thousands of summonses, before he was promoted to Sergeant. He was the type of cop who would give out summonses to regular working stiffs for smoking, because he knew he wouldn't have to wrestle those types of tags to the ground. After he'd initiated a summons for smoking, he'd write another one for littering when they stubbed the butt out on the floor. He was a real piece of work.

"That fucking Malaro is an asshole," Quinn said after he watched Tony board the train and leave the station.

"They should have fired his ass when he shot that broad. I got to tell him what to do all the time. I don't know who carried that prick through the DD."

Quinn then glanced at the body.

"Looks like a rifle shot to me." Quinn said. "It's a pretty small hole. Probably shot from the opposite platform."

Feuss and Jones just smiled at each other.

"Won't know for sure until the tests are back, Sarge, but that's what *Feussy* here thinks." said Jones.

Feuss shot Jones a dirty look, as Jones laughed behind Quinn's back.

Quinn bent down and started to turn the body over.

"Uh, Sarge?" Jonesy squirmed.

"Yeah, what?" barked Quinn, as his eyebrows furrowed, obviously annoyed as he looked up at Jones. Jones reluctantly continued.

"Uh... shouldn't we get pictures first?"

Quinn shot a glaring look back at Jones as he stood up slowly and took two steps to get in Jonesy's face.

"You know what I think?"

Quinn scowled and his voice grew louder.

"I think this is a crazy *skell* who fucked with the wrong person. I want you to get some identification, get him on a bus to Kings County Hospital or Jamaica, and the fuck out of here! We've got trains backed up to Lefferts Blvd."

The Transit brass loved Quinn; he was a real prick and he knew what was important. Get those trains moving on time, ensure that booth reliefs were being conducted, and have cops write plenty of summonses for extra revenue. Those were the important things, not some nothing *skell*. Technically, Jones was the lead officer in charge, because he was the ranking detective on the crime scene, but he'd worked with Quinn plenty of times and they occasionally went out drinking together off duty. He knew Quinn didn't want to hear it. Quinn also gave Jonesy additional overtime posts every week. Jonesy was processing quickly. He was visibly uncomfortable and looked over at Feuss, who was looking away, whistling.

This one wasn't going to be cleared anyway. Nobody saw anything. Who cares? Just one less skell *to worry about, right?*

He'd have to get busy with family notifications, anyway.

"Okay Sarge." Jonesy backed off.

The ambulance came, and the crime scene was gone within an hour of Malaro's initial contact. They loaded the body in a bag. When they went to zip it up, the zipper caught the victim's arm so they tucked it back in the bag. No one noticed the recent tear in the DOA's jacket. It was where the deceased had worn his Marine Insignia pin, until today.

Chapter Five

Six hours earlier
February 21, 2006

The cold air pierced his lungs and he was breathing so hard he could hear his own heartbeat. He alternated running and walking the ten blocks from the 80th Street subway stairs to his car, where he'd parked behind the PC Richards appliance store on Rockaway Blvd. He was wearing a scarf up to his nose. Even if he ran into someone he knew or knew him, he wouldn't be recognized. He was using his grandmother's car—also less likely to be noticed by anyone. He shot up 78th Street and zig-zagged to Atlantic Avenue, and though he walked calmly the last block and a half, he thought he was going to lose it.

Steady. It's over. Next time you'll be more careful. Next time stick to the women. The women are ones who make more skells. The women are the ones...Walk to the car, get in and drive home.

The newspapers had started calling him "Hunter" after he ice-picked the girl in Manhattan. He liked that name—felt it was quite appropriate. Now, *Hunter* was trying to figure out what went wrong. It had all happened so fast.

Number Four was at the 80th Street station like he always was at that time of night. The killer had previously scoped out his next victim three times. Each elevated station in Queens had two mezzanine areas. Some of the stations closed down one end due to lack of passengers. *Hunter* had climbed the stairs of the empty elevated station from the street. Using his cluster of keys, he entered the deserted booth area on the first level and went up the back stairs to the northbound platform. He opened the gate at the top of the platform, at the rear end of the station. Number Four was sitting there in all his filth, picking garbage out of a can on the platform.

Amazing. This skell *had some type of schedule, because he had been here at 1:30 AM three nights this week.*

Hunter was beginning to drift again, as he watched the man riffle through a sandwich by the dumpster.

Disgusting. Eliminating some of these wretched people was a service, though the Hunter would never get the credit that he deserved!

He shook his head to get back to the matter at hand. He looked up and down the platforms hovering fifty feet above the street on both sides of the tracks. He knew the schedule for all the departing trains going in both directions. He'd timed his entry onto the subway platform with the departure of two trains, going in opposite directions. There would be no more trains for at least twenty minutes, and the platform should be clear. There was always the possibility of a straggler just missing the last ride in either direction, but at this time of night, evening shifts were already in place and it was unlikely that there would be anyone around. Those facts and the recent cold snap made for a well-planned event. There were no passengers on either platform. There wouldn't be any cops around either.

Hunter had placed an emergency "officer needs assistance" call four minutes before he entered the 80th Street station. Any officer within a five-mile radius would be high-tailing it to Grant Avenue on the 'A' line, three stops away. He'd allowed enough time for any uniform or plainclothes cop receiving the emergency transmission from the Operations Unit to catch the outgoing train. Any officer who heard the call would have to go.

No need to take too many risks. Getting caught was not in the game plan. Seven skells *should do it. That also should be enough to surpass the biggest murder spree since Son of Sam...and be just as newsworthy.*

Hunter walked up to the homeless black man on the platform. He had seen him here several times. He looked familiar. He'd noticed it the first time he saw him. He remembered back to when he was a child.

She always had visitors. Some black. Some white. All with a bottle or a joint.

She'd party with them till the late hours. Hunter complained to his mother on occasion, and once took a terrific beating from one of the visitors. The visitor was black and he lived on the street. He was looking at him now...or so he believed.

The skinny man was eating what appeared to be a left over sandwich that someone must have discarded in the trash. If it had been thrown out today, the cold weather would act as a refrigerator. Number Four was taller than *Hunter* remembered. He was wearing an oversized parka with a fur hood, green camouflage pants, and black army boots. *Hunter* pointed the gun and then approached. Number Four appeared not to be concerned. He just continued to eat, his fur hood crumpled down around his shoulders, a mix of the hood fur and his beard resting on his neck and face. He was making a mess with the sandwich, and there was mayonnaise all over his mouth and facial hair. At first, Number Four looked up and saw the killer, but wasn't really absorbing what was about to occur. *Hunter* came closer with the gun, pointed it straight out, arm extended, about four feet away from the intended victim.

No time for mess-ups tonight. One shot to the head for "Tuna Boy."

He'd rehearsed doing Number Four over and over, as he had done with the others. He researched the times. He knew the post cop's routine. He was thinking too much again, and began to day dream.

49

Except for that one cop. I checked. He wasn't around, was he? He didn't have a routine.

Hunter had almost been jammed up by one officer at this very station last week. The killer was coming up the deserted back-end stairs and stopped, with his head and eyes barely above the top step, so he could just see the entire platform. Anyone walking on the platform coming towards him would not see him at all from a distance. He never ran to the top of any stairs without taking a peek first. He saw the officer about twenty feet away, with a flashlight, heading straight for him.

He was making an inspection of the closed end area! None of the cops did that!

Hunter had scampered down the stairs and out the back gate, sprinting back to Rockaway Blvd. He'd have to find out when that officer worked, and pull this off when he wasn't around. And that's what he'd done. He was getting better at this every time. Number Three had gone smoothly. The distaste and nervousness that he'd had prior to the third killing was dissipating. He knew he was becoming more proficient at the tasks, and hoped he wouldn't start liking it too much. As he was thinking about executing these last steps he'd rehearsed for Number Four, and how good he was getting, what he hadn't rehearsed happened quickly as he snapped out of his trance.

Number Four stepped forward in an almost combat-like maneuver. He was on *Hunter* in a flash.

Holy shit! Shoot! Shoot!

Number Four came up with a solid punch to the throat. *Hunter* dropped the gun and clutched his throat with both hands. The homeless man was not interested in the gun, nor was he angry that a gun had been pointed at his head. He was mad because he hadn't gotten to finish his sandwich. Number Four then delivered a gut shot right hook, while the would-be killer was still clutching his throat. *Hunter* doubled over and fell to the ground. The hungry, homeless man was done. He wasn't into whipping men who wouldn't fight back. In his mind he'd made his point.

Made him pay.

Now he could continue with his first solid meal in over twenty-four hours. He looked around for his sandwich. *Hunter* sat on the platform, holding his throat, with tears in his eyes. He was a ball of confusion. *Hunter* was normally clear-headed, except for his occasional drifting. Right now he was a frightened boy who had just got his balls handed to him.

He beat me again! He beat me when I was a boy and he beat me again! How do I explain this? How do I tell this story? My God, what am I going to do? Please stop hitting me...

He wasn't sure if he pleaded out loud or not. *Hunter* looked up, and Number Four had walked away from him. He quickly looked up and down the elevated station. The platforms were still empty. The gun had never been fired, so he didn't have to flee quickly. He recovered, now that he knew the crisis was over. *Hunter* had never been a fighter. He knew that. But he *was* back in charge now; quickly regaining the nerve he'd lost just a short time ago. He calmly got up and brushed off his pants. He walked over to get the pistol that was lying on the edge of the platform. He picked up the .38 caliber revolver and approached carefully this time, not preoccupied like he'd been the last two minutes before he was attacked. He was focused like he'd originally planned, with his gun-arm extended. Number Four had his back to the killer. He turned around while mumbling to himself about where he put his sandwich prior to the brief altercation. He looked up and met *Hunter's* eyes. The killer walked two more steps, came within two feet and shot Number Four at point blank range, one inch below the right eye.

Chapter Six

Tony Malaro, Ten years ago
May 23rd 1996
Halsey Street on the 'J' line

Many commuters tried to hold the closing train doors so friends wouldn't miss the train. Others held doors until the last minute in order to snatch a chain off a woman's neck, just as the doors were closing. Often, before victims even realized it, their chain or purse was gone, the doors were closed, and the train would already be halfway out of the station. Most victims wouldn't even report the crime. What would be the point? Some victims wouldn't even be able to tell police the station where the crime occurred, never mind a description of who did it. It happened that fast. But sometimes there were cops on the train. And those cops would mix in with other passengers and go relatively unnoticed. Two cops in that category were Tony Malaro and John Pulaski. They blended.

Tony hadn't always been painted a screw-up by Sergeant Quinn or any of the other bosses on the job. Early in his career, he was the hottest cop to hit the rails in the Transit Police Department. Most cops would say there was a lot of luck involved in making good collars. In general that was true, but Tony had a special knack for being at the right place at the right time. Some Anti-crime cops weren't even recognizable to other officers, and Tony was one of those. Sometimes he was a drunk, reeking of alcohol, bloodshot eyes and twenty dollar bills hanging out of his pockets. Other times, he'd dress as a conductor, Wall-Streeter or other anonymous sap. Nobody ever *made* him. Today he was reading a Newsday in his best construction outfit, complete with bucket of tools and lunch pail. His partner, John Pulaski, was good too, but getting burned out after just a few years on the road and a couple of failed marriages. Police Officer John Pulaski was one of the better cops, and Malaro chose him out of a dozen others in the command to be his partner. He had long, mangy blonde hair, a wrinkled shirt and worn-out jeans. He was not what an outsider would consider a "veteran," but the Transit Police Department was different. Cops like Pulaski learned quickly from the sheer volume of people encountered on a daily basis. Pulaski liked his beers a little too much, but Tony chose him over others because he was fun to work with and had a good eye for bad guys. But the edge that he'd once had was becoming increasingly duller. John not only played the part of a reeking alcoholic as a decoy cop, more often than not he had a real buzz on.

Tony and John were both seated in the second-to-last train car waiting for a chain snatch or some other ill-conceived notion. They were in the car by themselves, sitting opposite each other, so they could get a little closer and carry on a conversation when they had the chance. Their cover would not be compromised if no one saw them talking. Pulaski was laughing. The train was rocking back and forth as it slowed down for the next stop.

"Did you see that *schmuck*, Schoenstein?" Pulaski asked.

"No," Tony answered, knowing where this was going. "What was he wearing today?"

Pulaski continued.

"A butcher's outfit."

"A *what?*" Tony asked incredulously.

"A butcher's outfit. I swear that crazy Jew is squirrelly. And you guys are worried about us Pollocks? No one had the heart to tell him that *most* butchers wouldn't actually wear a bloody apron to board a train to go home."

"What would be the point of telling him?" Tony asked.

Pulaski responded angrily.

"He's a fuckin' embarrassment, that's what!"

Tony shot back, "He had more collars than you last month!"

"Fuck-o..."

Pulaski didn't finish his sentence.

The train had pulled up at the elevated station and the doors opened. Another passenger boarded the car. They went back to not knowing each other.

Tony gave a quick glance from his newspaper as the doors closed. He knew that the Halsey Street 'J' was a hot station. His partner got up and walked down another car. The conductor then opened the doors four inches, closed them, opened them four inches and closed them again. Somebody was holding the doors while the conductor tried to close up the train and pull out. Tony jumped up, put his foot in the door and waved to the conductor. The doors opened fully. Tony looked down the platform and back to the front. There was a young Hispanic kid in blue jeans and Reebok high tops with a gun in his hand, in an all-out bolt towards the mezzanine stairs. He was already near the doors to the street area and about three cars from Malaro. Tony ran out the door and gave chase. Pulaski jumped out and followed. "High Tops" ran down the stairs to the mezzanine area, leapt over the turnstiles and down to the street. He was gone.

Tony had been on the job for nine years now. He wasn't about to leap over anything. He didn't even look over the rail. No. It was better to let High Tops think that he'd made it without any problem. He'd stop running, drop his pants and throw them away, sporting another color on the bottom that he'd had under the first pair if he thought anybody had noticed him. Tony knew that occasionally a perpetrator would double back to the underground 'L' train that ran parallel to the 'J' line in some spots of Brooklyn. He took the robbery complaint from the victim, a black man, 42 years old. The victim reported that High Tops took his wallet and $40.00 dollars in cash at gunpoint. Tony completed his report quickly and called operations for a complaint number, which was required for all criminal incidents. Malaro and Pulaski then grabbed a ride from a street cop.

They drove straight down Halsey Street and were dropped off at the underground station of Halsey on the 'L' line. It was just four blocks away from where the crime had occurred. Malaro went down into the subway by himself, flashed his badge to the clerk, and stopped an outgoing 'L' train. He instructed the conductor to keep the doors closed as he keyed his way onto the train and walked slowly through the cars. High Tops was in the second car.

He approached High Tops, flashed his badge, speed cuffed him, recovered the wallet, cash and a .22 automatic, all felonies. Pulaski was upstairs in a *bodega* getting a six-pack while Tony "did his thing" underground and made the collar alone. They weren't supposed to separate, but sometimes John slowed Tony down, so Tony didn't mind. He liked John, and he'd been with him for a couple of years.

Most of Tony's career was just like the arrest at Halsey Street; a cake-walk. He never got hurt. He always knew what to do on a job or incident. He didn't last long in Anti-crime and was scooped up by Major Case Detective Squad in the Transit Police Department. His last big collar prior to being made detective was a string of robberies that had perplexed the Major Case Squad.

It appeared that the descriptions of the two perpetrators were mixed up by some of the witnesses, as noted in the investigation by Major Case detectives. Tony was asked to do a minor follow-up of the file. The other detectives had hit a wall in the investigation and they were beginning to catch some heat. Tony actually *read* all the witness statements which made him realize that the "mysterious" mopes and conflicting descriptions narrowed down possible suspects to the Hartnett brothers. Some would say that it was the foot work and doggedness of the Major Case squad which eventually led detectives to an arrest, which in turn, quietly propelled Tony into the unit. Tony would laugh and tell you how it was his identification of the brothers who had committed the crime spree. They were red-headed, albino, African-American twins. That helped narrow down the search, particularly because they had a lengthy record and they were the only such pair in the entire borough. They weren't hard to find. That case and a number of other record-breaking robbery and larceny collars in one year resulted in Tony getting into the Detective Division. Tony's whole career had been stellar until one incident put him back to uniform patrol duty and almost out of a job.

Chapter Seven

February 23, 2006.
NYPD Major Case Squad
370 Jay Street, Brooklyn, NY

Two days after Number Four was found with a bullet in his head at 80th Street, Detective Sergeant Michael O'Shea was reviewing the current report that Jones and Feuss had turned in about the crime scene and the investigation. The three detectives were sitting in the Major Case office on Jay Street in downtown Brooklyn. The detective squad was housed in a large room on the 6th floor with over a dozen twenty-five square foot cubicles. The little boxes were large enough for a chair, desk, file cabinet and a member of the squad. The partitions were just low enough for officers to stand and look over. Of the more than a dozen cubicles, only six were occupied at the time.

Sergeant O'Shea was sitting at Jonesy's desk while Feuss and Jonesy pulled two other chairs from nearby desks to have a meeting with their supervisor.

O'Shea was incensed.

"Can you tell me who moved the body before Greenfield and his CSU team got there?"

There was a long pause. The Sergeant's red face, barrel chest and crew cut made him look more menacing than he actually was. Jonesy shrugged his shoulders.

"Quinn wanted to ID the guy because the trains were backed up." Jones answered.

"Hey, Jonesy, what do we give a fuck about trains?"

He gave no time for a reply. The Sergeant continued.

"Who is in charge at a homicide, Jonesy?"

Jones replied mournfully.

"I am, boss."

"Not just you, Jonesy." Mike reprimanded. "We're the ones who are responsible to secure the scene, take pictures and do our shit. Right?"

Mike was not really trolling for an answer.

"Now if this gets fucked up, and oh, by the way Jonesy...it already is. I'll hear about how *we* screwed it up."

The rebuke was over now. O'Shea wasn't considered to be a prick by the men. He didn't have a reputation like most of the Irish police bosses historically had in the department. He was just fair. If one of his detectives fouled up, they heard about it. If they did a good job, they heard about that too. Regardless, Mike O'Shea always treated everyone with respect and nobody walked away from him irritated that they had been reprimanded. One thing was always clear with Mike, though...too many mistakes would not go unnoticed.

He was proud of his unit and the clearance rate. He did things the right way and his expectations for his people were high. He liked his beer when he was off, but he never drank on duty. He looked hung-over about ten times a year, but he was always sharp and never out sick. Everybody liked him, even the bosses. He was one of the few who knew how to play the game. He'd "yes" the bosses to death and straighten out cops who needed it. He wouldn't throw up his arms and give up and do nothing. It was a tough balancing act; not getting too involved with the job, to the point where it ate people up, but not bailing out completely. He'd been married for thirteen years and had two little girls at home.

"Now do me a favor, Jonesy...,"

He never barked orders.

"...try and ID the *skell* and make a notification before the midnight crew comes on. You know how that goes if we pass the ball. I'd rather clear up our own crap before we go home..."

Sergeant O'Shea continued.

"Have Feuss contact Troncoso about that other DOA from last week, the knocked up broad who rode the train for nine hours. Troncoso caught that case and processed the scene. See if anything turns up, compare notes, and cross check cases. You know the deal. It doesn't look like they would be connected, but ya' never know. But I don't believe in coincidences either."

Mike stood from behind the desk and walked by the two detectives. He wanted to make one more pointed comment.

"Two homicides in the same district in a week? That's bullshit."

"Okay, Sarge." Jonesy said.

Jonesy felt bad, but not that bad. After all it was Quinn who let him sleep in the back of the District for four hours at a clip sometimes when he had overtime, not O'Shea. But O'Shea didn't know about that.

O'Shea left the squad at Jay Street, drove forty-five minutes, and tracked down Sergeant Quinn out at District 23 in the Rockaways. He parked out front and walked through the station. The booth clerk recognized him, as he'd passed here about ten times a week for years, but the clerk made him show his ID anyway.

"Asshole," O'Shea muttered with a smile on his face as the clerk buzzed the locked gate open. He went past the turnstile area and onto the open-air, ground level island platform. To the left of the platform was the main entrance of the NYPD Transit Bureau, District 23. He tried the doors. They were locked. He looked at his watch. It was 12:30 AM and the first shift had turned out about an hour ago. Not many police stations in New York City would have had the front doors locked. District 23 was one of those that did. Quiet. The motto was "squash everything." O'Shea looked around.

Most all the NYPD Transit District stations were located within the confines of the subway system and adjacent to the track area near the end of a platform. The districts were part of the NYPD, and the officers were NYPD cops, but the patrol posts were strictly on train lines and bus routes. Many of the district stations were located underground. The Rockaway District, however, was located above ground at Rockaway Park at 116th Street.

The inside of most of the Transit commands was similar. They were dirty, gray, custodial looking areas with no windows; hardly noticeable by passersby. There was usually a small sign, no bigger than a paper plate, with the NYPD emblem on it, by the front door. Desk Officers and Commanders in Transit didn't want too many people wandering in off the trains to make a complaint. That would keep the complaint numbers way up. The commands were not exactly lit up for the public to notice ...they were subtle, and rather anonymous. Most people wouldn't know that the unexceptional looking structures or doors at the end of a platform were the entryway to a 24-hour police station, not unless someone told them.

Prior to traveling from Brooklyn to the Rockaways, O'Shea had looked at the computer roll call and knew that Lt. Harvey was on the Desk at District 23. All Districts and Precincts had the obligatory Desk Officer (DO), usually a Sergeant or Lieutenant, running the show for a nine-hour period assisted by an Assistant Desk Officer (ADO). Police stations in New York weren't like the busy places seen on television. Sometimes, Desk Officers could go the whole shift without an officer bringing in a collar or any other complaint at all. However, it wasn't always like that either. Occasionally, all hell could break loose, and there'd be twenty perpetrators in cuffs lined up outside the door. Desk Officers were responsible for the safety of all; the officers, victims, and perpetrators who entered the station house. The good Desk Officers ran a tight ship and barked orders when needed. Police Officers and most suspects didn't dare back talk.

Next to the Desk Officer, in most commands, were two cells. One cell was for male prisoners and the other for female prisoners or juveniles. In the back of the command was a muster room where supervisors conducted roll calls for each shift. Beyond the muster room were the cop's lockers. The Supervisors locker room was usually behind that in the back of the command.

Most cops who transferred out to District 23 in the Rockaways, went there as a warm-up for retirement. Their goal was to finish up their last couple of years without getting jammed up in heavy capers. District 23 didn't have heavy capers. Once every couple of years something considerable would go down, like a homicide or string of robberies, but that wasn't the normal routine on the peninsula.

Sergeant O'Shea banged on the doors of the command. After a minute, a police officer came to the door, shaking his head at being interrupted from finishing his "Newsday" late edition paper. He let the Sergeant in and locked the doors behind him. O'Shea signed in the big red log at the desk. Lt. Harvey was sitting down with his feet on the desk when Mike signed in. Harvey had been pretty good sometime in the past, but he was also here to finish out his last year without any problems. Or so he thought.

"Where the fuck is Quinn?" Mike barked as he signed his name. There was no time for pleasantries here; Mike was on a mission.

"Hey, O'Shea, I'm still a boss here, how 'bout a little respect?" The Lieutenant demanded.

"Okay, Lieu," replied O'Shea, trying a different tack with an Irish brogue and a small smile,

"Ah, and a pleasant good evening, Lieutenant Harvey. Is it possible you've stumbled about that ARSEHOLE SERGEANT QUINN?"

Harvey broke out laughing.
"That's more like it. How are ya' Mike? He's in the back."
O'Shea started walking back to the Supervisor's locker room.

Lt. Harvey called after him.

"How're those *Guineas* treatin' you up at Major Case?"

O'Shea laughed and kept on walking.

Lt. Harvey was mocking now in his best Irish sing-song voice,

"Now try not to ruffle any feathers back there Be-Jesus, I know what you might be discussin'. He was just trying to get those trains a runnin' now!"

Everybody in the police department knew everyone else's business. There were rarely any secrets. Cops were worse than old ladies.

O'Shea continued past the desk. Lt. Harvey and Mike had been uniformed cops together, shared in some heavy jobs and collars and hung out a few times. Mike would stop by and talk with his old friend on the way out.

The big grin slowly receding, O'Shea passed the clerical room toward the supervisor's locker area. The bosses had a twelve-foot room with about three feet of space between two rows of old, Navy-looking battleship gray lockers. Just prior to most shifts, no more than two bosses at a time were usually in the locker room. The District Lieutenants, Sergeants and Captain all changed from their civilian clothes into their uniforms there. One eight-foot bench stretched between the lockers for all to use. O'Shea walked in and put one foot up on the bench while Quinn was changing from his uniform into his street clothes. Quinn was about to go home, but it was already over an hour after his shift ended. He was in no hurry. There was no one to go home to. Quinn had his off-duty Smith & Wesson, .38 caliber, two-inch revolver in a shoulder holster, and a back-up weapon on his ankle. Most cops carried backup guns on duty... but not off. Quinn was a little quirky. He was buttoning up his white shirt and standing in his boxer shorts with his shoes and socks still on.

"Hey Billy, what was with 80th Street and Hudson?" Mike asked.

Quinn answered testily.

"Whadddya' mean?"

O'Shea replied with a direct question and raised eyebrows.

"Well, it was an obvious homicide, why didn't you secure the scene and take care of business like you're supposed to?"

Quinn looked up as he pulled up his pants. Quinn had what other cops called a "thermometer face." Perps and cops who liked to get a rise out of him knew they were on the right track when his face turned red. It was getting red now.

"Look, O'Shea, I know the drill. Don't get all pissy on my ass. You're not in no elite unit. You're starting to sound like your buddy Malaro, a fuckin' know-it-all..."

He paused, trying to regain his composure while explaining this away like it was no big deal, then continued.

"Jonesy and that red-headed moron took their sweet-assed time wrappin' that shit bag up."

O'Shea shot back an answer, but backed off a bit, using a *'we're all on the same side'* voice.

"Billy, you *know* what to do, you've been here long enough. Don't give me any shit about those two fuckin' it up either. I checked with the Operations Unit. That call went through for the crime scene unit before they even got there. You didn't wait!"

Quinn was a little defensive now and beginning to glow.

"Yeah, I didn't wait. So what? And yeah, I have been doing this a long time."

There was a short pause while he shook his head.

"Mike, how many times have we moved trains so we could process a crime scene at the train yards?" Quinn waited for an answer.

Mike shrugged his shoulders.

Quinn continued.

"What police department does that? We've done that in the past plenty of times, and you know it. There was nothing on the tracks. The mope was on the platform. We wrapped it up and only one train was cancelled. Everyone gets what they want. End of story. You're not the one who has to hear it from the Duty Captain, not to mention the Trainmaster about late trains."

It was O'Shea's turn now, the anger quickly returning.

"Billy, I'll tell you what I just had to tell Jonesy... Since when do we give a fuck about trains on a homicide? The *Trainmaster*? Give me break!"

Quinn didn't like this exchange and was going to finish it.

"Mike, you know how it goes around here and if you don't... grow up! This is not a high profile case. He was a nobody, a *skell*. And since you never were a patrol sergeant for that long, I'll spell it out for you, we *do* keep the trains moving. That's been the gig since I've been here. We were a separate department for a reason, *Transit Police*... Remember? As far as the *skell* goes, I got news for *you*...who gives a fuck? If you ask me, that's one less dirt bag to be cleaned up by the Bus Squad."

Mike knew there was no use keeping up this conversation. Billy was right in his own way.

Nobody gave a shit, unless the train was late or the mope was a white "somebody."

O'Shea gave a last ditch effort for future reference.

"Billy, just wait for the pictures next time, okay? That crime scene was all over the place and there might have been some stuff on the tracks. The trains came through and blew everything all over. We haven't got it all figured out yet, but the shot came from the same platform, up close."

He paused.

"It's Jonesy's call anyway. He was the ranking Detective on the scene"

Quinn looked up puzzled. The argument was over.

"Well he didn't object much. Not at all in fact...What made you think the shot was so close anyway?"

O'Shea explained.

"First glance looks close range. The preliminary pictures show burns from a close range discharge. If he dropped where he was hit, which it looks like he did, thirty feet from the other platform is too far for a pistol or rifle shot. It also looks more like there was a little scuffle with the bad guy and that would put him on the same platform. We're doing prints on the closed end. The clerk didn't see anyone going out her way."

"You don't think it was a random thing? Like he pissed someone off or something?" Billy asked.

Mike replied.

"I don't know what to think yet. I think it was planned. The shooter just disappeared afterwards. He didn't board another train and he never passed the clerk downstairs to exit the station...and that points to thinking ahead. I gotta' feeling this one won't be the last."

Chapter Eight

March 1st, 2006
District 23
Far Rockaway, Queens

O'Shea was required to report any ongoing investigations weekly to the District Captain. The Captain was a real buff, but with no real experience. He'd spent most of his career as an inside-the-precinct administrative police officer, usually known as a "house mouse." Captain Alan Reitman had been a house mouse his whole career and everybody knew it. He wasn't a bad guy, just out of touch and always listening to other cop's stories with eager enthusiasm. Sometimes he'd add to the conversation, a bit of his own prior experiences, most of which were imagined or originally attributed to somebody else's good collar but became, along the years, his own story. Mostly, no one would know it wasn't him he was describing in the spectacular collar he had made "some 20 years ago." Occasionally, an old-timer would remember the incident from way back when, and share with everyone, other than the Captain of course, that the Captain was, in fact, full of shit.

But he was one of the more harmless supervisors. He was no different than most of the Transit Police bosses; he was no exception. He rarely addressed the officers at all and was content to hide in his office all day. His idea of keeping a tight ship was to create memos. Sometimes he'd develop ten policies a month and send out a memo for each one. Nobody ever followed them or enforced them. There were too many to take seriously. It was a district joke.

Many times his posted memos in the muster room were adorned with additional hand-written comments, or trinkets put there from cops within the command. The trinkets would somehow be related to the memo. The current memo addressed members wearing unauthorized socks. The official policy was that cops were supposed to wear dark socks when in uniform. The hand written response that some anonymous officer had written on this official memo read "fuck-off." There was also a Boston Red Sox pin attached to the memo. It was a new memo, so there were just a few things attached to it by the rebel officers. By the end of the week, it would be covered with sarcastic remarks and items related to socks. When a memo had come out last month about cops not wearing hats while on patrol, there were a bunch of novelty hats on the board surrounding the memo. One of the hats read "Honk if You like Tits"... and so on. Cop humor.

O'Shea reluctantly went to meet with the Captain to give him a run down on the latest two homicides. O'Shea pushed the door open, stuck his head in the door and saw Captain Reitman cleaning his nails while seated at his desk.

"Now a good time, Captain?" O'Shea asked.

"Yes, yes, Mike. Come in."

High profile cases solved quickly made Captains look good. But in general, Transit bosses didn't like serious things happening in their district. It made them look bad. Not only that, the new Chief of Patrol had insisted on reviving the weekly administrative meetings called COMSTAT. (Computer Statistics) At these meetings, all of the Transit District and NYPD precinct Captains were required to meet with chiefs of the department to review "activity" in the commands. Activity typically meant summonses. That's what cops were supposed to do, write summonses. As the Captain often put it, if the district or precinct wasn't measuring up, a "thorough ass-chewing" would be delivered to the respective Captain.

Captain Reitman began by complaining to O'Shea about his last COMSTAT meeting. He was a thin man with a pencil mustache, equally thin lips and a very large bald spot.

"Ya' know, Mike, some of the news people are critical of 'quotas' or activity or whatever euphemism the papers want to call it, but the reality is, if you're a cop in New York City and work an eight or nine hour shift...you're full of shit if you say you didn't observe violations on a daily basis. It would be like a Department of Sanitation crew coming back from a full day's work, reporting they didn't see any garbage on their route that day."

Mike didn't answer. He knew from experience that it was best to nod and be polite rather than get into any conversation with the Captain, even if he sometimes made sense.

"Nevertheless..."

The Captain looked up for a response. There was none. He continued.

"...as you know, activity also looks at the number of felonies or misdemeanors happening in my area. Those are the items to be kept down and if there's some serious shit that would hit the papers, like now, heads will roll if we don't deal with it swiftly."

The Captain knew all this to be true and he needed to cover his ass and have somebody handle this mess quickly. The last thing he wanted was attention drawn towards him or his command at any meeting. He was extremely agitated that his district had to "eat one" because the first victim had been riding on the train for over nine hours. More than likely, the crime could have happened in almost any of the districts along the 'A' line. He didn't appear concerned about the homicide at 80th Street being connected to the ice-picked girl, even though 80th Street was clearly within his command boundaries. The Captain continued.

"What's going on with this anyway, and what happened with Quinn earlier Mike?...Ya' know I do get wind of some things back here..." he said with a slight chuckle.

O' Shea didn't mind the Captain too much. Reitman had been in District 23 for over twenty-five years and anyone who lasts that long without being divorced, alcoholic, or dead, can't be half bad, or so he thought. The Captain had always admired Mike O'Shea for the good cop that he was. He looked after him and had been reasonable with Mike's requests in the past. Mike knew the Captain had always wanted to be a great detective, but he also knew Reitman never really put in the time to become one, and was referred to frequently as being somewhat of a wimp. He certainly had shied away from ugly crime scenes in the past, but the Captain had never treated O'Shea poorly.

"Well, I gave Quinn a little shit for moving the train at 80th Street," O'Shea began.

The Captain looked puzzled.

"Why?"

"Captain," Mike reasoned, "I realize we need to keep trains moving, but we got to do our thing. We would've wrapped things up quickly. It was uncalled for ...everything was all over the place down there..."

The Captain interrupted.

"Look, Mike, clear this case and let's not drag it out. I heard talk about connecting these two dead *skells* and I'm not interested. We're not going to eat two homicides in this district, in one year, never mind in one week."

O'Shea exercised restraint. After all, Reitman was a Captain and he'd displayed that he had balls on a couple of occasions.

"Okay, Captain, but I think you should know we're looking into missing items from both bodies."

The Captain jumped up from behind his desk, brushed past O'Shea quickly and quietly closed the door.

"Sit down, Mike."

He sat down and the Captain returned to his desk.

"Listen ..."

The Captain sounded concerned and lowered his voice.

"I've been doing this a long time. These are not the kind of cases we make huge deals over. You know were gonna' get lucky in a few weeks, catch a break, or something will come our way and boom...you'll know what happened and make a good collar. But if you start with this 'missing things' shit, we'll have newspaper people down here, NYPD homicide and those Chief of Patrol pricks all over our asses. And as you know, they'll send shoo flies, Internal Affairs, and duty Captains, making sure we're all doing our part to make passengers safe out here... It just wouldn't be a good thing for any of us. Let's wait and see what your investigation turns up"

Mike just stared out the window for a few moments. Captain Reitman looked down and started cleaning his nails again. The Captain had made his point, cold and callous, but a point none-the-less. Years ago he would have argued with him, but Mike was becoming a consummate Irish politician as the years passed.

Better to grease him over and do what I gotta' do anyway.

Maybe he'd get more information first.

"I see what you're getting at Captain," Mike finally answered.

"Good," the Captain continued, "And Mike, let me know when you've got anything. I'd like to be kept posted on this. Let's catch this motherfucker."

O'Shea stood up. The Captain rarely used profanity. He sounded silly when he did, but Mike knew that, deep down, he just wanted to be one of the guys. As the Sergeant walked out and shut the door, he was shaking his head, smiling to himself.

Two skells *not connected my ass!*

Chapter Nine

Eleven years ago
April 1, 1995
Bushwick and Aberdeen on the 'L'

Kevin McCaffrey had now been on the job a few months short of a year. It was the evening before the big merge between the NYPD and the Transit Police Department. City officials had been working on this for years and it was about to finally take place. Kevin had been rewarded for his felony and misdemeanor collars by being accepted into the Anti-Crime/plainclothes unit three weeks ago. He was doing well and on a fast track. Not many officers made it into plainclothes so quickly, but the arrest numbers he'd achieved in the short period of time he'd been in uniform were staggering. While working Anti-crime, Kevin thrived even more .

An influential Inspector named McHale took notice and used Kevin occasionally on uniformed overtime assignments to secure crime scenes for incidents with a lot of people traffic. The department didn't want anyone wandering in and contaminating a crime scene. The Inspector also wanted Kevin to be exposed to some solid Detectives within the department. That's how Kevin met Tony Malaro.

Kevin watched Tony whenever he worked, and he ran into Tony at a number of crime scenes. He would pick Tony's brain anytime he could. He asked Tony a lot of questions about processing scenes and what should be done first and last. He learned plenty and enjoyed working with Tony. Kevin knew he'd go the Detective Bureau route. He also knew if he was paired with a guy like Tony, he'd be one of the best after a period of time.

Tonight, Kevin was back in uniform to perform a four-hour overtime shift for extra money. He had just left roll call and was traveling alone on the 'L' line on his way to Myrtle Avenue. It was 8:00 o'clock at night, and he was just rolling into the Bushwick-Aberdeen station. Kevin hated the station. It gave him the creeps. There was a graveyard directly across the outside platform and the station always appeared abandoned.

The doors opened and he peered out, like all cops did at stations, and what he saw was a blur, and totally unexpected. The train had pulled right into the middle of a gang fight involving about twenty kids. Some of the teenagers had bats and sticks. Others had chains. He didn't see any guns. Usually in Brooklyn, if a gun was involved there wouldn't be twenty people hanging around to see who got shot.

He stepped off the train, grabbed his radio, and called his first '10-13,' *an officer needs assistance*, emergency signal. Nobody involved in the brawl noticed him. Kevin stepped off dead smack in the middle of it and no one saw who, or recognized what he was. He came upon a Hispanic with a black "doo-rag" who was beating another Hispanic kid with a bat. The one being beaten was on the ground and his white Yankee T-shirt was covered with blood. Kevin pulled out his gun and ordered *Doo-Rag* to put the bat down. *Doo-Rag* stopped, looked over his shoulder and saw the gun. He lowered his arm and was about to drop the bat when Kevin felt the hair tingle on the back of his neck.

Kevin quickly turned and saw a tall black kid wearing a big kitchen clock around his neck. He was about to come down on Kevin's head with a two-by-four. *Two-By-Four* was on a mission. Kevin already had his gun in his hand, so he turned and shot him in the left shoulder. The boy dropped like a slab of granite. Kevin froze; he'd never shot anyone before. He was in shock for about three seconds, then remembered the one with the bat.

Doo-Rag!

MAN UNDER

As Kevin turned back to look, he put his left hand up, just in time to deflect the bat blow that crashed down and cracked his left elbow, breaking something. Kevin still had his gun in his right hand. He was on automatic pilot now, and some good training from the weapons unit up in Rodman's Neck kicked in. As he was getting hit with the bat, he pointed the gun at *Doo-Rag* and let another two rounds go, one into *Doo-Rag's* chest and the other grazing his shoulder. *Doo-Rag* went down too. Kevin shook his head to shake off the dizziness; the beginning stages of shock.

They knew I was a cop. I had the hat on with the shiny shield on top and the badge on my chest. It's a well-lit area. They must've got caught up in the brawl. What the fuck are they thinkin'?

The gravity of his actions in the last twenty seconds would not come to him for hours. After *Doo-Rag* hit the ground, most of the remaining brawlers took notice of the multiple gunshots and ran. Some darted into the graveyard across the platform, others to the end of the platform, onto the tracks, scattering in different directions.

Two gang members remained. Recessed in the middle of the outdoor platform was the token booth area. There were no stairs there. The booth was on the same level as the northbound platform and the street. The last two were caught up in their own activity and hadn't heard the shots from the platform area. Kevin staggered up the platform headed towards the booth. He came around the corner unnoticed and saw the two thugs. The bigger one had on a white muscle tee-shirt, tattoos on both arms, and appeared to be Hispanic. The shorter one had a turned-to-the-side white baseball cap and was more middle-eastern looking. Kevin immediately thought of *Of Mice and Men*, Lenny and George. They were accosting a middle-aged black woman passerby. She was an aide at a nearby nursing home, on her way home from work.

The two teen-age gangsters were unaware of the carnage that had just taken place on the platform, or the two bodies that still lay there writhing. *Lenny and George* had other plans when the fight began. They were attempting to pry open the turnstiles to steal tokens when this lady stumbled upon them. They both had knives and already had cut the pocketbook off her shoulder and were holding her face up against the wall. Each had one of her arms pinned. The shorter one held a knife to her neck and the taller of the two held it to the middle of her back. The taller one was tearing a slit with the knife down her pants, following the crease of her buttocks, when Kevin came around the corner. They weren't going to rape her, they didn't have time, but the big one wanted to have some fun and it was later found out that, in prior robberies, he'd usually carved his initials in the victim's buttocks. He wouldn't have that opportunity this time.

Kevin was exhausted and barely conscious. He walked as if his shoes were filled with concrete. He stumbled along the platform, rounding the corner towards the booth and the ongoing criminal activity, seemingly without purpose. He was about to pass out from the pain and trauma of the past few minutes. Kevin was confused at what he then observed.

This should be over!

He continued to walk towards the figures by the booth. He was not fully aware of the situation now occurring just a few yards in front of him. As he approached slowly, his gun already reloaded, he pointed it at the three near the wall. When he was closer, he pointed the gun at the tall one who had the knife at the lady's butt. He could hear her whimpering as the shorter mutt giggled and whispered something nasty in her ear. Kevin was mentally and physically spent. His left arm was throbbing. Shock was closing in on him from the injury to his arm and the totality of the events of the last five minutes. Kevin ordered the tall one to drop the knife. It was more like a raspy whisper. He hadn't noticed his mouth had gone dry. He almost gagged when the words first came out. After a small struggle to swallow, Kevin called again a little louder.

"DROP IT!

The tall one looked over, saw Kevin, and was startled. He was a two-time loser named Jesus. Jesus knew if he was caught in the commission of a felony, the consequence would be that of a three-time convicted felon: twenty years to life. As Jesus was thinking this, the sirens were on top of the station, one of the few stations where the exit was level with the street. The little one dropped his knife and stood with his hands up. His name was Robert and he wasn't going to fight. He knew he'd be out by tomorrow, two days tops.

Jesus was quickly assessing his options, running for the booth area out to the street where he knew over a dozen cops were pulling up, or sprint past this, what appeared to be, walking dead man. He was deciding to take his chances. The cop wouldn't shoot if he dropped the knife, and he didn't appear to be in good shape to fight. During this instant, Kevin was walking closer. He didn't want to hit the civilian. He didn't want to take a center mass, deadly shot either. For all he knew he'd already killed two people in the last few minutes. Kevin spoke.

"I'm tired. I don't think I can kill one more person tonight."

He aimed from three feet away and shot the hesitant, three-time loser in the right thigh. Jesus dropped the knife and collapsed on the ground, clutching his leg in agony. The *Cavalry* arrived, and Kevin slumped against the wall as a handful of cops came to help him, while four others put a beating on the two that had assaulted the woman. The responding police officers thought the two gangsters by the booth were the ones who had inflicted the injuries on Kevin. If they had an open chance, cops threw beatings to anyone who injured another cop. This was Brooklyn. The cuffs weren't on yet and the fight wasn't over. Robert was cuffed after half dozen punches had landed. He didn't fight back. He was smart. Kevin's eyes closed as he watched four other cops give a terrific beating to Jesus, who shouldn't have put up a fight when they arrived, but couldn't help himself because he was so angry for not taking off in time.

Chapter Ten

March 4th, 2006.
111th Street and Liberty Avenue on the 'A'
Queens, NY

"*Man under...*111th Street on the 'A'...any unit to respond?"

The voice squawked from Central Command over the radio. "23-04, come in 23-04."

There was no reply.

"Any unit to respond to a *man under* as per train dispatch, we need a unit to respond..."

"23-Adam to Central...we are responding to 111th Street, ETA approximately seven minutes."

23-Adam was one of the two Suburban trucks District 23 had to cover the entire Rockaway area, including Lefferts Blvd. on the 'A' line, up to 111th Street, where Queens meets Brooklyn. Vincent Venera was driving. He was a Major Case Squad Detective and usually worked all the boroughs, but had been weaseling into some uniform overtime in districts for years. District 23 was closer to where he lived in Ozone Park. A few of the uniformed officers were jealous of him because he dressed like a pimp, talked junk to everybody and made more collars then anyone cared to admit. He was good and he knew it. He was also what some cops considered a "fat-mouthed guinea bastard." But most of the cops loved him because he said whatever he wanted, no matter who was around.

Vinnie had been a police officer for twelve years and was one of the few who had actually made headline collars to get into the Major Case Squad as a detective. He would go no further than his present rank. He was known throughout the department not to "bullshit" much, either. He could back up whatever came out of his mouth. And he was funny. At 5'9," and well over two hundred pounds, he was a menacing enough looking character, but he also took care of business and had a lot of *street* in him. He got the overtime because bosses loved him and he played the game. He kissed their butts and made great collars.

He had no business being in the car, though. He wasn't a great driver and his reputation with a pistol was larger than he was, and not too flattering. He also should have been serving his overtime on a foot post. Vinnie got away with everything. Riding along side him was Stephen Kopf. Stephen was scared to death to be riding with Venera. He had eight years on the job and gave his required fifteen summonses a month to remain anonymous on the midnight shift. He had not made any arrests in over seven years, and had a total of about nine for his career, all of which were misdemeanors. Not an easy feat for a cop in New York City.

The two uniformed officers were traveling at high speed on Cross Bay Blvd., heading towards 111th Street. Stephen had replied to the Operations Unit that they'd arrive at the station in seven minutes. They were there in three. The officers parked their car and walked up the elevated station to the booth area. The booth clerk was on the phone and pointed to the southbound platform. Vinnie asked her if she'd seen anyone pass. She cupped the phone and told him 'no'. At the top of the stairs they met the conductor and the motorman, who were both obviously shaken. There was no sign of Malaro anywhere, and this was his assigned post. He hadn't responded to the radio earlier.

Tony showed up on the next train on the opposite platform. He went down to the booth area and met Venera and Kopf on their way up the northbound platform stairs. When they got to the top they noticed that the train was more than halfway pulled out of the station. They were on their way to view the dead body at the back of the train.

"Where *you* been you old *geep*?" Venera asked.

"On my meal at the Grant room lockers, fuckhead, where you been? White Castle? Ya' fat bastard." Malaro answered his own question.

Venera laughed and Malaro smiled.

"What's going on?" Tony asked.

Venera filled him in on the radio call from Operations as they walked down the platform with the motorman.

"Man under, I guess."

Kopf got busy separating and attempting to get statements from two people who had been in the last car when the incident happened. He always jumped on something mundane at heavy scenes. He didn't want to get his hands dirty...or his clothes, either, for that matter. Both witnesses were Ecuadorian men, coming back from a late shift somewhere in Manhattan, and didn't speak English. Venera and Tony took a quick look in the last car while Kopf was trying to get information from the witnesses. They walked to the end of the train and glanced out the back window. There was a hunk of twisted metal and wheels ten feet to the left of the train. The body was about 30 feet from the last car on the tracks.

Venera spoke.

"Come on, let's take a look."

They walked out of the subway car back onto the platform, both grinning directly at Kopf, who was obviously getting frustrated from the lack of progress with the Ecuadorians.

"That should keep that annoying Jew busy for half an hour. Do you know he hasn't made a collar in a decade?" Vinnie stated emphatically as they walked.

"Only seven years, but who's counting?" Malaro shot back.

"And what's that got to do with him being Jewish, moron?" Malaro continued.

"Hell, I haven't made a felony collar since I unofficially retired out here myself." Tony had transferred to District 23 after he left the Detective Bureau.

Vinnie responded.

"Yeah, but I hear you're sucking up the overtime..."

He stopped in mid-sentence as he looked down at the tracks, just past the end of the train that was halfway out of the station. They were in the middle of the platform.

Venera gasped and shielded his eyes with his hand as he noticed the dead body on the tracks.

"Holy shit it cut her legs clean off. The pants even look seamed together."

He was half-kidding and half-repulsed. He never got used to this part of the job, but he was still good for a chuckle, even now.

Tony laughed and added.

"You're some great detective material. Didn't you see the mangled wheelchair up there on the tracks?"

Malaro was pointing to the twisted metal lying next to the train.

"The mope was already missing two legs before this happened."

"The jeans looked sewn together because they are; looks like she was a double amputee in a wheelchair, and apparently got caught up in the train."

Kopf had already asked for the Crime Scene Unit, an ambulance, and the Duty Captain, at Venera's direction.

"Want to see what we can see before the *real* cops get here?" Tony asked Venera.

"Sure, why not, we got some time to kill. I think I heard over the radio they were at District 20. That should give us twenty minutes."

Major Case Squad was considered by the brass to be the "best of the best." Vinnie was a member of the Squad when he wasn't doing overtime in uniform. Malaro was a former member. Some argued that

Major Case was the top of the food chain, although most cops would acknowledge that the ESU (Emergency Services Unit) NYPD and Transit ESU were the real deal. Emergency Services went to *every* major incident, repelled off bridges, climbed under trains for *man unders* to get the bodies, dead or alive, etc. Major Case came afterwards, in suits. They really didn't get their hands dirty, but some of the best, sharpest investigators were in the Major Case Squad.

The motorman told Venera that he'd seen the wheelchair lady at the end of the platform as he was pulling the train into the station. He reported he had caught only a glimpse of the victim in the wheelchair and couldn't tell if anyone else was on the platform with her. Like most of the elevated stations in Queens, 111th St had one open end mezzanine area and a closed one. At the closed end of the station, the gate was locked to the street area. Vinnie remarked to Malaro that if anyone was with the victim just prior to the train entering the station, they didn't exit out of the open end and pass the booth clerk. The motorman was a little distraught because of the fatality, and reported that he couldn't understand how the wheelchair lady was struck or how she wound up on the tracks.

Vinnie and Malaro went to the end of the platform and climbed down the back-end access stairs onto the track area, but not before confirming with the Operations Unit over the radio that electric power to the third rail had indeed been turned off. They walked back up the tracks towards the train. There were four cars in the station with the last car in the middle of the platform. The tracks were littered with garbage.

"It looks like the inside of your car down here, shit all over," Vinnie remarked,

"Hey" Tony answered. "Don't make fun of a man's ride. That car is a classic."

Tony and Venera made it to the area where the body was lying. They both exchanged comments that there were no severe injuries normally associated with a *man under*. All the limbs were intact, or rather what she'd had when she came to this station. There was a head injury above her right eye that looked like she had been hit with a bat, but that was about it. They looked around some more.

Vinnie made additional comments.

"Looks like she was dragged more than anything else...don't look like she was smacked or run over, she looks too damn good."

Tony observed the scratches and tears along the middle of the torso, across both arms and chest, like someone had drawn a straight line along the front of her body with a thick marker. There were also grease marks on her pants and the back of her shirt.

"Let's look up the tracks...by the end of the train," Tony added. "I want to get a better look at her wheelchair."

They walked slowly on the tracks, being careful not to fall. They approached the last car of the eight-car train. The trains are sizeable when observed from the ground up. There are about six feet of undercarriage that passengers don't normally see, below the platform. They are massive, impressive machines, and eight of them connected are formidable. Tony and Vinnie looked up at the rear end of the train, but the glare from the platform lights made it difficult to examine anything from the tracks. They turned their backs to the platform and the light. They were looking under the train and the platform area for evidence.

The motorman was standing on the platform. He was a short, round black man with a full beard and glasses. He was wearing the gray one piece outfit topped off with a motorman's cap. He looked like something out of a 1940's movie. He yelled from the platform down to Vinnie and Tony.

"Nobody told me anything. One of those Spanish people pulled the emergency cord."

Vinnie and Tony listened with their backs to the motorman, but continued their observations.

"Yeah...and?" Vinnie prodded.

The motorman continued.

"Like I said, the Spanish guy was frantic and tried to tell me what happened and that something was wrong in the back of the train...they kept on banging on the window and making gestures that they were the ones who pulled the cord."

The motorman explained that he barely understood the men and initially was a little anxious to get back to the Lefferts Blvd. terminal station. He couldn't move the train until he reset the cord and attempted to figure out what had happened. When he followed the witnesses out of the train onto the platform, he discovered the wheelchair on the tracks and walked back farther and saw the dead body.

Venera and Tony nodded to the motorman; the talk was temporarily over. They walked up to the chair. It was a manual standard, silver wheelchair that looked as if someone had pulled it apart with a giant pair of pliers and stretched it along the tracks. It was seven feet of twisted metal. Everything was intact, but elongated.

"Man...it looks like concertina wire all spread out like that," Venera said.

Tony got closer and put his face about twelve inches from each part of the chair and scanned it slowly from front to back. It didn't take him long to find what he was looking for. Three feet from the chair he observed a lasso-type hoop made of metal chain.

Tony addressed Venera,

"Let's go take a look at the back of the train. I want to check something out."

They both decided to hop up on the platform, rather than walk all the way back to the end of the station to take the access stairs. Malaro climbed back up near the end of the train in the middle of the station. He creased his pants with grease from the underside of the platform.

"Fuck! I just got these back from the cleaners...son of a bitch!"

Venera laughed as he moved farther down to climb up in an attempt to find an area where he wouldn't get dirty.

"Come on, I didn't know you were such a fag about your clothes, Tony...Fuck!"

Venera stopped in mid-sentence. He'd gotten the same grease six feet farther down the platform.

"These aren't even my pants, I borrowed 'em from Faisano," Venera complained.

"Serves you right, dumb-ass." Tony rebuked.

Tony stopped abruptly on the platform, looking at the back of the last car.

"Will you take a look at that *shit!*" Malaro said.

Venera tabled his chest and upper torso on the platform, swung his legs around and stood up wiping his pants and further smearing the grease.

"Look at what I did! That fat, red-headed prick is going to be..."

Tony grabbed Vinnie's arm to stop him from talking.

"Oh, man." Vinnie uttered.

Vinnie looked at the back of the train while he tried to brush off his pants.

Tony and Vinnie stood dumbfounded. Both seasoned veterans working out a probable scenario of events that led to the death of the victim on the tracks. Neither spoke for a full minute, coming to the same conclusion. There was a large "S" hook in the rear of the train with a thick chain attached.

Vinnie spoke.

"That looks like something you'd see in a warehouse, hauling crates or some heavy shit."

The thick metal links were severed at about ten feet from the top of the "S" hook; the wheels of the train had cut the chain in two.

Malaro explained to Vinnie what he'd seen: the other end of the chain on the tracks.

"It was a lasso, like in a rodeo, around the main body of the wheelchair. The chain was cut all right, but not before pulling the chair with this *skell* off the platform for half the station, about 200 feet."

Vinnie asked slowly.

"How fucked up is *that*?"

Malaro looked up and down the platform.

"This is a first for me. Our cowboy dropped a hoop over the *skell* just as the train was pulling out."

"Yee Haa" Vinnie uttered flatly.

Chapter Eleven

March 5th, 2006
Queens, NY

Hunter woke at 6:30 AM. He walked to the bedroom window in his briefs and opened the long ceiling-to-floor curtain. There were no leaves on the trees and the sky was gray. No identifiable clouds, just one giant, granite slate. There was a whiff of cold from the windowpane. He hadn't been sleeping well for a number of nights. Number Five and the wheelchair was easier than the beating he had taken two weeks ago from the homeless veteran. *Just a few more weeks and this will all be over.*

The news had thoroughly covered his escapades since Number Three, and at first he enjoyed the attention. After a while, the reports on the later victims painted the killer in a less flattering manner. This he did not enjoy. After the information leaked out that the ice pick victim was pregnant, words like *freak* and *animal* kept popping into his head. It was beginning to become unnerving. The wheelchair incident was a stroke of genius. He'd have to get back to the basics though.

His objectives were becoming increasingly more confusing in his head and he feared, after the last killing, the comments in the newspapers were now becoming true. He had to admit to himself there was a part of him that was starting to enjoy the killings. The plots to eliminate his victims were becoming more elaborate, and with that, riskier. That was the part he was beginning to take pleasure in. However, the payoff would be the biggest reward.

They didn't know me. And what about that shithead doing an interview on channel five profiling me? You don't know me!

The previous night he had been glued to the set while he watched the former FBI profiler go through *Hunter's* supposed past. The ex-profiler spit out the usual hypothesis they always put to the media...

"...between the ages of 25-39, white, lived alone and was abused as a child..."

"Okay, they got the "white" part right...not even close with anything else.

He began to think about the relationship he had had with his mother. He quickly re-directed himself to his morning routine. He put on a robe and went downstairs to have his coffee. The house was empty. He'd never married and had no children. The rare companionship he had was purchased. His grandmother had raised him, for the most part. She'd died seven years ago from lung cancer. He kept going over things in his head, both from the past and the future. *Hunter* had overheard people talk about him plenty of times. He never really did fit in. That would be different now.

There is a purpose to all this. This is a culmination of a lifetime's work. I'm not deranged. Are they trying to draw me out so I will make a mistake? No, No, that won't do. I've got to stick with the plan and then stop. I'll kill who deserves it. Do my seven. I owe it to the bitch.

Hunter finished his Raisin Bran and coffee, went back upstairs, showered and shaved, got dressed in his gray suit with a solid tie. He'd work out later. He pulled the subway map from his briefcase and laid it out on the kitchen table. He looked over the times and dates of his last two capers and tried to make sure there was no particular pattern. He watched the A&E channel all the time. When other killers did this stuff, they fell into patterns and then they got caught. That much he did know, and he was going to make a conscious effort not to fall into any discernible routine. *Hunter* was almost done.

A few more articles in the paper, maybe an article about how perplexed the police were.

He was determined not to screw it up at the last minute. He headed off to work in his car and was listening to 1010 WINS news station on the radio. There was another interview with the Police Sergeant in charge, Mike O'Shea.

Someday they'll be interviewing me on the radio.

The reporter, John Fontane, had just asked a question. O'Shea sounded confident.

"We have over twenty detectives working on this, and we are following some leads as we speak."

There was a short pause.

"This guy is a sick individual and some preliminary forensic work indicates a strong possibility that he or she is HIV positive..."

The reporter continued with another question, but *Hunter* didn't hear it. He almost drove straight into a telephone pole on Cross Bay Blvd. He was numb. A sudden lump swelled in his throat.

What was that? Where did they get that information? I'm not a queer! Goddamn them!

He quickly pulled over in front of a parking meter. *Hunter* was enraged, banging his hands on the steering wheel. The news on the radio continued about the weather in the region.

What forensic evidence? Did I bleed on the platform? Why did I hesitate? Wait a minute...AIDS? I got to get to a doctor, I bet that nigger had AIDS...I hope he didn't give it to me...what about work?

Hunter was starting to sweat. The previous newspaper articles had annoyed him, but the AIDS comments had an unnerving effect. This latest information set an unexpected panic upon him.

MAN UNDER

I know I didn't get any disease from those whores. I always used protection and I never touched them. Grandmother had been right about a lot of things including that bit of advice.

Hunter had worked himself up into a frenzy. He was feeling dizzy and like he was about to vomit. He opened the door and stuck his head out without getting out of the seat. A car horn blared as he pulled the door half shut. The blue Mazda flew by, narrowly missing his driver side door.

"*Bendejo*!" screamed the irate driver as he drove by *Hunter*.

He opened the door again and drew in some cool air and was feeling a little better. He thought there had to be some mistake and he'd get checked out as soon as he could. This was not something he could tuck away in the back of his head like he could the murders. He had to settle this quickly.

Who was that? Oh yeah, O'Shea. Detective O'Shea. Where did he get information like that? I'll have to find out.

His senses were coming back and the lump in his throat was going away. *Hunter* hated when the tantrums came. They clouded his vision. When he was upset, his emotions drove him rather than his usual, methodical, thought process and he knew he'd have to monitor that trait.

Chapter Twelve

Seven Years Ago; Tony Malaro and Kevin McCaffrey
April 26, 1997
Kings County Court, Downtown Brooklyn

Tony and Kevin had been paired together for over two months. Kevin continued to learn from Tony, who occasionally demonstrated a wild side against authority. Today, Tony brought Kevin along to witness a judge make a *prima facie* decision on evidence that Tony had recovered after a long chase with a booth robbery suspect over three months ago.

Just prior to the arrest, Tony had been interviewing a booth clerk at Ralph Avenue on the 'A' line, when the robbery suspect mistakenly walked into the very same station he'd robbed a day earlier. The clerk screamed to Tony, "Holy shit! That's him..."

Before the clerk finished her sentence the suspect was back up the stairs onto Fulton Street in Brooklyn. Malaro gave chase to the top of the stairs, but the suspect had already disappeared. Tony made his way back to the Major Case Squad computer and went through about 250 mug shots until he found the picture of Ronnie Coleman. Ronnie had been previously arrested four times for larceny/chain snatches and one robbery with a knife. Tony jotted down the address and proceeded on his own to 1449 Broadway in the Williamsburg section of Brooklyn.

He'd waited for an hour and a half when he finally observed Ronnie walking down the street. He got out of the car across the street from where the suspect was walking. Ronnie turned his back to Detective Malaro, who was secreted behind his car, and walked up the dozen steps into his apartment building. When he got to the top of the steps, he turned around, as he always did, only to see the Detective leaping onto the first two steps of the building. Ronnie entered quickly and ran up to the second floor with Tony hot on his heels. He made it to the second floor walk-up and opened the door to his apartment. He was trying to shut it when Tony gave the door a straight-on kick, which sent Ronnie flying backwards.

From his back on the floor, Ronnie reached for his hidden weapon on a belly-band, just over his belt line under his shirt, when Tony stepped up closer and kicked him square in the face, knocking him unconscious. Tony recovered the gun and arrested Ronnie. The gun was later tied to another robbery at Halsey Street on the 'L' line that had occurred six months earlier. At the Halsey Street incident, the weapon had been discharged and a round recovered from the wall behind the booth. The forensic ballistics test matched the weapon Malaro recovered at Coleman's apartment with the bullet that had been recovered from the Halsey Street robbery. The hearing was a *prima facie* decision. "At first look" or "on its face," the evidence would normally be considered a shoo-in for an indictment.

The Judge presiding over the case came into the courtroom with a swagger. He was sixty years old and had a full head of unnatural-looking sandy hair. He was a tall man with a large frame and stylish glasses. He hobbled a little under his robes, as if suffering from a long-ago football injury. He was definitely intimidating to Kevin. His name was Francis Mahoney, II. The cops called him "Turn Him Loose Deuce." The entire courtroom stood up. The Judge waved everybody to sit down, obviously not comfortable with the tradition that has endured for hundreds of years, its roots in British jurisprudence. He read the folder in front of him. The gun recovered was on a table where the court officer sat to the right of the judge. The weapon was in a vouchered evidence bag. The bullet recovered at Halsey Street was in a separate bag, as was the ammunition from the Colt .45 automatic retrieved by Malaro when he made the arrest.

The judge spoke, his voice gravelly from too many cigarettes.

"Ronald Coleman. Please stand and approach the bench."

Ronald, wearing a brown business suit and glasses, stood up from the defense table. He had been cleaned up a great deal since his arrest three months ago. He looked like part of his own defense counsel.

"Ronald," the judge bellowed.

"As much as it pains me to say this, under New York State law, the seizure of the weapon found in your possession is under question."

"BULLSHIT!" The shout came from the scant audience in the court. People began laughing immediately.

The judge was instantly irate and banged his gavel three times.

"I know that's you, Malaro. Get your butt up here now!"

Malaro stood up.

"You got the wrong guy your honor, but I'd be a liar if I said I disagreed with the statement uttered here today, sir."

There were more snickers from the courtroom. Kevin just sat there behind the prosecutor's table and sank deeper into his seat. He wanted no part of this. Ronnie Coleman grinned and sat back down at the defense table.

"Shut up, Malaro. I almost cited you for contempt the last time you were here, so keep your fat mouth shut."

The judge directed his attention to the prosecuting attorney's table.

"Will the people representing the City of New York approach the bench with Detective Malaro, please?"

Malaro walked up to the judge's bench, which was two feet higher than the group of people standing below it. The judge continued.

"The defense attorney may approach as well."

A short, well-dressed man with receding brown hair, a pale face and round spectacles approached the bench. Malaro looked at him as if he was something one would distastefully wipe off the bottom of a shoe.

The defense attorney spoke.

"Did you have a ruling on that, your honor?"

The judge now spoke in a whisper. He was no longer being recorded by the court reporter.

"Shut up you little shit...I'll get to it."

The defense attorney stepped back one step, with an embarrassed grin. The judge continued and pointed his finger at Malaro.

"Tony, you better cut the crap. I don't take none of that fucking nonsense in my courtroom, and you know it. I've got a set of rules to go by and you're gonna' eat it and that's it."

Malaro rolled his eyes and didn't respond.

The judge looked down at the folder on his desk and opened it.

"The motion before the court requested a review of precedents involving a continuous hot pursuit. Your case doesn't meet those requirements. You broke off the chase at the booth when you lost him. Under hot pursuit arguments, too much time elapsed. When you ID'd Coleman, you had time to get a warrant and pick him up at his house."

Malaro chimed in with an unsolicited and exasperated response.

"He woulda' got rid of the gun by then! We wouldn't have shit, your honor."

The judge shot back.

"I got news for you, stupid. You don't have shit now. The weapon is dead...it's out...inadmissible."

Malaro knew he was beaten, but asked anyway.

"Are you telling me I had no right to take his gun from him when he was about to draw down on me?"

"You're way ahead of yourself, hotshot." The judge answered as he closed the folder in front of him. He pulled off his glasses and looked at Malaro disapprovingly.

"You didn't have any right to even be in his apartment."

Malaro continued in what was beginning to sound to the rest like a pointless argument.

"So legally, I shouldn't have taken the gun away from him then, right?"

"*Now* you're getting it, smart guy." The judge answered snidely and put his glasses back on, seemingly ready for the next case.

"Well then..."

Malaro answered with a small smile and walked away from the group.

The judge was surprised by Tony's sudden departure. He thought he'd get a vehement argument from him and was prepared to dismiss him immediately. He watched Malaro as he walked away, but became distracted when he answered a question from the prosecuting attorney. He looked back and forth from the attorney to Malaro's back while he was talking. The judge then became engaged in an argument with the prosecutor.

Tony walked over to the evidence table and picked up the Colt .45. He ripped open the numbered, plastic evidence bag slowly but deliberately. The court officer looked up in surprise and shot a look over at the judge, who was beginning to forget Malaro while starting another heated debate over the evidence with the prosecuting attorney. Malaro left the evidence table with the weapon. He walked over to the defense table, pulled the gun out of the bag and handed the .45 over, butt first, to Ronnie Coleman.

"I'm sorry Ronnie, this must belong to you."

The judge caught this maneuver at the last minute, as Tony was handing the weapon over to Coleman. Coleman, with an extreme lack of judgment, accepted the weapon from Malaro, and for a brief moment was standing in a Brooklyn court room with a gun in his hand. He looked around smiling. He was still under the giddy effects of realizing he'd just escaped fifteen years of hard time.

"MALARO...WHAT THE FUCK IS WRONG WITH YOU?"

The judge screamed as the court officer jumped over the evidence table, not really thinking whether the weapon was loaded or not. He and two other officers by the door just reacted. Malaro casually walked down the aisle and motioned to Kevin to leave. Meanwhile, the court officers jumped a surprised Coleman and began beating him until he dropped the weapon.

Coleman dropped the gun, but started to fight back. The entire courtroom was in upheaval. Tables were overturned. People were knocked over from both the defense table and prosecutor's table. Tony and Kevin walked past two charging court officers who'd responded from the hall into the courtroom and dived into the melee. Tony was laughing as he and Kevin walked out.

"That was almost worth it, seeing the judge lose it like that."

Chapter Thirteen

March 4th, 2006
St. Albans, Queens

Jonesy was driving by himself in the department-issued, silver Chevy Caprice. His partner, Billy Feuss, had called in sick because he was taking a three-day weekend and a quick trip down to his condo in Florida. Jonesy was on the Belt Parkway enroute to interview the dead *skell's* mother in St. Albans, Queens. He was doing about forty-five miles per hour, and had the window down, smoking a Newport.

It had taken Jonesy three days to identify the victim who'd been shot at 80th street. A number of merchants in the area saw the homeless man frequently picking up bottles and cans for money. He had been a regular in the neighborhood and, as all reported, caused very little trouble. He bought his bottle of "Olde E" everyday from the same liquor store on Liberty Avenue, near the station where he was killed. He sucked beer down, and slept here and there in the neighborhood. Often, he got on trains to go one or two stops in either direction before being ejected by a police officer or thrown off by the train crew. He had rarely ventured any farther than three stops from 80th Street in either direction for the last three years.

After hearing the *skell* was a regular around the train stations and vicinity, Jonesy went back to District 23 to review the ejection reports to get a name. According to the NYPD procedures manual called "The Patrol Guide," if cops threw anyone off trains or ejected a passenger from the subway system, the officer was required to fill out an ejection report. On that report there was to be an identification and general condition of some sort describing the person they tossed off the system. Jonesy did a computer query on the stations that the victim frequented. There were about twenty hits, which were further narrowed down by description and sex. Jonesy found what he was looking for. The reports indicated that the victim had been ejected from the system three times in the last year, and there were three records to verify. His name was Brian Addams.

He never produced ID, but he always gave the police the right name. Cops didn't care; sometimes they got credit for activity by kicking the homeless out and keeping the stations safe and clean. If they had ever bothered to ask Brian, he always had in his possession an expired New York driver's license and his Marine military ID, although neither had been on him when they found his body.

Jonesy did some further digging. Brian had served two years in the Gulf War and was decorated three times for bravery. He'd received a Purple Heart in 1991, after getting shot in the shoulder by a sniper during a recon mission in Iraq. He was a decorated war hero, but not many people knew about that, with the exception of his mother, who Jonesy talked to briefly on the phone when he set up an interview.

Mrs. Loretta Addams lived in a duplex on 280th Street and Francis Lewis Blvd. The neighborhood was on the edge of Queens, bordering Nassau County. She shared a front porch that was divided by a white split-rail fence, with the adjoining family next door. There were Big Wheels and small bicycles piled on the porch next to hers. The house with the neighboring family begged for a paint job on the trim and porch railings. Mrs. Addam's half of the two-family home, however, was impeccable. A broom stood by the doorway, next to the bell. The porch and the trim on the door and step railings gleamed with fresh paint.

Mrs. Addams had the front door open with the screen door closed. Jonesy rang the bell, cupped his hands over the screen to see better, and observed an old black woman wearing a cooking apron hobbling to the door. She was a heavy woman with black orthopedic shoes, pull-up stockings that went just past her calves, but under her knees, and a plaid dress.   Her hair was in a tight bun, and her glasses hung around her neck, probably for reading recipes. A big smile came over her face. Jonesy could tell from his phone call, and now the look on her face, that human contact and having someone to talk to was a rare treat.

They exchanged pleasantries as Jonesy glanced around, taking a brief snapshot of the living room. A picture of Adam Clayton Powell hung in the middle of the wall, along with one of Martin Luther King, Jr. Jonesy laughed to himself, because he knew Powell had hated King. Each famous historical figure was eclipsed only in size by the picture of her son, Brian, in his Marine dress uniform.

The living room was as crisp and clean as the porch. A pea green couch and matching chair were covered with plastic.   The fabric underneath looked as new as the day it was purchased, probably twenty-five years ago. Jonesy remarked on how fine the house looked, and that it reminded him of his Grandmother's house in Georgia. Mrs. Addams was clearly enjoying the conversation.   She was the type of person who was very polite and courteous, but direct. She liked to receive direct talk as well. She was seventy-two years old and showed no signs of slowing down soon. Jonesy liked her immediately.

"What's a sharp-looking black man like you doing with all those white cops?"

Jonesy wasn't going to be surprised by anything this woman said or asked.

"Well Ma'am, who else is going to be around to make sure the brothers get a fair shake?"

She smiled, knowing he was half-kidding, as she gazed at the picture of her son on the wall. She made the transition to the discussion of Brian, painfully aware that this was not purely a social visit. Jonesy was an experienced investigator and remembered quickly about talking to witnesses.

It's been a while since I gave a shit though...

He didn't push. He just listened as the smile faded from her face and her gaze continued to linger on the picture of her son. Jonesy looked at it as well. Unlike the skin and bones DOA he'd observed at the crime scene, the picture caught Brian Addams at his prime, right after boot camp at Parris Island. He looked more like an All-American linebacker. He had a large neck, with an appropriately proportioned head neatly cropped in a crew cut. Mrs. Addams began.

"When Brian came back from the Gulf, he was not the same boy that left."

She paused and then looked directly at Jonesy.

"I'm no fool, Detective Jones, and I know the temptations that surround us. Brian had his alcohol and occasional weed before he went into the service, but overall he had his head on right and he was a good boy. He went to church with me every Sunday after his father died, when he was fifteen."

Jonesy continued to listen, and for some reason he would never be able to articulate, was actually interested in what the old lady had to say.

Mrs. Addams went on.

"It was a tough time after Clarence died, but Brian didn't stray too much. After a year of hanging out with the wrong crowd, he knew what direction they were headed and where he would be if he hung with them."

Another pause.

"...dead or in jail. So he joined the Marines."

She stopped talking, not wanting to rush this visit too much. She didn't get many visitors, except the local Pastor occasionally. And she knew the Pastor only came for some tea and cookies because she was among the biggest givers to the church.

"Wait a minute," she said.

Mrs. Addams got up and went into a small bedroom on the same floor. She didn't take long to get the large photo album she was looking for. She looked at it often, Jonesy guessed. She sat back down, now on the same couch as the Detective, opening the album on the coffee table.

"He was a second team, All-State running back in high school," Mrs. Addams continued, briefly forgetting her son was dead, just relaying some information as if he had moved to another state, an obvious beam of pride on her face.

"Clarence only saw him play when he was in 10th grade, then he passed on, God rest his soul."

Mrs. Addams went on for fifteen more minutes, Jonesy careful not to interrupt, as this was probably one of the few brief moments in a week that she hadn't thought about her son's death. Jonesy would normally breeze through interviews as quickly as possible. In the past, it wasn't unlikely that he'd have interviews completed within five minutes, then onto a nap, lunch, or a cocktail at a local pub. But he didn't do that this time. He let the old lady bathe in a sort of suspended pleasant memory. He did not want to break the quiet, fragile trance she was in. He thought to himself as she talked about Brian.

What is it, the southern accent or the deep-fried smell still hanging in the air?

Jonesy could not quite pinpoint the origin of the familiarity.

"I bet you're hungry" she interrupted, but didn't notice he was off somewhere else.

"I...sure am, Ma'am, but I better be gettin' to my next interview...Well, I...er..." Jonesy stammered.

She looked disappointed.

He spoke again, noticing the look on her face.

"But that sure does smell good. What is it?"

The smile slowly returned to her face.

"Baked macaroni and cheese, fried pork chops, and a little beans and ham hocks... I always cook like that, much too much. Brian used to love it."

Jonesy looked at her face. He couldn't say no and he *was* enjoying her company. He had a feeling he hadn't experienced in many years. He'd been divorced for four years now, hadn't seen his two girls in months, and Grandma long-since dead.

"All right, Mrs. Addams, ya' got me, the ham hocks was the clincher."

She smiled and got up, summoning him to follow her into the kitchen.

"The ham hocks are what always gets 'em..." she laughed.

Jonesy enjoyed his next ninety minutes with Mrs. Addams. He had just finished his coffee and large slice of pecan pie she'd made earlier in the day. She was right.

Much too much.

But she must've known he'd stay. Most of the conversation was about the South and cousins and distant relatives they knew from the same county in Georgia. He was just about to leave, when he remembered to ask her about personal items that were to be returned to her from the morgue. She reported that she got everything except his marine insignia and his military ID card.

"He always wore that pin, even when he was sleeping on the streets...and he always had his card on him. He was always proud of that. He'd come visit me from time to time, maybe about twice a year. He'd clean himself up some...he still stunk of that smell, but he tried and he always had that insignia, like in the back of his mind he knew what he was and was proud, just went a little touched in the head, I guess."

Jonesy left after making her a promise on the porch that he would do his best to find Brian's killer. He always made those promises. But this time it wasn't the empty one that he usually gave.

"I know you will boy, God Bless now." Mrs. Addams answered, believing him.

Chapter Fourteen

Tony Malaro and Kevin McCaffrey
Five Years Ago: April 26, 2001
Cypress Hills, on the Brooklyn/Queens border on the 'J'
Line

Tony and Kevin were parked in a van two blocks from the subway station. They had been parked there for over three hours. The two detectives were part of a stakeout team that was positioned along the 'J' line in an attempt to catch a serial rapist. Using the pin board at Major Case and a computer program that specialized in probability, they chose an area on the 'J' line from the border of Brooklyn to 121st Street in Richmond Hill, Queens. The team strategically placed uniformed officers at all the stations along the suspected line of attack except for two stops, Cypress Hills and Woodhaven Blvd. They had used this strategy in the past with limited success.

The plan revolved around the data gathered. The perpetrator had only carried out attacks at stations where there was no police presence. However, tonight, at each of those two "open" locations, there was a team in a car close to the station, and another team positioned in a room directly across from the booth. Tony and Kevin were in the car near the Cypress Hills station, and Feuss and Jonesy were in a room upstairs. Sergeant O'Shea had borrowed four Anti-Crime officers from District 33 to cover the other station at Woodhaven Blvd. Temporary surveillance cameras were also positioned on all exit stairs of the two stakeout stations.

The research from the last three attacks indicated that the perpetrator probably entered and departed the subway system from the street. The last victim fought back and was nearly thrown from a platform. She sustained a variety of injuries, including a broken jaw from the attacker punching her in the face. Tony and Kevin had visited her yesterday at her home. She had just spent ten days in the hospital. Kevin noticed a change in Tony when they left the victim's apartment. He had rarely observed Tony display any type of emotion in most investigations, but he was visibly agitated.

Kevin was sitting on a bench in the back of the van, drinking a cup of coffee, smoking a cigarette. There was a small, silent, roof fan that dispersed the smoke on the inside and drew it out of the vehicle. He was wearing a pair of Nike's, blue jeans and a gray, pullover sweatshirt. He was ready to run. Tony was sitting in the driver's seat wearing Dockers, buttoned white shirt and a pair of loafers. He was ready to drive.

"Hey, guess who I saw in Central Booking yesterday?" Kevin asked randomly as he sipped his coffee.

"Yeah? Who?"

"Ronnie Coleman."

Tony squinted.

"Who's Ronnie Coleman?"

Kevin smiled.

"Remember four or five years ago when you gave that mutt back his gun in the courtroom?"

Tony let out a small howl and nodded his head.

"Hah...I coulda' been really jammed up with that one. Good thing that judge and his court boy there didn't know dick about evidence procedures in a court room."

Kevin finished a sip from his coffe cup and responded.

"You act as if you knew they wouldn't have made a stink because of their failure to safeguard weapons."

"No, I'm not saying that...I was stupid...could have been busted back to patrol for sure. I was just *so* pissed off...What was good ole Ronnie doing back at Central Booking?"

"Armed robbery."

Kevin continued.

"Hey did you hear that fuckin' judge was caught up in an internet predator sweep three months ago?"

"Get the fuck outta here!" Tony burst out laughing.

Kevin went on.

"Swear to God. They kept it out of the papers, but he was picked up in Jersey lookin' to bone a twelve-year old boy who turned out to be a forty year-old state special investigator."

"That's priceless." Tony smiled.

"3319 to Central."

The voice interrupted the two in the van, crackling over the radio. Tony and Kevin stopped talking. Thirty-three nineteen was the patrol post number for 121st Street on the 'J' line. It was one of the stops where the team had placed a uniformed police officer for the squeeze play.

The dispatcher responded.

"Go ahead 3319."

"Central, be advised a possible suspect came to the booth area, bought a card and then departed the station. Stand by for a description."

About twenty seconds elapsed, as if the dispatcher needed to leave her radio to go get a pencil.

The post cop continued over the radio.

"Okay Central. We have a male, white, 5'10, 190 lbs. He's wearing a tan, waist length jacket with blue jeans. He has a trimmed beard and is wearing a brown baseball-style cap...can you advise all other units standing by?"

The dispatcher relayed the information to the stakeout teams and the uniformed participants.

"Whaddya' think?" Kevin asked.

"I don't know. Maybe nothin'. But it's pretty close to the description that two of the victims gave, minus the beard....the facial hair might be new."

Kevin finished jotting down the description, then put his book and pen away. He reached over behind the bench he was sitting on and pulled a milk crate from under it. He retrieved a folder from the crate, which appeared to have a dozen other similar folders readily available. The one he pulled had the second victim's case file and he read the description the officer at the scene had recorded on the complaint form three weeks ago. Kevin read the incident report out loud.

"Male, white, 5'10, 200 pounds and blue jeans."

"Pull those other ones outta' there and read me the same section for a couple more, will ya'?" Tony asked.

Kevin read two more; the descriptions were very close. One of the reports also had the perpetrator wearing a "tight beard." As Kevin read the last information, the radio crackled again.

"3320 to Central."

"Go ahead 3320."

The uniformed officer on the radio was at the next station down from the previous call.

"Central, be advised, the same individual who was seen ten minutes ago at 3319, just came here and did the same thing, bought a fare card and left the station."

Post 3320 was at 111th Street. The next station down the line from 111th Street was Woodhaven Blvd. Woodhaven was one of the two squeeze stations where the District 33, Anti-Crime teams were located. The perpetrator was coming down the line, apparently right into the trap. Tony and Kevin heard the officer's transmission directly. Malaro started the car. They were about three miles from the other team at Woodhaven Blvd. Tony began a slow drive under the elevated tracks down Jamaica Avenue. Kevin left the back seat area, climbed over to the front, and buckled himself in on the passenger's side.

Kevin got on his cell phone to Feuss, just upstairs in a room at Cypress Hills.

"Yeah?" Feuss answered.

Kevin spoke.

"Looks like we have a possible hit at Woodhaven. We're taking a slow ride down the block if something pops up. Stand by will ya'?"

"Gotcha." Feuss answered.

Tony and Kevin parked two blocks from the last stairway at the Woodhaven Blvd. station. The elevated tracks above them periodically showered sparks where the electrified rail caught garbage or arced from the third rail connection to the train. Kevin watched as a cluster of sparks rained down about ten feet before it dispersed in the air. He looked at his watch. Thirty minutes had passed since the last transmission from the officer at 111th Street. Tony spoke.

"Hey..."

Kevin read his mind and completed his sentence.

"Let's get back to Cypress Hills. He would have been here already."

Tony started the car, made a 'U' turn on Jamaica Avenue, and headed back to Feuss and Jonesy's station. They drove for five minutes and had just passed 76th Street, about five blocks away from Cypress Hills, when they heard a frantic radio transmission from Feuss.

"10-13...10-13, officer needs assistance at Cypress Hills on the 'J'."

Tony punched the van up to eighty. They were two blocks away when Feuss' squeaky voice came over the radio again from just above them on the elevated station.

"Suspect is heading northbound on the platform area towards the closed end."

Tony and Kevin arrived at the station with a squeal as they heard Feuss give the direction of the suspect. The closed end was two blocks farther up. Tony punched it again, and nearly lost control. He regained the van quickly and sped up into Brooklyn, continuing on Jamaica Avenue. When they were about two hundred yards from the closed end staircase they saw someone scurrying down the roof of the subway exit stairs across the street. Tony stopped the van. He wanted to get closer before he spooked anybody into bolting. They heard Feuss again.

"Central, advise units, suspect jumped over the platform and onto the stairs roof at the closed end of Cypress Hills and will be on foot at Jamaica Avenue and Cypress Hills station."

From the van, the two detectives observed the suspect drop from the end of the staircase onto the sidewalk. He stumbled and fell on his butt. He regained his balance, got up and walked quickly to a parked, dark green Jeep. Its front end already pointed in the direction Tony and Kevin were coming from. Tony pulled the van over to the curb. They weren't sure if the suspect had noticed them flying up the avenue or not. Tony was waiting to see which way the perpetrator was heading, and briefly contemplated hitting him head on.

Kevin interrupted his thoughts.

"I know what you're thinkin' and don't forget that's Feuss giving these transmissions; could be the guy just hopped the turnstile and didn't pay his fare!"

Tony snapped out of his trance and laughed nervously.

"Shit...how right can you be with that one?"

Tony grabbed the radio mike, as his eyes were locked on the suspect's car. He wasn't interested in radio etiquette right now.

"Feuss, FEUSS!" He yelled into the radio.

"What?" Feuss responded.

"Is that our guy or what?" Tony asked Feuss as he watched the green Jeep pull away from the curb and drive right towards him and Kevin.

Feuss answered sarcastically.

"What do you think?...uh, we lost him on the street. I ain't jumping over no roof and neither is Jonesy."

The Jeep slowly passed the detectives parked at the curb. Tony watched in his rearview mirror. As he was looking, they overheard Jonesy in the background, too. It sounded as if he was talking through a tin can.

"...you tell him Billy, I ain't jumping over nothin'!"

Tony yelled.

"Billy, is it him or not?"

"Affirmative Tony...he made another attempt on the platform. He must've come in on a train. We have a victim here with a ripped shirt. He didn't get a chance because we heard her scream and came right up the platform. He was dragging her to the end of the station and bolted when he saw us at the stairs. I'm gonna call central and ask for a bus. Male white, 5'10, 190 lbs."

Tony threw the radio down.

"Those fuckin' morons!"

Then he yelled again. "Call it in!"

Kevin grabbed the radio on the dashboard as Tony spun the tires and made a 180 degree turn on Jamaica Avenue. Cars stopped in both directions. Tony didn't even notice when he nearly hit a flower delivery truck as he pulled out. The smell of burned rubber and smoke permeated the air in the van. Some people on the sidewalk jumped and ran when they heard the wheels screech.

"Hit the lights!" Tony barked.

Tony now wanted the suspect to bolt, hoping he'd make a mistake or run into traffic on the unyielding Jamaica Avenue during a panicked escape attempt. When Tony completed his turn, he was fifty yards behind the suspect. The Jeep took off heading east on Jamaica Avenue. When the suspect got to 76th Street, he made a left, going the wrong way down a narrow, one-way street. Tony followed as Kevin gave directions for responding units over the radio.

Tony observed a minivan coming toward both speeding cars. It was at the top of the hill, which was 76th Street. If the bystander's minivan kept moving forward, it would block access to the only street exit, 85th Drive. The suspect would be trapped.

"Come' on... keep coming." Tony begged.

Both Tony and the suspect were approaching fifty miles per hour when the oncoming driver, headed towards the chase, reacted to the police lights from the detective's car. He stopped in the middle of the intersection of 85th Drive. The suspect didn't slow until he was nearly on top of the van. The Jeep slammed into the van's front left headlight, and then completed the turn onto the short street. Tony followed, and was accelerating when he saw the suspect make a left onto 77th Street.

Kevin spoke.

"He knows where he's going..."

Tony made the left onto 77th Street, too. It was only thirty yards to the next block. Forest Park was directly ahead of them.

"I know where he's going, too. The question is, which way will he go on the Parkway?"

Kevin called on the radio again as the suspect in the green Jeep made a right turn.

"Central be advised, suspect is on Park Lane South. He's headed for the Interboro Parkway."

Tony casually corrected him as he made a right onto Park Lane South.

"They call it the Jackie Robinson Parkway now."

"She knows what I'm talking about." Kevin answered.

There was silence for about five seconds.

The radio crackled with the dispatcher's voice.

"That's Jackie Robinson Parkway, officer, and let me know which direction—east or west—when you get there."

Tony laughed.

"Bitch," Kevin said before pushing the transmission button. Then:

"Thank you Central, duly noted."

Two marked vehicles were responding from the opposite direction on Park Lane South, so the suspect made a left onto the uphill portion of Forest Park Drive and Tony followed.

This section of Queens looked more like upstate New York, with large boulders, steep hills and sharp turns. They flew by the golf course and onto the eastbound lanes of the Jackie Robinson Parkway. Kevin called in the update.

The terrain was a natural deterrent to speeders, with frequent curves and sharp turns. Tony caught up quickly and was right on the bumper of the suspect doing eighty miles per hour. The van they were driving was noisy, with empty cans and gear falling all over the back each time they hit a sharp curve. Tony was braking intermittently to keep from losing control and to make the turns without flipping the van. He was about ten yards behind the suspect and closing when the Jeep hit one of the cement dividers. The suspect nearly lost control, but turned into the skid and recovered. Kevin held his breath.

"This guy's no joke at the wheel."

Tony looked in his rearview mirror for the other responding vehicles. There were none. He spoke casually.

"Time for a *pit maneuver*."

Kevin looked at him.

"On the Interboro?...Are you out of your fuckin' mind?"

After losing some ground to a sharp curve, Tony caught up to the suspect as they approached a straightaway just past Metropolitan Avenue. The Jeep was in the right lane when Tony appeared to be trying to pass on the left. The suspect braked hard and cut Tony off, forcing him to brake. He almost flipped the van trying to avoid a collision with the suspect at eighty miles per hour.

Tony caught up quickly again as they approached an exit for Union Turnpike. This time Tony remained directly behind and gave the Jeep a nudge with the van. The suspect kept going. Tony approached a second time and gave another nudge. The suspect's vehicle lurched forward. The road would come to an end soon, with two choices for drivers: The VanWyck Expressway, a sharp right, or Union Turnpike, which contained traffic lights and heavy traffic. Tony approached the Jeep once more, but darted to the left before he was about to nudge him and crept up quickly on the left side. The van's right front fender was near the left rear tire of the Jeep when Tony made a sharp turn into its left quarter panel. Kevin gasped.

The Jeep fishtailed right while Tony braked and slowed. The suspect almost recovered, then fish-tailed left, over-compensated, and the Jeep flipped and tumbled four times before it sailed over the three-foot cement barrier into the woods and down a sharp ravine.

Tony pulled over where the tire marks on the road indicated the vehicle's departure from the parkway into the woods. The two Detectives got out of the van, stood at the cement barrier, and looked over. The air was thick with burned rubber. The suspect's car was overturned and smoking about twenty feet below them.

Kevin went back to the van and called in the location, requesting a supervisor, Duty Captain, ambulance, and the fire department. After his transmission, he went back to the wall. Tony had already gone down into the ravine. Kevin hopped over the cement wall and looked for a clear path down to the vehicle. After sliding part of the way on the uneven terrain, he saw Tony standing by the driver's side window of the upside down car. Kevin was on the opposite side.

Tony had his 9mm Glock drawn, pointing it at the suspect in a controlled combat stance. Kevin crouched down and drew his weapon. He looked in the passenger side window. The suspect lay, strapped in upside down, with his left leg caught in an unnatural position between the steering wheel and the dashboard. It was clearly broken. He was out cold, looking near death. His nose was smashed on his face and there was a large gaping wound on his cheek. Half of the left side of his face, from under his eye to his jaw, was hanging off. The wound was about two inches wide. His eyes were closed tight.

Kevin looked away.

Why is Tony in a combat stance?

Kevin stood straight up and holstered his weapon. He could hear the approaching sirens.

He looked at Tony and was suddenly frightened. Tony was about to discharge his weapon. Kevin spoke calmly.

"Okay Tony. It's over. He's unconscious..."

There was no response. Tony still stood with his gun straight out in a combat stance.

"Tony. Tony. It's not worth it..."

Kevin then made an unconscious move. He put his hand on the butt of his own holstered weapon.

When he did that, Tony looked up and snapped out of it. He shook his head.

"I'm good...I'm good...all clear. Thanks Kevin. I don't know what's the matter with me lately. This fuck just pissed me off, is all."

Kevin casually took his hand off his own holster.

EMS and the firefighters had already arrived and jumped over the cement barrier. They were each bringing down heavy equipment and a cage stretcher from the rescue unit.

The two men slowly walked back up the hill.

Kevin talked in a low voice as he placed his hand on the back of Tony's neck and lightly squeezed it.

"Okay partner. It's over." He smiled. "I coulda' done without the *pit maneuver* though."

Tony laughed out loud nervously. "It worked good though, didn't it?"

Kevin answered sarcastically.

"Oh yeah...that was great! Let's do it again right now...you crazy fuck!"

Chapter Fifteen

March 7, 2006
Long Island Expressway

Sergeant Mike O'Shea was tagging along for lunch with Detectives Vinnie Venera and Kevin McCaffrey and catching a ride for a meeting at Borough Headquarters. Vinnie and Kevin were on their way to Manhattan to canvass the Chambers and Fulton Street subway stations. A downtown merchant had recognized the ice-picked girl from the newspaper as a local vagrant and called Police headquarters.

Mike missed hanging out with other cops after he made supervisor, and he liked Vinnie and Kevin. They were top-notch plainclothes officers and the best detectives in the squad. Kevin had originally been partnered with Tony Malaro when he'd first come to the squad. After Malaro's shooting incident, Mike paired Kevin up with Venera. They made a good team, but Malaro had taught Kevin everything he knew.

Mike had made all the assignments for the multiple murders case. Jonesy was assigned the 80th Street homicide. Feuss had the girl who was ice-picked, and Vinnie and Kevin were investigating the wheel chair victim. They'd had no luck contacting anyone related to the double amputee; nothing from witnesses, either. Their piece of the investigation was a dead end, except for the coroner's report that they hadn't reviewed yet.

They were driving a blue Suburban because all of the unmarked cars for the Detective Bureau were either being used or were inoperable.

"This truck is a piece of shit," Venera muttered as he drove the unadorned vehicle on the Long Island Expressway from Queens into Brooklyn.

O'Shea was in the passenger seat reading the Daily News, eating the second of three hot dogs they'd bought at Woodhaven Blvd. Kevin was in the back, finishing his second hot dog, with a Styrofoam cup of coffee between his feet. O'Shea and Kevin were dressed in similar brown sport coats, with white shirts and ties, and both wore comfortable, black Rockport shoes. Venera was dressed as if he were attending a wedding. He wore a double-breasted tan jacket, matching pants, and a lime green shirt with a white collar. He also had on $300.00 Italian leather shoes. Venera's socks and tie cost more than O'Shea's whole outfit. But he did look good. Venera was also sporting a trendy, neatly trimmed beard, just enough to show the shadow. He was about fifty pounds overweight, but carried it as if he were a muscle-bound Olympic athlete. When he walked, his stride matched his attitude.

Number Three, the homeless girl found two weeks ago who had ridden the train for over nine hours, had recently been identified as Kathleen Prodski from the Greenwood section of Brooklyn. Kathleen got into drugs when she was a young teenager, and had been arrested for minor offenses all through her life; shoplifting, jumping the subway turnstiles to beat the fare, disorderly conduct, assault, all just parts of her sad resume. Detective Feuss had notified the parents two days ago. Kevin and Vinnie were doing a follow-up informational in Manhattan to close it out; seeing if there was any connection to the other victims, and maybe get lucky and discover the father of the baby. They had time. Their wheelchair assignment was a solid Jane Doe.

O'Shea had just finished his second hot dog from the stand near the cemetery.

"Those are the best dogs in the city..." he exclaimed.

Venera cut in.

"That's bullshit...you say that every time we go there. You ever been to Karl Ehmer's? They got the best *everything* on that stand on Metropolitan Avenue."

O'Shea was shaking his head in disagreement, while chewing.

"I don't go to Karl Ehmers—they hate everyone who's not German. I swear, I thought Irish people were a cold race, but those fuckin' Germans...they're like ice."

"You all should take a lesson from us Italians, we're very warm people," Venera answered.

"That's cause you're all fags who sleep with your mothers until you're twelve years old. When are you moving out anyway, it must really cramp your sex life." O'Shea laughed.

"Fuck you, you Irish prick!"

Vinnie paused.

"It's only temporary till I find my own place. Besides ... Hey what do you get when you cross an Irishman with a donkey?"

"I don't know...what?" O'Shea answered.

Venera belted out his answer with a loud laugh.

"ONE STUPID DONKEY!"

All three cracked up laughing. Kevin was out of the line of fire in the back seat and knew enough to stay out of this and enjoy the show. It was generally known throughout many precincts that it took brass balls to take on Venera.

"You're a moron," Mike replied after he stopped laughing.

Venera continued with another joke.

"...how about the two Irish, gay guys, named Phil McCracken and Pat McGroin?"

Kevin interrupted.

"That's enough. I heard that one from you three times this month...speaking of which, what was with the AIDS remark on the radio the other day Sarge?"

Mike answered.

"Pure bullshit...I wanted to see if we can rattle this squirrel's cage a little bit—maybe make him come out and do something stupid, like go to his doctor and record his visit."

Venera changed the subject and asked his Sergeant.

"Why are *we* going down here anyway?"

"I want you two to close this out right. Feuss is getting sloppy. A flower stand guy located in Manhattan called two days ago to report that the Prodski girl was a regular around Fulton Street. And Feuss, the jackass, called in sick today. I'll have to slap him around soon. After you drop me off, go ask a couple of questions, see if she was a Queens regular or a Manhattan *skell*. High profile cases necessitate the big guns like you and Kevin here. Tomorrow, if Feuss is still out, I want you to check back with her family, then go ahead to the morgue and see if anything turns up."

"Why do we have to go to the morgue to clean up their shit?" Venera asked.

O'Shea responded.

"Cause your end of this is a dead end anyway. We need more info on Wheelchair Lady and I don't like coincidences. See if there's something else to tie them together."

"That Feussy couldn't do dick without Jonesy helpin' him out and tellin' him what to do." Venera added.

Then Kevin spoke up.

"What's going on with Jonesy lately? The last couple of days he's been on fire with this investigation. I've never seen him work witnesses so quickly."

"Ya' got me...looks like he's finally out of his coma," Venera answered.

"Maybe he got religion," Mike added.

The three the detectives were very comfortable around each other. Mike went on.

"Jonesy's been working this hard. I think that Addam's old lady really got to him."

Venera chimed in.

"Well it's about time he started carrying his weight around here. Maybe he can wrap this up and we can chill out a while. Been a lot of pressure on this one."

O'Shea nodded as he finished the third hot dog and washed it down with a black cherry soda. He swallowed and spoke.

"It would be a good thing if we can make some headway and have this *skell* offed in Manhattan instead of Rockaway. The Captain thinks so, anyway. Besides it would be better for Malaro if we can throw that out there, even though it looks like the District is most definitely gonna' eat that one."

Mike took another sip of soda and continued.

"I don't give a shit about the Captain digesting a heavy felony in his district, but because it was Tony's post, he could get jammed up."

Venera sat driving, one hand at the bottom of the wheel, a newly lit Kool sticking out of his mouth, "You think so, Sarge?"

Mike answered.

"There's been some talk. He's not the favorite son anymore, and it was his post where the Prodski girl was found."

Kevin just shook his head in disgust.

Venera looked at him, puzzled.

"Oh, that makes sense. This fuckin' broad rides the trains for a full day all over the city into the Bronx and back. Somebody happens to find her scraggly ass on his post in Queens, and now it's *his* fault she's dead? That makes a lot of fucking sense!"

O'Shea laughed.

"You're a pisser; I've long-stopped questioning why this job does anything. All's I know is that someone's gotta get one. You don't have a DOA take a nine hour subway version of the Circle Line tour and not stick it to someone. I guess they think it might as well be him. They all think he's a fuck-up anyhow."

119

Venera's anger was subsiding.

"Why is that? Huh? He was a hot shit a few years back."

"Grow up," O'Shea answered. "You've been on the job long enough. You of all people should know how this works. A cop catches *Son of Sam* and he's a hero. The next week, that same cop bangs up a Radio Motor Patrol car, he gets written up. The bosses are just scared pussies. They go to these Chief's meetings now and pray they're not the object of ridicule in front of the rest of the other *schmuck* commanders. So if something good happens in their command, they pat themselves on the back. If something bad happens, they want heads to roll so they can tell everyone at these meetings how they straightened out the problem back in their command. Right now, people are dead and someone's head needs to roll and it's gonna' be Malaro's."

Mike looked out the window.

"You're right about one thing though, Vinnie. Ask Kevin here. He was a hot shit. A few years back he was the best, but not after that shooting. He got a raw deal and they hung him out to dry. He was lucky to have a job after that."

Chapter Sixteen

Tony Malaro, Four Years Ago
2:00 AM, April 12ᵗʰ, 2002
Knickerbocker Avenue on the 'M' Line

It was early into the midnight shift and Malaro was drinking his coffee and smoking a Kent on the mezzanine when he heard screaming on the northbound platform of the elevated station. He was one of the officers who didn't sleep when he did his overtime shifts in uniform. From a career standpoint, Tony Malaro had it made. He was a second grade detective in the NYPD Major Case Squad, just about the most elite unit that existed in each borough. He had been a Transit cop for a few years, finishing up there as a detective. When the NYPD merged with the Transit Police Department in 1995, he transferred into the NYPD Detective Bureau. The Transit Police Department no longer existed, but the subway Police Districts and boundaries still were in place under the new Transit Bureau and there was plenty of overtime.

He periodically worked in uniform for his old buddy, Lt. Gaetano out in District 33. *"Guy"* hooked him up with four hours once a week on a "tit" post like the 'M' line. Malaro would be a fixed officer at an assigned station, read a paper on the turnstile and smoke cigarettes. Easy money. He needed a pool this summer for the wife and teenage boys. He was doing his crossword when the screams started

They wouldn't have heard shit. Even if they did, they would ignore it and go back to sleep, he thought to himself as he bounded up the northbound stairs two at a time, faster than most *hair-bag*, midnight cops.

When he got on the platform he couldn't see anything. The light was out at the far end, and he suspected someone might be down

121

there. He walked slowly down the platform. It was dead quiet. A figure was beginning to emerge by the sand box. It was some junkie woman, Hispanic-looking, about five-foot nothing, crying by the box. She looked about forty years old, but was probably more like twenty-seven. He quickly looked around. There were no other passengers on either platform. Malaro made an intentional throaty noise from quite a few feet away. It was best not to sneak up on anybody around New York City subways. Nobody liked surprises...whether they were homeless, criminals or cops. Tony asked her name. There was some vague recollection on her face as she attempted to remember. Her blue jeans were filthy and she wore an equally dirty blue hooded sweatshirt with *University of Michigan* on the front. Her nose was leaking clear liquid on her face, and it ran down all over her sweatshirt. It also looked like she'd wet herself.

"Look honey..." Tony began, "...I can't help you if you don't tell me what the problem is—"

She mumbled a low groan. Tony circled her, keeping his distance. He'd seen situations like this get ugly real fast, and he had an uneasy feeling in his stomach. Tony now had his back to the end of the platform and was standing ten feet away from the unstable woman. He patted his leg as he went for his nightstick, but he'd left it in his locker tonight.

It was supposed to be a slow tour.

He decided he would call it in and try to get a female cop on the scene. It was obvious by now, with the unintelligible responses from the woman, that he wasn't about to successfully communicate with her.

"3314 to Central."

As he was calling, she staggered closer to Malaro.

"Stay right there sweetheart, we're gonna' help you out," he said.

She looked up now, no more tears in her eyes. The tears were replaced by rage. Who knew what or who she saw now.

"3314, go ahead," replied Central over the radio.

Tony's radio was already back in its holster. He had his hand on his mace, because she'd closed the gap between them another five feet. The girl straightened out a bit and stood erect, unlike the apparently drug-induced stupor she'd been in a few short moments ago.

This bitch isn't harmless anymore.

She cleared a box cutter from her sweatshirt pocket with her left hand and, with a determined look on her face, began to approach the fifteen-year veteran. Tony couldn't even step back; he tried, but he'd circled her earlier, and now found himself at the end of the platform. Malaro didn't have time to call for a 10-13, so he maced her instead. She would slice him before he could call for help.

The mace had little effect on the deranged woman. She wiped her eyes with her sleeve and kept coming, with a new purpose in her step. Tony finally managed to call a 10-13 emergency call on his radio, after he maced her, but Central Operations never acknowledged his request. He had seen mace fail once before, on an *angel-dusted* high school football player. It took five cops to pull him down. Sometimes it just didn't work. Sometimes it made them angrier.

He went left. She went left. He went right. She went right. She was beginning to lunge with the box cutter, with strafing arm sweeps. This was no joke. He was about to be cut. Most cops realize that there is no reason for equal opportunity or a fair fight when you want to go home at night. Tony knew better. He'd seen more cops get serious injuries because they didn't act when they should have, because they were dealing with women or someone smaller.

Bullshit.

Anyone who had ever witnessed two Brooklyn girls really go at it knew they made men look like pansies. Hair would be flying, blood squirting, eye gouging, anything goes. A different world. A tough broad in this neighborhood would put a hurting on a cop worse than most men could. He dodged her two more times, then removed his gun from its holster. He crouched down in his controlled stance. He told her to back off or he would shoot. She came right at him with the box cutter. He slowly squeezed off one round with his 9 mm Glock. The shot caught her in the neck. She dropped immediately. What Malaro didn't notice was that the box cutter also dropped...off the platform and onto the street.

An hour later the whole platform and booth area were swarming with cops. Someone called the news, and by coincidence, a mobile unit from channel five was already on the scene before the NYPD Crime Scene Unit. Malaro was sitting in the ambulance being treated for emotional distress. It was a courtesy to leave cops alone after something like this, but some people wanted answers. From the academy, cops were told not to say a word until you went to the hospital and a PBA lawyer showed up. Experienced cops, however, knew enough to get their own lawyer. Sharp guys weren't going to let their careers or lives ride on some twenty-five year old lawyer with bad shoes, on a minimum retainer from the PBA, determine their future. Malaro called his cousin, a hot-shot attorney from Queens, and he was going to meet with Tony back at the command. Sergeant Quinn approached Tony, who was sitting on a stretcher in the back of the ambulance.

"We can't find no box cutter, Tony. You better tell us what really happened before the Duty Captain gets here," Quinn said.

Tony didn't even look up.

"We looked all over the platform." Quinn continued, getting antsier now. "We didn't find anything. You sure she had something in her hand?"

Tony looked up, with a twisted face, but responded without emotion.

"Quinn, go fuck yourself. I'm waiting for my attorney."

Quinn left Malaro in a huff, wrapped up the station and got everybody off the platform as fast as possible. He did have officers search the platform, but no one considered the possibility of the weapon falling to the street area. By the time Mike O'Shea arrived at the scene with other detectives and searched the street, the box cutter was nowhere to be found. The only witnesses reported that the girl was unarmed and had her hands on her head when the officer shot her, even though it was later verified by the booth clerk that the "witnesses" were by the booth area when they all heard the gun go off. It didn't matter, except that the discrepancy of their statements was enough to prevent him from being fired.

They never found the weapon, and the department brought administrative charges against Malaro for not requesting back-up in a situation that involved deadly physical force, and failure to have proper equipment during uniformed patrol duties; his nightstick. Tony's Malaro's Detective career was over.

Chapter Seventeen

March 8, 2006
370 Jay St.
Brooklyn, NY

"I'm not getting in the car until you tell me where you wanna' eat." Vinnie demanded.

He continued his usual rant.

"The last time the radio car stunk of hot dogs all day. I want to sit down, and I don't want to eat it in a car, period!"

Kevin looked up from his coffee and Kent in the Major Case Squad room at Jay Street.

"Jesus Christ, Vinnie, it's eight o'clock in the morning! I'm not really thinking about lunch right now."

Vinnie began whining.

"Be that as it may, we do this all the time. We don't talk about lunch at all, and then drive around talking to people, getting all hung up and shit with witnesses, statements and interviews...two o'clock rolls around and we're starving! Then we pull over to the nearest shit-hole and cram greasy fries in our mouths. I'm not doing it today, damn it!"

Kevin just stared at him.

Vinnie changed tack, and instantly became softer.

"Now, how about that China-Rican place on Broadway, near Myrtle Avenue?"

Kevin gave up.

"Fine...whatever...China-Rican it is. Stop breaking my balls about lunch!"

Kevin loved Vinnie, but like all people who love and are loved, he wanted to punch him out occasionally.

Today, both detectives had to go to Kings County Morgue, and then back to Steinway Street in the Greenpoint section of Brooklyn. They wanted to interview Kathleen Prodski's parents, to see if there was anything that Feuss might have missed in connection with the other murders.

The detectives had already talked about this at length, and figured these killings weren't as random as originally thought. They also agreed that they should gather additional information. Sergeant O'Shea had a point, though, about two homeless girls being pregnant. It sounded more than unusual. The dead Prodski girl had some ligature marks on the back of her neck, which were found during the autopsy, but she hadn't been strangled. The ice-pick had done the trick, but there was certainly a struggle to get something off her neck, and they assumed it was after she was dead. They wanted to know what it was.

Kevin drove. Neither of the detectives actually liked the morgue, but of the two, Kevin had a better stomach for it. Kevin could last up to an hour. A visit to a morgue didn't usually extend past an hour, anyway. He didn't like the after-stench. The most troubling to Kevin was the feeling the morgue odor remained with him the rest of the day. He knew it was probably all in his head, but could swear he smelled that combination of formaldehyde and antiseptic overpowering the stench of death until he changed his clothes and showered later on in the evening.

Vinnie was another story. He *hated* the morgue; and although he was somewhat used to it after a decade, he never lasted more than ten minutes. He *played* like he was ill or going to vomit, but he really just couldn't take it. Kevin and the Medical Examiner people loved to tease him, because Vinnie gave them grief sometimes by just being Vinnie. Kevin wouldn't miss the opportunity to laugh at him, and rode him every time they went.

Most civilians believed that doctors were the ones cutting bodies open and performing delicate autopsies in a morgue, but that isn't accurate. At any given time, unless it was a high profile case, the lab techs did all the work. An odd bunch, they were often adorned in baseball caps and sunglasses. They tossed bodies here and there to examine limbs and weigh organs. It was not as dignified as one would have hoped.

The indifference that permeated the air was as strong as the formaldehyde. There were over a dozen stainless steel tables, five of which had bodies on them—stiff mannequins that were no longer recipients or givers of comments such as "please" or "thank you" when they were flipped back and forth, naked, on the tables. There were loose snickers and remarks that were bandied about like "*Nice tits*" and "*Wow, look at this.*"

Vinnie and Kevin put their masks on and clipped their detective shields on a chain that hung around their necks. They weren't going to talk to the regular ghouls today. They wanted to speak with an ME, and they were hard to find. Kevin walked around the large room with Vinnie slowly following. Vinnie was shielding his eyes, when he inadvertently observed one tech carve a "Y" section on an old man in his eighties.

After five minutes of walking around, Kevin recognized an Assistant ME he'd worked with before.

Kevin approached him and shouted in his best Rodney Dangerfield voice.

"Hey Huang, put the camera away, will ya', it's a parking lot!"

Martin Huang turned around, laughing loudly through his mask. In his hand was a four-inch circular skull cap belonging to the body he was examining. He was inspecting the top of the brain for blunt force trauma.

Huang was of average height with black hair, and had on his white lab coat. His father was Korean and his mother was Jewish. He had been working at the Kings County Morgue for four years—about two years past the average for competent doctors, and he was more than competent. But he liked the hours and the time off. He was getting overtime whenever he wanted it.

"Hey Kevin, what's up? I haven't seen you in a while."

Martin looked over at Vinnie, who was obviously feeling less than par.

"Hey Vinnie, come here, I got some nice '*Cervala al Napoletana*'for you."

"What's that?" Vinnie asked.

Martin replied, matter-of-factly.

"Brains with capers and olives, what else?"

Kevin laughed.

Vinnie looked up with a queasy expression on his face. As he followed Kevin to Huang's table, Vinnie finally noticed the rest of the techs were hacking through five bodies at the same time, and it was a little more gruesome than usual.

"You're a lotta' laughs, *Huangstein.*" Vinnie answered. He didn't have the stomach for the usual banter.

"I'm gonna' get some coffee," he muttered and walked out of the large room by the side door.

"What's the matter with the *Big Ragu*?" Huang asked.

"He's really a big pussy, ya' know." Kevin said. He watched the door close on Vinnie, then refocused on the purpose of his visit.

"Hey, Martin, I need you to look at a DOA for me. She's on ice over in the Jane Doe room. We ID'd her, but she's still in there till the parents make a decision on what to do with her."

The two walked over to the separate room where the girl was located. She was in a dark drawer, and had been in the Jane Doe room for over a week, along with about twenty other bodies waiting to be carved up or shipped to a funeral home, or in some cases, Potter's Field. Huang pulled opened the body length tray and drew back the sheet. The techs had cleaned her up a little bit. She actually looked beautiful, and

Kevin was somewhat startled. He spoke, as Huang was pulling her hair back from her breast to get a clear look at her neck.

"Wow, she's kinda' pretty, huh?" Kevin said.

Huang answered.

"We got a name for that you know...Hey..." Huang said suddenly, changing the subject. "...did I tell you about the security guard who was banging some of the dead women on the four to twelve night shift?"

Kevin answered in disgust.

"Get the fuck outta' here!"

"No shit," Huang continued.

"Last month. Some attendant caught the guard in full thrust, on top of some fifty-year-old dead lady. The attendant forgot to pick up a load of laundry at his usual time, and caught this squirrel right smack in the middle of his date."

Huang was telling the story as he was turning the female body on its side.

"Oh, here it is." He pointed to the right side of her neck.

He grabbed the camera from under the gurney, and placed the extended cone from the lens on her neck. Huang had taken plenty of pictures when she first arrived. These were for the visiting detectives. He took three pictures with the contained flash in the cone, and flipped her back over quickly, taking three more close-ups of the marks on the front of her neck.

"Looks like some sort of friction burn from a strap, or something leathery. A regular metal chain would make a cleaner, thinner pattern. It looks like it was pulled back and forth, and then probably yanked off. I'll take a look at the x-rays again, but I'd probably say it had nothing to do with her death."

"Thanks, Martin." Kevin said.

"This is the second *skell* who's missing something. The marine was missing a pin, and this one's missing a necklace. I don't know about the Jane Doe in the wheelchair."

Martin's eyebrows furrowed as he interjected.

"She was missing something too ..."

"What's that?" Kevin asked.

"Two legs!"

Martin burst out laughing. Kevin smiled but didn't think it was *that* funny.

"Hey..." Kevin asked. "How far along was that Jane Doe, anyway?"

"She was about four to five months."

Kevin rubbed his face. He no longer felt the cases were disconnected.

"I think we got some sort of freak on our hands ..."

Chapter Eighteen

March 8, 2006
370 Jay Street
Brooklyn, NY

Four days after visiting Loretta Addams, Jonesy was going over train runs the night of Brian Addams' murder. He also plotted a map on the wall in the Major Case Squad room and pinpointed all of last year's open DOA's from the entire system. He used color-coded push pins to highlight approximate death times, rather than the time of the reports. He included the two pregnant girls, as well. This would give him a better picture of when the victims died, and reveal a pattern, if one existed.

Jonesy had put more time in the last four days working on this case than he had in any case over the last four years. When Feuss came back from Florida, Jonesy had him run officer's memo books. Feuss's task was to review inspection times at stations from post cops, to narrow the time of death of each DOA. The most interesting item Feuss found was the 10-13 call, prior to the discovery of the dead Brian Addams at 80th Street. There hadn't been a 10-13 call in months in District 23, and those that were called in the past year were actually called by cops who needed assistance.

Jonesy added that piece to his hypothetical scenario, and came up with an accurate time of death estimate for Brian—between five and ten minutes after the 10-13 emergency call. Jonesy was sitting in the interview room at Jay Street in downtown Brooklyn by himself, going over the last data from Feuss. He was smoking a Kool by an open window, his third one this morning.

This wasn't random. This was well planned.

As he went back to the train schedules, he also realized that the timing, if everything went right, placed no trains in the station *and,* by a good chance, no passengers, either, at the time of Brian's death. Feuss came in while Jonesy was recording some significant times in his own notebook, and reminders of what to check next.

Feuss interrupted, without noticing that Jonesy was busily entering his notes.

"Faisano had the post from Rockaway Blvd. to Grant Avenue on the 'A' line when that *skell* was offed."

Jonesy looked up, annoyed.

"His name was Brian Addams...and he was a war hero from the Gulf War, for Christ's sake."

Feuss looked at him, surprised.

"*Really,* Jonesy?" mocking him now. "That's great!...Who gives a fuck, ya' prick? Ya' catch religion or something?"

Jonesy didn't answer. He just shook his head and entered more information in his notebook.

Feuss interrupted again.

"Let's take a ride to Rockaway. We can kill time and eat at that Deli on 116th Street."

Jonesy wasn't about to explain his recent interest to anyone. He couldn't explain it to himself. He decided not to share his thoughts with his partner, and certainly did not want to share that he'd spent almost two hours with Mrs. Addams. He'd never hear the end of it. They put on their suit jackets and full length overcoats. Jonesy put on his fedora, and had an unlit Kool dangling from his mouth as they walked out of the office building in Downtown Brooklyn, on their way over to the Rockaways.

Jonesy drove. The ride was relatively quiet. Halfway there, Feuss asked if they should touch base with Malaro and bounce some things off him like they'd done in the past. Jonesy thought about it for a second. Malaro was sharp, and had put him in the right direction for other capers. Jonesy liked Tony, too. But he was on his 'A' game now, and could be just as sharp himself.

"Nah, let's see what we turn up on our own." Jonesy answered.

Feuss looked at him sourly. Usually, if there was a short-cut to something, Jonesy and Feuss would take advantage of it, and take all the credit anyway.

Feuss thought it over, and then replied.

"I get ya'. We can do this on our own. Tony can be a little bit of a know-it-all sometimes, anyway."

Jonesy looked at him and laughed.

"He knows more than you do, ya' dumb-assed motherfucker."

"Yeah, that's true, but I got more money and a condo in Florida."

Jonesy chuckled. "Hah, I'm sure *he's* jealous of *you*."

They were approaching Jamaica Bay, which separated the rest of Queens from the Rockaway peninsula. There was silence for a moment in the car as Billy fished in the glove compartment for the NYPD parking placard that would get them a free ride over the Cross Bay Bridge out of Broad Channel and over to the Rockaways.

Feuss asked. "Whatever happened to him anyway?"

"Who?" Jonesy asked as he continued to drive and occasionally looked out over the water.

"Tony! Who the fuck have we been talkin' about? Tony...What happened to him? I heard rumors and shit...weren't you already in the DD when he got busted back to patrol? I heard he fucked up big time."

Jonesy answered.

"That's bullshit. The only person I ever heard talk that shit was Quinn. He never liked Malaro. Quinn was just another jealous shit who didn't do much on the road. Just like the Captain who works out here."

Jonesy continued.

"No. Malaro wasn't a fuck-up, just got screwed as easily as

anyone else would have, being in the wrong place at the wrong time. He was the top guy in the Major Case Squad. Nobody could touch him. A string of good luck and some solid police work. He closed some of the toughest capers. It was more than the luck, though. He was good. He was good with the brothers and he was good with '*Ricans*. He treated everybody with respect and they respected him. Tough when he had to be, but he never went overboard, like everyone else did."

Feuss interrupted. "So what happened?"

Jonesy continued. "Tony was painted a *skell* cop because he shot some mutt. A shit-load of protests started because nobody found the weapon."

Jonesy stopped and thought for a while, as he lit up another one of his Kools. He blew the smoke out slowly through his nose and mouth and went on.

"Quinn fucked that one up. He wouldn't know how to do a crime scene if it bit him in the ass. The protests brought up all that other crap about another shootin' in the *Black* community, even though she was really Puerto Rican. The media didn't care about the facts, though. It sold more papers, made people watch the news on TV. Everyone was in an uproar cause a white cop shot a black girl."

"Holy shit!...Don't tell me—she was '*getting her act together*,' right?— was going to enroll in NYU in the fall."

Jonesy just shook his head. "Yeah, something like that."

Jonesy continued, a little angry from Feuss's last comment.

"Ya' know, Billy, not every shoot is a clean one. I tell this to the Guardians all the time, and I'll tell you. What it is, is what it is."

Billy interrupted.

"Let me write that one down," as he patted his breast coat pocket, pretending to look for a pen.

Jonesy went on, becoming increasingly agitated, even though he knew Billy was just attempting to get a rise out of him. Jonesy had worked with Billy for years and they were tight.

"Billy, every incident can't get the same treatment. It takes away from the few bad shootings that need serious attention, and lumps them all together. When the protests start and the call for an independent investigation is all over the papers, it makes it hard to sift through genuine *nigger*-shooters, Billy...and they do exist."

Billy answered, sarcastically.

"Okay—calm down, *Reverend,* I just asked about Tony."

Jonesy caught his breath and flicked his cigarette out the window. He liked Billy a lot, but he was sometimes a moron.

"Ain't you listening, motherfucker? It was a good shoot and a bad shake for Tony. He made out all right. If it was a brother that'd killed somebody, not only would he a' been kicked out of the Detective Bureau, he would have lost his job, too."

Chapter Nineteen

Jonesy and Billy entered District 23 at 7:30 PM. They were following up on the police memo book entries connected to the DOA at 80th Street. Jonesy also wanted to check his overtime that weekend, and make sure his cousin, a police officer in the command, was on the right track and staying out of trouble. He'd heard from his sister that Erica was getting a little lippy, and he wanted to smack her around a bit.

Jonesy also wanted to run something by the Captain. As they entered, there was some commotion at the desk. A Hispanic woman, attractive, about thirty-five years old, with long hair in a pony tail and a fresh black eye, was rambling in half Spanish and broken English to the Desk Officer about her boyfriend, who had apparently just beaten her up. She was wearing a long overcoat and had her hands in her pockets. She had just finished her story, and there were three uniformed officers standing right next to her with big smiles on their faces.

"Jonesy," Lt. Harvey yelled to the two detectives as they were trying to squeeze by the front desk.

"Yes, Lieu?" Jonesy asked.

With feigned concern, the Lieutenant continued.

"You won't *believe* what some son-of-a-bitch did. Tell him your story, Ms. Suares, he's a Detective."

Ms. Suares began her story again. From what Jonesy and Billy could decipher, her boyfriend had come home drunk, accused her of fooling around with his friend and started beating on her. Jonesy couldn't figure out why the Lieutenant had called them over.

Why did he drag us over for this bullshit? It happened in an apartment. They'd have to call the local precinct to handle a street job, anyway. Transit's area was strictly the subway.

137

Billy didn't mind, though. He loved a good story, and she *was* pretty.

The story went way too long, and Jonesy and Billy were getting anxious. The cops that had already heard this story once still remained. Apparently they were in no hurry to get back to whatever they were *not* doing anyhow. They stood with exaggerated looks of concern on their faces as they listened to the whole tale a second time. Jonesy was starting to figure out what to say and how to get out of there to take care of his own business, when she apparently got to the end. Jonesy reluctantly focused in again.

"...and after dat he poonch me in the ribs and left dees."

Ms. Suares opened her overcoat with her hands still in the pockets and posed; she had no clothes on underneath the coat. She just stood there, showing the small bruise below her magnificent left breast, and held the coat open for about five seconds.

"Holy shit!" Jonesy gasped, suddenly realizing why the Desk Officer had called him over.

He'd have to thank him later. Billy just stood there with his mouth open, and the other cops refreshed their grins again.

"Somebody better get on that right away, Lieutenant." Jonesy stated plainly as he brushed by the giggling officers, grabbing Billy by the arm and dragging him into the back muster room.

Billy was shaking his head in disbelief while Jonesy escorted him away. Jonesy dropped Billy off with the clerical man to retrieve some memo books and archived post assignments from the night Brian Addams was murdered. He then went to the roll call man to check on his overtime post scheduled for after his shift. After that, he looked for his cousin, Erica Wheeler, in the locker room. He couldn't find her and asked the radio room officer, Ben Tripp, a black cop in his late forties, how she was doing.

Tripp told him. "She *could* be a little more 'low key,' man."

Jonesy talked to him some more and then left. He'd make it a point to sit down with Erica and discuss long term goals and the big picture.

She's young and stupid, just like everyone else her age.

Jonesy then went to the Captain's office, knocked on the half-opened door, and was summoned in even though he was already halfway into the room. Captain Reitman had just put a copy of Newsweek in his top desk drawer and Jonesy caught a glimpse of it before he briskly put it away. Jonesy dreaded this conversation, as he did when he spoke with most bosses.

He approached the desk and the Captain directed him to take a seat. The Captain sat at a 100 year-old mahogany desk that he'd brought into the command when he was promoted. He'd had it lifted a subtle extra four inches from the floor in order to gain some type of psychological edge when he met with underlings that were seated in his office. He'd heard something about J. Edgar Hoover doing the same thing, and didn't get that it was slightly disturbed. The Captain also had a number of thriving plants he maintained daily, and some expensive window treatments. As a boss, the Captain spent a lot of time in his office. He preferred it that way, and he wanted to be comfortable. Jonesy thought, as did most of the cops, that the Captain was a bit of a wimp. He maintained impeccable reports and he color-coded files and just about everything else for organizational purposes. His office was a sterile place, and although cozy for the Captain, plain uncomfortable for everyone else.

He began by asking if there was any progress on the homicides.

Jonesy pulled out his memo book and gave a recap of events, most of it uninterrupted. He spoke for four minutes about the research he and Billy were conducting. He was approaching the part of the investigation where the Captain was most interested, and he knew why.

Jonesy went on.

"Well, the dead girl found at Far Rockaway was ID'd by Feuss and followed up by Kevin and Venera. She was a *skell,* too. It doesn't look like it happened there, though. From interviews that Kevin and Vinnie conducted...ya' know, from the family and other *skells,* it looks like she hung out strictly in Manhattan."

Jonesy looked up from his notes for a response from the Captain, but didn't get one.

"Assuming the memo books are right and they match the car numbers from the rookie's Tactical Patrol Force runs..." Jonesy continued. "The ME has her dead for no longer than ten hours. Looks like she bought it somewhere in Manhattan, arrived here once, went all the way up and back again to Far Rockaway."

Jonesy closed his book, then went on with his report. He knew it by heart now anyway.

"The timing's pretty close. There were no reported delays or interruptions of service." Jonesy waited yet again.

The Captain finally spoke.

"Shit, Jonesy, a dead *skell* rides through three boroughs for ten hours and nobody notices? I don't want to eat that one, damn it! Put it in Manhattan where it belongs!"

Jonesy looked up.

"I can't *do* that, Captain. The crime scene was here, the DOA was here, and she was killed on the train. Unfortunately, you own it."

The Captain looked out his window at the parking lot, flustered and red in the face.

"There's more," Jonesy added.

"Oh, go ahead, get on with it." The Captain sighed. He was obviously agitated, and continued to stare out of the window into the parking lot as Jonesy resumed.

"There was something missing from Brian Addams after he was shot...a Marine insignia on his shirt lapel. His mother told me about it.

Then I went back to all the merchants and other *skells* who knew him in the area. They all remember it being on Addams. I didn't tell any of them what it was I was looking for, either. I just asked if he ever wore anything familiar. They all said either the Marine insignia or they described the eagle and globe emblem."

He paused.

"The dead girl with the ice pick in Rockaway was missing a necklace her mother gave her. Kevin was at the morgue yesterday and followed up on the marks on the girl's neck. She always had on a leather necklace with an ivory face on the end, according to her friends and family. I don't think it's gonna' be a surprise if the Jane Doe wheelchair girl turns up missing shit, too. So far, we have two victims missing items, after they were killed, and both women were pregnant."

Jonesy paused again for a moment, then went on.

"Our boy we're looking for is taking things now...like souvenirs..."

Jonesy waited again for a response, but the Captain didn't give him one. Jonesy was getting annoyed that he was doing all the talking.

Phew. All right, here it goes.

"Captain, I think this guy killed three people over the last month or so. The Prodski girl first with the ice pick, Bryan Addams with a gunshot to the head, and this last woman he lasso'd at 88th Street. I'm thinking there might have been more. I'm lookin' over all the homicides on the system for the past twelve months. There's one more thing. I didn't even tell my partner about it, because I don't want this floatin' around and originatin' from me..."

Jonesy hesitated, his voice lowered slightly.

"I think it's a cop."

Jonesy just tossed that out there as a trial balloon. It floated heavily in the air. The Captain continued to stare out the window, but turned around slowly after a long ten seconds and met Jonesy's eyes.

"Jonesy, let's be careful here. You remember when we had that nut, Caprianis in District 33?"

It was a rhetorical question.

"He killed...or we thought he killed two *skells* on the 'L' line. He was dating the girls from the shelter. We took a lot of shit on that one. The problem was, Jonesy, we knew he did it, we just couldn't prove it. So, politically, and I know you guys don't dwell on that too much, but politically, we took a major hit on our screening process, training, the quality of the people we hire, and so on. Transit wound up getting shit for years. *And,* if you remember, Caprianis didn't even lose his job, never mind being arrested. He just resigned and went to Florida. Did us a favor, if you ask me."

The Captain, who had been pacing while he talked, walked slowly back to his chair and sat down behind his desk.

"Anyhow, what I'm saying is...Jonesy, you better be more than 100% sure before we throw anything like that out anywhere. If you're wrong, *"we'll"* –and what I really mean is *"you'll"*– be in some knee-deep shit."

Jonesy knew the Captain was a jackass, but if there was one thing the Captain was good at, it was keeping off the radar and not getting jammed up with the higher ups. Jonesy thought about what he'd said, and he knew the Captain was probably right. It could be someone else who had access to train schedules, cop's schedules, and knew about 10-13's.

Bullshit, It might not be a cop, but I don't believe in coincidences.

"Well," Jonesy said, "here's a couple of things I got. Brian Addams was killed at 80th Street. About five minutes before he gets whacked, an emergency 10-13 is called at Grant Avenue, one stop away. That pulls any cop within a five mile radius, street cops included, down to Grant and away from 80th Street at the time of the murder. The timing of 80th Street also puts two trains pulling out of the station at almost exactly the same time, leaving the station dead-empty, except for Addams and the mope who killed him. I already checked out the trainmaster's office to see if anybody's work schedule matched and could put them at the station at that time. I didn't find anyone from the Transit Authority. The next thing I'm looking into are all the shifts and officer's posts, and the uniformed TPF runs throughout the 'A' line on both nights the *skells* out here were killed."

Jonesy paused. This time he was going to stick with the uncomfortable silence and wait for the Captain to say something. He waited a full minute.

The Captain sat back in his oversized desk chair and clasped his hands behind his head.

"That sounds like a real gamble with the trains pulling out at the same time, and this mutt hopes nobody remains on the platform or comes up the stairs?"

Jonesy answered quickly, having already considered this.

"This guy is in no hurry, Captain. He waits for an opportune time after careful planning. The way I figure it, if something doesn't pan out, or even if he gets a bad feeling, he'll wait for another time or pick someone else. He's patient."

The Captain considered this.

"Okay, Jonesy, you do what you gotta' do. Just keep it to yourself and don't repeat this to anyone else until we're sure. The last thing we want to be is embarrassed. At some point, and *you'll* be sure to let me know when that is, because we ain't there yet, we'll need to notify Internal Affairs.

We also need to look at all the other responsibilities when there are pattern killings. I might be out of practice, but I think we probably need to contact someone from the FBI. If you get anything concrete, come see me and we'll map out a game plan. Sergeant O'Shea and I already talked about the souvenir bullshit... He and I agreed to keep this quiet for now. I advise you to do the same. This way you're off the hook for now, you notified the Precinct Commander and your immediate supervisor is up to speed. And by the way—no newspapers. It's going to be hard enough. Having the papers involved might just spook someone, and then we won't have anything."

Chapter Twenty

March 11, 2006
District 23
Far Rockaway, Queens

Jonesy had just finished his 4:00 PM to midnight shift in the DD. Jonesy maintained a locker at the Major Case office and another in District 23. He changed into uniform for his overtime post at Broad Channel. Feuss's assigned overtime was in District 33 in Brooklyn, a few stops from Jonesy's assignment. Jonesy was supposed to patrol the stretch from Rockaway Blvd. to Mott Avenue, riding trains back and forth. He'd already talked to Sergeant Quinn for ten minutes. He was not supposed to share any of his ideas about the case, as directed by the Captain, but nobody listened to the Captain anyway. Over the past three days, he'd told Sergeant Quinn, his cousin Erica, and Officer Tripp what he felt about the case. It was just too big to hold in all to himself.

Quinn didn't believe that the killer could be a cop, and told him to keep looking. Officer Tripp was skeptical, too, but Jonesy's cousin, Erica, was interested. Erica made a comment about that type of crime being "strictly for *whitey*." Jonesy agreed.

Jonesy picked up his radio and headed to his post. He knew no boss ever noticed him missing when he took his usual three hour nap. But this overtime shift, he was going to work the case and review roll call assignments for the last few months. He left the command and stopped in at Broad Channel to let the clerk get a good look at him so someone could verify he was there at least once during his overtime tour. He then boarded the northbound 'A' train and found his usual room at Euclid Avenue, in Brooklyn. Euclid was underground within the confines of District 33, about four stops away from his assigned post. Cops knew it would be ill-advised to goof-off near or at the assigned post. Most accomplished pails were even better at this than Jonesy. The real smart ones stayed clear of the subway system altogether. But Jonesy didn't have a broad to coop with for this shift, and he had work to do anyway.

The room at Euclid would be perfect. He got off at Euclid Avenue station at 12:20 AM and went up the stairs to cross over to the other platform. As he passed the clerk, Jonesy asked when the next southbound was coming, just to make it appear he was going to be on it, then shot down the other stairs. In the middle of the platform was a room that most of the rookies didn't know about. He hurried down the platform, unlocked the door and locked it behind him. Jonesy then walked down a narrow hallway with no lights, and saw the lighted room ten feet in front of him.

Some of the Transit Authority rooms were fairly decent. Not the Plaza hotel, but this was one of the better areas to kill time. There were long gray benches; a broom-swept concrete floor, some narrow lockers, and a small refrigerator. A couple of old desks were against one wall, with ancient black rotary phones on top of them. Behind both desks were large bulletin boards with thumb-tacked notes covering every inch of the cork. Dozens of plumbing pipes of varying thickness hung from the ceiling. He took off his gun belt, which also carried his radio, nightstick and mace, and hung it on a hook between the bulletin boards. The equipment became heavy when cops went to plainclothes and usually didn't carry it every day. He looked around. Normally he'd already be into his nap. He had an alarm clock feature on his cell phone. It wasn't a good idea to oversleep and turn up missing after four hours of overtime. That would be a dead giveaway. He wasn't going to let that happen again. He'd been half an hour late once, about six weeks back, but Quinn had bailed him out.

He took off his shoes and was just about to stretch out and read some assignment sheets, when he heard a slight shuffle in the entrance hallway.

Damn that Feuss! He thought. *He's gonna' fuck it up for everyone...two guys at the same spot!*

He scurried over to the door in his socks and opened it. He looked up at *Hunter*. But Jonesy couldn't quickly process what was directly in front of his face: a silencer that was attached to a .45 caliber automatic. Concluding the inevitable, all rational thoughts left his mind. Acting on instinct, Jonesy turned around to look behind him. He could see his gun hanging on the hook about fifteen feet from where he was standing. For a split second, he thought he might make it.

Chapter Twenty-One

March 11, 2006
Euclid Avenue Subway Station
Brooklyn, NY

A porter found Jonesy in the small room on the Euclid Avenue platform. The detective was expected to return to District 23 at 4:00 AM. Since he'd missed return roll call recently, Sergeant Quinn later told O'Shea he thought Jonesy had overslept again. A search didn't go out until 5:00 AM. Mostly those officers looking did so with snickers. If he *was* sleeping again, what a *schmuck*! The men agreed he would've deserved to get his balls busted. A few cops knew about the room at Euclid. They let Quinn know where he might be.

A short conversation occurred between Quinn and the assistant Desk Officer. Quinn decided to save someone from trekking all the way out there to wake him up. He still had three more hours until the end of the midnight shift. Quinn called the booth directly and asked if there was anybody at the station who could go wake up a possibly "sick" officer down in the platform room. The clerk assured him that he had seen Jonesy earlier in the night, but he could have sworn he saw the police officer run down to catch an outgoing train. Quinn rolled his eyes while he was receiving this information, telling his assistant desk officer afterward that he knew exactly what Jonesy's ploy had been; making the clerk believe he'd left the station. Quinn asked the clerk to send someone down anyway. Ten minutes later a porter showed up at the Euclid station and the clerk directed him to wake up Jonesy. The station exploded with activity after that.

Police Departments take on a different personality when one of their own is gunned down. Outsiders wouldn't see more somber faces after a fellow officer was shot, especially faces that had worked in the same command as the deceased. The Euclid Avenue station was swarming with cops within half an hour. Sergeant O'Shea himself handled the crime scene, along with the Commanding Officer from Major Case, Inspector Gavin McHale.

McHale was an old salt and top notch in his day. He resented being a boss, and had always been a cop's cop. He was well liked, but had little or nothing to do with ongoing criminal investigations. The Inspector hadn't attended a crime scene in eight years, but he'd been Jonesy's patrol Sergeant when he was a rookie cop almost twenty years ago. Nobody minded him being there. Even though his appearance was shoddy, with his old trench coat, handlebar mustache and moderate beer belly, he had a presence about him. The Inspector had always commanded a healthy respect from everyone, but was humble and wise enough to stay out of the way.

Kevin and Venera were called, too. They were going to need everyone for this one. Even Malaro was on his way in from home after receiving a call from Pulaski. His old partner was on duty in District 33, had heard what was happening on the radio, and called Tony. Nobody would mind Malaro showing up, either. He was the best among them and they all knew it. He'd also known Jonesy for a long time.

The first cops to arrive at Euclid station were so distraught when they saw the crime scene, they had to be relieved of duty. It was their first homicide, never mind their first victim being a cop that they knew. They did a good job before leaving, however. They taped-off the area, called for a Duty Captain, ambulance, and crime scene unit. They didn't really lose it until the rest of the onslaught arrived. There were over one hundred cops in a one block area. Many were standing around. Quite a few were canvassing for TA workers who had been working the shift, or they were knocking on doors upstairs at six o'clock in the morning. Not many witnesses would be expected at this time of day, but in New York, there could always be someone who saw something. Whether they would bother to report it was a different story. It was startling the amount of information some witnesses had, but for lack of a direct question, didn't give to the appropriate people.

Kevin swung by Vinnie's mother's house and picked him up on the way to Euclid Avenue. Venera was in jeans and looked like he'd just rolled out of bed. Kevin was in his tie, tan slacks and clean-shaven. When they arrived at the station, Vinnie and Kevin spoke briefly to a couple of uniformed cops who had turned out of roll call with Jonesy earlier. Kevin and Vinnie walked down the stairs to the platform area, casually nodding to most of the uniformed officers as they passed. Mike O'Shea and Inspector McHale were waiting at the doorway to the room where Jonesy lay.

McHale and O'Shea had been the first detectives on scene. They'd peeked in the room quickly before Vinnie and Kevin arrived, but Mike had decided to wait five minutes and have all four of them go in together. If there was going to be any initial assessments, Mike believed that four solid investigators were better than two. The Inspector had agreed. Mike was in no hurry to go running in there anyway. Although he had been on the job for fifteen years, this was his first case involving a member of the force.

The Crime Scene Unit was also on the platform, about ten yards from the four Major Case Detectives. They had on the standard suits and trench coats with contrasting, colored, fedora hats. They'd been on duty from the midnight shift, and had been catching some shut-eye before they were called out of Borough Headquarters. They were talking to each other about the delay, but would wait patiently until the Inspector gave them the go ahead. They knew not to say a word. Frequently, at these types of investigations involving examining one of their own, some thoughtless officer would utter something inappropriate or insensitive and an instant brawl would break out among cops.

Unlike most crime scenes, this morning there would be none of the usual banter or wisecracks by detectives. That talk was reserved for DOA's who were strangers. Prior to the arrival of Kevin and Vinnie, McHale had instructed the Crime Scene Unit team to take pictures, but told them not to touch anything in the crime scene. He wanted the photos taken before the four went in and started poking around. They were finished taking pictures in twenty minutes. The Inspector then directed them out of the room and told them to wait for print-taking and other evidence gathering until after the four detectives were done. This was not the usual protocol, but they weren't going to argue with an Inspector at the scene who had known the dead officer.

Kevin and Vinnie walked up to the two older detectives and nodded.

"Ready?" Mike asked the rest of the team.

Kevin, Venera, O'Shea and the Inspector bent under the yellow crime scene tape and walked down the short corridor until the narrow passageway opened up to the main room. Jonesy was lying face down, sprawled out on the floor, with a two-inch hole in the back of his head. He was halfway in the room, his gun belt still hanging on a hook by the desk with the bulletin boards overhead. His service revolver was missing from the holster. The four seasoned detectives divided the room into quarters and each examined every inch. There wasn't a detective in the room who didn't have a tear dripping down his cheek in the first two minutes. Not a word was spoken.

After the initial shock and the subsequent emotions discreetly displayed by all of the detectives, they began their methodical search of the room. When they were done, they'd review each other's observations while still in the room and piece together the scenario. It was Kevin's turn to take notes and record important information and to leave out comments that would be considered "off the record." Everything a detective recorded in note form could be used in court.

O'Shea spoke first.

"The clerk didn't see anyone cross over to this platform after Jonesy went down the stairs at about 12:30. Our mutt must've come in on the train on the same platform, or walked up the tracks to get here without being noticed. If he knew Jonesy was here, I'd bet he walked from the nearest emergency exit up the tracks. To tell ya' the truth, I'm wondering if Jonesy was porkin' somebody's wife."

It was a thought that had crossed all their minds, and one that Kevin did not jot down. A lot of cops were dogs like that. Mike looked around at all of the men in the room. No one responded. They would go from one to the other without being interrupted. No one wanted to trigger anyone else by interrupting or contradicting. Not this morning, anyway. O'Shea continued.

"He's either got his own keys or Jonesy let him in when he knocked. Jonesy didn't expect any mope with a gun. He wouldn't have been answering the door in his socks if he thought he was in any danger. At some point, and I'm guessing early on in the meeting, Jonesy tried to make it back to his weapon...with no luck. This fucker has his gun now, too. Inspector?"

The Inspector answered.

"I don't see anything else in my quad that doesn't support your version of how it happened. That being said, I don't think we should be talking anymore about a jealous husband or boyfriend, though, until we get some more information."

The Inspector didn't care if he stepped on anyone's toes. No one was going to punch him out, no matter what he said. He continued, somewhat puzzled.

"But what's Jonesy doing here? He's four or five stations off post. I don't know... It's your show Mike. Just let me know what you want me to do. You name it, you got it."

O'Shea gave a nod of appreciation.

"Thanks Inspector...Kevin? What do you think?"

Kevin sighed heavily.

"Everyone knew he hung out here on overtime. He usually slept. But that's why he's here, Inspector." He looked back to Mike. "His memo book is gone, too. I don't know why anyone would want that. I can see taking the gun, maybe even as an after thought, but the memo book doesn't make sense if this is somebody's man that got pissed off. And this doesn't look to me like Jonesy was at the wrong place at the wrong time. No. Jonesy was the target."

Kevin said this with conviction. He didn't care if he was called on this observation. He assumed they all would arrive at the same conclusion sooner or later, but Kevin knew he was right. He continued.

"We need to go get his notes back in his locker. We need to look at both of his lockers. He had one at District 23 for his uniform and overtime shit, and one back at the Major Case locker room. We should look for all his files on these *skell* killings, computer entries and everything else."

"Where's Feuss?" Vinnie finally realized.

O'Shea responded. "They called him at his house in Staten Island. He should be here in a little while."

Vinnie then spoke.

"Anyway, I guess I'll throw in my two cents. He wasn't sleepin'. He's got his flashlight in his back pocket. I know he liked his "Z's" every once in a while, but he was working these *skell* murders hard lately, and we all noticed it. A couple of the midnight cops said he had a thin, zippered notebook with him tonight, and I don't see that anywhere. I'm with Kevin. We need to be all over the shit he was working on and start from there."

Some footsteps were coming from the back where they'd entered. They all turned around hoping it wasn't Feuss, Jonesy's partner. It wasn't. It was Tony Malaro with an unlit cigarette in his mouth. He stopped at the doorway and looked down at Jonesy.

"Mother-*fucker*" he said, emphasizing the last half of the epithet.

Tony went straight to business. He walked directly over to Jonesy's body and crouched down.

"What've you got so far?"

O'Shea began to fill him in. Before O'Shea got to Kevin's observations, Tony cut him off.

"We got to get to his shit. See what or *who* he was on to..."

O'Shea looked up at Kevin and half smiled for the first time in hours. He then said to Tony.

"You trained your boy well. That's what Kevin suggested."

Malaro displayed a slight glimmer of pride and stood back up.

"Ya' think you can use me, Mike? I'd like to help out if I can. I'm getting a little bored doing those token booth relief assignments."

O'Shea knew he could use him.

"What do you think Inspector? You got enough juice to bring back Tony here? Anything you could do, remember?" O'Shea asked.

The Inspector nodded in the affirmative.

"Special times call for special considerations. Don't you think so, Michael?"

After another twenty minutes of gathering information around the room, and a few additional brief conversations, they all inspected the body. Venera noticed two smaller holes in Jonesy's back that were obscured by creases in the shirt at first glance. Vinnie pointed it out to the rest of the Detectives in the room.

"He took two in the back as he ran for his gun and one up close in the head when he was stopped."

They left the room, and the Inspector had the Crime Scene Unit finish up what they needed to do. They all agreed to meet back at

District 23 in the Rockaways to review assignments for the investigation, and to go through Jonesy's locker. Another team would cover both platforms and examine the tracks and emergency exits on both sides of the tracks.

Chapter Twenty-Two

Hunter sat at his kitchen table drinking a cup of coffee. He was up early for work and had been day-dreaming again, attempting to work out what he was going to do next. Officer Jones was a no-brainer. If he hadn't done him, things were going to unravel quickly. It was not in the plans though, to kill a cop. That wasn't part of the plan at all.

But, what's done is done. Think, stupid! What was the original plan? I have to step this up and finish ahead of schedule. Jones is gone. One more. One more will be the key to solving the whole thing and I'll be at the top of the food chain, where I belong. I can wrap this up and show everyone. Grandma would be proud. Mother can rot in hell.

He continued to daydream. Thoughts were rambling into others, past and present coming together.

Everyone thought I was too young to remember. That's because I never talked about it. It never happened. Bullshit. I remember everything. The men. Her sitting me in a chair. Her Pall Malls. When I tried to cover my eyes and she'd yell. Her sickening perfume. I don't know where she found the sick bastards who didn't mind that shit. I hate them all. She deserved to die the way she did. They all do. Skells having babies...*Fuck that!. What was the term I used...retroactive abortion. Those two* skells...*Prodski and the other one in the wheel chair...sick.*

Cops saw him around the command almost everyday. *Hunter* had access to all the roll calls, muster room, memo books, etc., and complaint reports. That's how he knew they were pregnant. They had been ejected from the subway on several occasions and it was noted in the police reports.

No one would even question why he was in any of the rooms or even reviewing patrol records. In the back of the command was the officer's locker rooms. There were no windows and twenty rows of battleship gray lockers. Each row had eight-foot benches for cops to change.

Two days ago, he'd overheard Jonesy in the hallway. *Hunter* was just inside the locker room when he heard Jonesy talking to another cop. He recognized the other cop's voice. It was Jonesy's cousin, an angry young black woman with two years on the job. Jonesy had pulled some strings and used a "hook" to get her out to District 23 so he could keep an eye on her from time to time.

"What makes you think it's one of us?" Erica Wheeler asked.

"Look, rookie motherfucker." Jonesy reprimanded. "Keep it down. And I didn't say one of us. I agree with you. This guy's a stone-cold cracker. Brothers are never into this type of shit." Jonesy paused. "We may rob and steal people's shit, but we draw the line!" Both of them cracked up laughing at the same time.

Hunter continued to listen from behind the locker room door. He was always casually waiting in spots, listening, when people didn't realize it. That's how he got most of his information. Jonesy continued.

"I'm onto the fucker, too, I just hope he ain't from this command, but I'll know soon enough. Keep your mouth shut and your eyes open. It could be a porter, secretary, whatever. I doubt it though. Some of the information this mope needed to carry out these killings can be gotten from other places, too, but not *all* the information. All those schedules and shit this sucker needed to be successful are right here in the command."

Hunter was surprised by the speed with which Jones had come to these conclusions. He'd heard that, for the past few years, Jonesy was a bucket of shit. Normally, when assigned a case, Jonesy would go through the motions, occasionally get lucky, but always with minimal effort. This was different. He was actually looking into this. *Hunter* was thinking while the two he was listening to continued to chat.

I'm gonna' have to do something about this. I don't need some spook screwing up everything I planned.

Hunter walked by, relatively unnoticed by the two black officers talking, and went into the muster room to take a quick glance at the week's assignments. He got his information, jotted down the times, and knew where Jonesy would wind up during his overtime shift. The rooms where cops hid weren't as much of a secret as they would have liked them to be. He'd just have to wait and plan. That's all.

Hunter knew Jonesy would be at Euclid Avenue in two nights to sleep off most of his overtime tour. It was a matter of reviewing train schedules again. Timing. As always, timing was everything. He couldn't walk through the station. He'd be seen. Getting on and off trains would also be too risky, not to mention the possibility of actually bumping into a cop on the train or platform. No. *Hunter* would have to walk up the tracks from the emergency exit between the Grant Avenue and Euclid Avenue stations. He had the maps and schedules, and reviewed them ten times. The night before Jonesy's overtime shift, he went over the route and drove between the two stations. It wasn't easy finding the exact spot where the emergency grate on the ground was, but after half an hour driving around, he found it. *Hunter* made mental markers.

Past the green house with the decorative rails on the basement windows. About twenty feet in from of the fire hydrant.

After he drove by the first time and found the grate, he went to get something to eat, then drove back to the emergency exit at about eleven at night. He parked on the same side of the street. Luckily there were no houses directly in front of the hidden entrance to the subway. Quickly, but casually, he got out of his grandmother's car and tried the key. It worked. He'd practice this whole process two more times, except there was no need to take chances and actually get out of the vehicle again until he was ready to go down. *Hunter* didn't want to take any risks, so he wanted to make sure he knew exactly where the grate was. When he went down tomorrow night, he'd park his car a few blocks away. He knew what kind of heat would come from this event. If he saw *anyone* out that night, or even in a window, he'd think of something else and change his plans. He was looking to take even fewer chances as he approached the end of his dangerous journey.

One more day passed, and Jonesy's scheduled overtime day arrived. *Hunter* was anxious. He called in sick and watched TV into the night. He waited until he was sure Jonesy would be tucked away nicely in the room at Euclid Avenue, then drove up Fulton Street, made a right, and parked the car. He walked two blocks to the emergency exit. The neighborhood used to be all Italian, but was now a mix of Blacks, Puerto Ricans and, more recently, a heavy dose of people from the Middle East. He walked by some store fronts with rolled shutters covered in graffiti. He also passed some old, narrow, center hall row houses, about five feet separating them. Some of the homes were better maintained than others. He had just past the green house with the decorative bars on the basement windows, when he began thinking again.

Maybe I should have done this somewhere else. Nah, how would I sneak up on this spook in his own house? That would be ridiculous.

Hunter knew his limitations. This was best. Jonesy would be alone. He'd also be sleeping. *Hunter* was lost in thought when he heard a dog bark and snapped out of it, upset that he was not paying attention about something important again. He turned around quickly. He'd walked twenty yards past the emergency exit. The dog stopped barking and by then he was back to the exit again, past the green house with the bars.

He pulled out his keys, walked up to the lock and popped it open, then lifted up the heavy gate. At first it stuck due to lack of use. He pulled hard the second time and it released. It was on a gliding spring that made extremely heavy and unwieldy items easier to handle. He stepped onto the vertical ladder and went down four steps, then pulled the grate back down, being careful not to latch it so he could get out easily. The steps were very steep and his gloved hands gripped the rail that was marred by grease and dirt. He walked down the first set of steps in the dark, then used his flashlight to look around. It reminded him of the narrow ship ladders from the Navy, where he and other sailors had to squeeze between levels to get to lower parts of the ship. *Hunter* turned off his flashlight as his eyes adjusted. He could see one bulb covered by a yellow protective case, two more stair levels down, directly above the tracks.

According to his train records, a southbound 'A' should be passing by shortly in the direction of Euclid Avenue. He'd go down one more level and wait just above the tracks. After the train passed, he had about half an hour to walk down the tracks, take care of Jonesy and make it back out to the street. *Hunter* waited and waited...three, four, then five minutes past the time he'd recorded for the next train towards Euclid Avenue. Something was wrong. There must have been some delay.

A crime up the line? No. That would be too much of a coincidence. Switching problems. The trains were always having switching problems.

Hunter had to walk 200 yards down the track to get to the back end of the Euclid Avenue station. It was a long walk.

Well, I'll hear the train and duck into a room or space if it comes. Got to get going.

He was growing anxious. He climbed one more short-stepped

160

ladder attached to the tunnel wall and he was on the narrow walkway, three feet above and alongside the tracks. He could see the line of emergency lights up ahead, every hundred feet, curving around the tunnel. The tracks were full of small bits of garbage; a liquor bottle, crumpled empty pack of Newports, rocks and gravel, a small river of dirty water between the rails. There was a perpetual light breeze in the tunnels. Sometimes those small breezes were interrupted by strong periodic waves of wind pushed along by trains.

Hunter had gone about half way to the Euclid station when he heard the tracks click. He turned around but didn't see anything. He would have to check behind him frequently, while he picked up his pace. *Hunter* thought about finding a space to climb into if a train approached. It was true that there were hundreds, if not thousands, of abandoned, unused rooms and alcoves in tunnels throughout the city, but there were a lot of "dead" spaces as well. A person could be pushed up flat against the wall, and still be caught by a moving train. For just these situations, at intervals there were two-foot wide recesses, about 10 inches deep, but they were not the safest places, particularly if the trains were moving fast. *Hunter* continued with increased trepidation. The train would be approaching this curve slowly, and a room had to be near. If not, he'd have to use the recessed wall and ride it out.

It wouldn't be that bad. Unless the train was deadheading, empty of all passengers, and making up time.

He had traveled an additional thirty feet when he turned and saw the lights behind him. It *wasn't* coming up slowly like he'd expected.

Hunter's heart was in his throat as he cursed himself for not waiting.

I don't know what my hurry is. That fucker will be asleep for hours!

He started jogging in the tunnel and glanced behind him again.

The train had covered half the distance since the first time he'd looked.

"Oh shit!" He yelped out loud.

Hunter tripped and fell on the walking platform, cutting his gloved hand on a broken liquor bottle. He cursed again. He could just cross the tracks, but at this point the motorman would see him, blare the horn, and call the trainmaster to report a man on the tracks. It was too late to cross the tracks unnoticed. *Hunter* quickly rose, running on all fours at first to try and get to his feet. As he reached his feet, he saw the red striped paint indicating a recess in the wall ten feet in front of him. The train would catch his clothes or body if he didn't make the recess. And it still might grab him even if he did make it. He looked one last time over his shoulder. The train was doing about 50 mph and was twenty yards away.

He reached the recess and pressed his back up against the wall, pushing with his feet and toes with all his might. He pressed as though if he pushed hard enough, he could melt through the concrete slab to safety. The train whooshed by, wind riffling his clothes, nearly sucking him along. *Hunter* turned his head and pressed his cheek flat to the wall, letting out a scream. With the deafening noise of the train speeding by, no one would hear. He then clenched his teeth and closed his eyes tightly as the train flew by, seeming to have no end. When the last car passed, he collapsed and crouched like a little boy who'd just hurt himself on the playground. His hands were cupping his face and he was now laughing nervously with tears streaming down his face. He got up, shook it off and calmly continued the walk towards Euclid. The motorman hadn't seen him. He would have stopped or sounded the horn if he had.

Hunter arrived at the platform stairs and took two steps, stopped short of the platform to make sure no one was around, and then made a quick walk to the room where Jonesy would be. He pulled the .45 out of his coat pocket and attached a silencer. He wasn't as accomplished with weapons as he'd like to be, and it took him three attempts to thread the attachment. He then looked up and down the platform and across the tracks to the other platform. There was no one around. He moved to the door and got out his key to open it. Jonesy would be sleeping, but he had the gun in his hand just in case. He opened the door. Jonesy was coming toward him, cursing something about his partner, Feuss.

No problem. I knew this was a possibility.

Hunter stepped through the door and closed it behind him before Jonesy could figure out what the deal was. Jonesy stopped and stared in disbelief. He then turned quickly, made a run for his gun belt hanging across the room. *Hunter* raised the .45 and began squeezing off rounds. The first one hit the wall. The next two found Jonesy's back. *Hunter* walked up to Jonesy, who was still barely conscious. Jonesy was breathing heavily, rasping actually, as his face pressed against the floor. Jonesy heard *Hunter* walking slowly up behind him.

Jonesy turned his head sideways, rapidly losing strength, and boldly stated,

"I would have got to you sooner or later, motherfucker."

Hunter smiled and said matter-of-factly, "No shit," as he leaned over and put the last hole in the back of Jonesy's head.

Chapter Twenty-Three

March 14, 2006
District 23
The Rockaways

Two days after Jonesy's murder, just before the second shift at 7:00 AM, Kevin, Mike and Vinnie were in the smaller interview room at the back of the District 23 command in the Rockaways. Malaro called. He wanted to stop by District 33 in East New York and then go to downtown Brooklyn to get more train records. Tony would be on his own most of the day, while Vinnie and Kevin would visit Mrs. Addams. Mike would call the shots and work out of the command. The three detectives were sorting out information re-cap sheets to be handed out to all the detectives working the case. The only physical evidence at this point was the blood a team of detectives found on the tracks in between Grant and Euclid Avenues. The blood evidence would be useful only if they had a suspect to match it with. Mike, Vinnie and Kevin were wrapping up a short meeting when they heard a scuffle and some shouts coming from the hallway outside the locker room. Nobody was going to bother getting up until it sounded like it was getting serious. Sergeant O'Shea got up and walked toward the locker room.

Venera shouted to him "Take care of that, will ya' Sarge?" laughing as he finished his sentence.

Mike walked into the hall and found two cops holding back Jonesy's cousin, Erica Wheeler. John Pulaski was standing in front of a new black police officer named Bryant.

"What's going on?" Sergeant O'Shea yelled.

All the cops by the locker room were relatively new to the job, except for Pulaski. A Sergeant yelling like that had impact. They all immediately straightened up and stopped their aggressiveness.

Pulaski spoke up.

"It's okay, Sarge, just a little harmless remark that didn't go over too well."

"Yeah, what about?" O'Shea asked.

Wheeler then spoke.

"He said something about my cousin sleeping in rooms."

"You big pussy," Bryant interjected. "Why don't you call your Mama too!"

The scuffling broke out again, but stopped quickly when O'Shea barked and grabbed Bryant by the necktie.

"STAND DOWN, OFFICER," he yelled at Bryant.

O'Shea then directed Wheeler to the supervisor's office and got in Bryant's face.

"What are you on the job for, all of five minutes? I'm not in the habit of nursing titty-mongers like you. The next time I even hear your voice, you'll be up in the Bronx doing midnights. And by the way, ask around. I don't bluff. AM I MAKING MYSELF CLEAR?"

"Yes sir." Bryant's lip was trembling as he spoke.

"And just for the record..." Sgt. O'Shea added. "...if you tried real hard, you could be half the cop Detective Jones was, and don't let anyone tell you different! Got that rookie?"

"Yes sir."

Mike walked out of the locker room, poked his head in on Vinnie and Kevin, and told them he'd be right back.

"Hey Sarge?" Kevin questioned.

"Yeah, what?" Mike answered as he was walking out.

"Titty-monger?" Kevin and Vinnie broke out laughing. Mike gave them the finger as he left.

Kevin yelled to Mike as he walked down the hallway.

"Come on, Sarge, let the day bosses take care of that bullshit."

O'Shea kept walking. He knew Kevin was right. He had better things to do, but he wanted to touch base with Wheeler anyway. Losing family wasn't easy.

Sergeant O'Shea walked into the supervisor's room and the slight, dark, wiry woman, with her hair in a tight bun, was pacing back and forth. She was attractive, but did her best to hide it. She wanted attention for her abilities as a cop and nothing else. Mike had heard that she was a collegiate athlete, a track star. Wheeler had a reputation as a hothead and many cops, black and white, didn't care for her too much. Jonesy had told Mike over a month ago that he got her down here to keep her out of trouble while she was still on probation. Mike also heard from others that Wheeler had the makings of a good cop, but just needed the edges ironed out a bit. What she lacked in social graces toward fellow officers, she made up for by dealing well with the public and making good collars. She was hard when she needed to be, and soft when necessary.

"Calm down, Wheeler. It's over."

Mike pulled up a chair and sat down.

Wheeler engaged in the conversation right away as she paced the room. She didn't want Bryant in trouble, so she began openly talking now, trying to verify or refute what Bryant told her.

"Was he a pail of shit, Sarge?"

Mike was ready for most things, even this grown woman breaking down and crying over her cousin, but he wasn't ready for this.

"Sit down, Wheeler."

Erica pulled out a chair from the supervisor's table and sat down. Mike took a pack of Kents from his shirt pocket, lit one, and sat across from her.

"Did Jonesy ever talk about the squad?"

Wheeler was now equally surprised. She wanted a straight answer.

"Yeah, he talked a lot about it. He always emphasized the importance of keeping your mouth shut and paying attention to the world around you. Not just the witnesses or the mopes, but the people you worked with. He said most of the assholes on the job had an agenda, whether it be the Guardians or the Guineas or whatever. He said you had to be very politically aware. I didn't get that part. The only guys he talked about with respect were you, Vinnie, Kevin and Malaro. He thought the rest in that unit were assholes, who would hand you over on a platter in a heartbeat. So with that respect my cousin had for you, I'd appreciate it if you'd answer my question... Was he a pail?"

Mike told her all about Jonesy. How he was a hot shit detective and how he slowed down after a few years in the unit. He also told her how he was revived by the murder of Bryan Addams, and how he was as sharp as he had ever been these past couple of weeks.

"When we bust this thing...and we will, it will be because of Jonesy's hard work. We're pretty sure he was onto something or somebody, and that could have been why he was killed."

Wheeler stared at the wall. She knew her cousin's ways. She had caught Jonesy herself a couple of times, sleeping or smelling like booze.

"I appreciate you not sugar-coating it for me. I respect that. It sounds like you liked him, too."

Mike answered.

"Nobody's perfect, Erica. But everyone has value, too. He was a good cop...and a good friend."

Mike changed direction.

"Listen, I gotta go." He stood up.

Wheeler got up too and shook Mike's hand and thanked him.

"Look Sarge, if there is anything I can do to help out...I know I ain't got the experience like you and your boys, but you know I'd work hard. Just let me know."

"Thanks Erica. I'll keep that in mind."

Chapter Twenty-Four

March 15, 2006
Jackie Robinson Parkway
Brooklyn, NY

The third evening after Jonesy's death, Kevin was driving home to Woodhaven, Queens. The sky was clear and full of bright stars that peaked through the trees as he sped along the Jackie Robinson Parkway. He usually drove home with a clear head, but tonight his mind went back and forth between his two worlds, the one at home and the one at work. Each had different characters and settings, and different personalities, including his own. He liked the drive home. It gave him time to transition. And he needed that. He didn't like thinking about work or cases when he was with family. It made him different.

Two pregnant homeless women. What would have become of the children.... Future senators? Star athletes? Doctors? No. That wouldn't have been their future, would it? He knew the answer.

It was best to wash it off when he came in the door, like the garbage man would. No sense stinking up the house or tainting his family with that other world. Kevin was always good at making that transition. He knew it would be a long time before he could wash out the recent images, though. He was cruising at 75 mph. It was about forty-five degrees outside, and his window was half-way down with the heat on low. The outside air was clean, cool, rejuvenating. He was on his second cigarette in fifteen minutes. The obtrusive, wretched pictures of his dead friend kept coming back at him. Something else was gnawing at him about Jonesy. He believed it probably was the same thing that had been driving Jonesy...*when he was alive.*

Kevin had just finished working sixteen hours straight with Venera, Malaro and a host of other detectives on the Jonesy case. After they left the crime scene, they met in the muster room at District 23 and pooled information. There were chairs and tables, coffee cans filled with butts and no cloud hovering tonight, just a smoky haze from floor to ceiling. A "No Smoking" rule had been established in commands since 1992, but no one was going to enforce that rule these first few days after Jonesy's death.

There were a lot of cops who had liked Jonesy, and even more who knew or worked with him from time to time. Everyone was on edge, even the Captain, who normally didn't take any interest in even the most significant capers. There was a giant whiteboard with designated assignments for the detective teams. The board was always there, usually used for cops who were studying for the Sergeant's test. Overstuffed notebooks crowded the table along with a few Mac and IBM laptops used by the younger detectives. The command was buzzing with people. Reporters were outside with their news vans and giant antennas.

Captain Reitman had just given the department's official statement to the news crews, and they were wrapping up. The reporters and their equipment people were heading back to Euclid Avenue to get some additional shots outside the station and on the platform. The department brass had decided they would put it out that Jonesy was on his lunch break in the room. They didn't need to release details that he was on overtime and was hanging out in a room instead of being on post. They all felt there would be no point in letting that piece of information out.

On each shift there was a recap of assignments as the day came to an end. Another shift of detectives was coming on as Kevin and others departed. Kevin, Mike, Tony and Vinnie wanted a seamless transition, so that the evening shift detectives could continue without any major gaps in time or effort. Those directly related to the case would not rest much, work twelve or fourteen hour days, and not take a regular day off until this was resolved. The *skell* murders were on the back burner. Kevin, Venera and Malaro would work together. There were three other two-man day teams, two four-to-twelve teams and one midnight team, which included Billy Quinn, who had begged the Captain to be temporarily re-assigned.

Feuss, Jonesy's partner, was completely out of the picture for now. He'd gone home on medical leave, having broken down at Euclid Avenue after insisting on viewing the crime scene while Jonesy was still sprawled on the floor. He'd taken two steps into the room, seen the hole in the back of his partner's head, and nearly collapsed. It was heartbreaking. Two uniform cops drove him home to Staten Island, while another followed with Feuss's car .

O'Shea began the first meeting, outlining the investigation. He had a set way of administering meetings and it was very effective. Mike, having observed many a conference misdirected by errant comments or a particularly strong personality, knew the most effective way to manage, and that was to lead them. He was not a typical NYPD boss. He began by outlining the assignments to the teams, and then explained how the transition meetings would take place one-half hour before every shift change. Up-to-date information would be gathered from all teams and put on a recap sheet prior to the end of each shift and disseminated to all the teams. When he was done with his portion of the initial briefing, he gathered input from all the detectives. Each one would have a turn, and they were requested to contribute at least one observation to be discussed by the team. No one would interrupt another.

They were all familiar with how the Sergeant's brainstorming sessions worked. Items would be further expanded by the contributing Detective or at Sargeant O'Shea's discretion. If anything was worthwhile, it would be added to the recap or assignment sheet, or put on a secondary sheet to come back to later. His team knew that even the small things could later turn out to be something valuable.

Kevin repeated what he had said earlier at the crime scene about Jonesy being a specific target. Venera spoke about the missing gun and the two gunshot wounds to the back, and ran over, step by step, how the incident probably occurred. Malaro had gathered some additional information that Jonesy had kept in his locker about train runs and the 10-13 call just prior to the Bryan Addams killing. Tony said he went through Jonesy's lockers at both District 23 and back at Major Case, and it looked like he had a lot of information printed out from a computer as well. The last computer command that Tony found indicated Jonesy printed out twenty-four pages the night he was killed. The last two pages of the printout were all that remained. The data on the only two pages appeared to be a cross-reference query of train schedules. Tony was back-tracking to find the server or printer that had processed the original command in an attempt to obtain from the computer memory a repeat printout of what Jonesy had queried.

Other detectives ran down the emergency exit, and verified it had recently been used, after what appeared to be a considerable amount of time in disuse. Recently disturbed mud cakes and overgrown grass and moss around the edges had been dislodged. The area maintenance records were reviewed and also supported the one conclusion they all agreed on. The killer had entered and exited the subway system using the emergency exit.

The crime scene officers processed the entire area, from the exit on the street all the way to the Euclid Avenue platform. Trains were re-routed to by-pass Euclid station, using the express tracks only. There was blood found on a broken piece of glass on the walkway. The crime scene guys were looking for anything on the entire path where the killer had walked. They were using a luma light for other trace evidence. The blood on the glass and the three drops on the walkway were barely enough to use for DNA testing. They normally only used that technology on high profile cases. But now, after Jonesy, the murders were in that category. It would take weeks to get results. A match against the database was unlikely, but DNA evidence would be extremely beneficial if a suspect was apprehended. This was the first concrete piece of evidence from any of the homicides to date, but still no help at all.

Kevin was in the interview room getting ready to go home with his large folder containing the train schedules, maintenance records and porter assignments for reviewing, when he stopped and looked up at Malaro, his old training partner. When Kevin had first arrived at "The Squad," the older detectives, including Jonesy, initially resented the fact that Kevin made it into the unit faster than anyone else remembered. Tony had talked to Jonesy at length on a number of occasions, as he did with other skeptics, when Kevin came to the squad. Finally, it was Kevin's reputation, and immediately-evidenced talent, that won over the rest of the detectives in a few short months. Kevin and Malaro were tight, like brothers. The admiration and respect was mutual, although Kevin did feel that Tony occasionally made critical errors in judgment. The gun in the courtroom was one, and Kevin believed Tony would have shot that suspect on the Jackie Robinson Parkway, if he had not been there to stop him.

Malaro was going over train master schedules of all the homicides and running down the dead-head train from the other night.

"Something missing." Kevin said to Malaro in a low voice.

Kevin got up from his seat and walked over to Tony, clearly uncomfortable about sharing his latest intuition. He sat down in a chair next to Tony and dragged it closer to talk to his former mentor. He spoke in a whisper.

"For whatever reason, we all know Jonesy didn't have his head up his ass for a change."

He looked at Tony for some type of expression, but didn't get one. Kevin knew he shouldn't be talking like that about Jonesy. Comments like that could set people off. Kevin proceeded.

"He's got all this shit in his locker and he's looking at everything and everyone. Same shit I'd be collecting and the same shit you'd be collecting, except for one thing."

"What's that?" Tony finally asked.

Kevin lowered his voice even more.

"...roll calls, overtime assignments for cops in the command, Tactical Patrol Force assignments for the rookies that ride the trains."

Kevin stopped and looked around to make sure no one walked into the room while he was sharing his thoughts with his long-time friend and partner.

"For my money, Jonesy's being thorough, and if you're on the right track, you're looking at everyone...you're looking at cops too."

Tony looked up at Kevin and reached into his front jacket pocket. He pulled out a stack of vertically folded papers, stapled together in bundles. He handed the bundle over to Kevin and spoke as Kevin was going through them at the table.

"There are the roll calls." Tony quietly confessed.

"He *was* thorough. I found those in Jonesy's locker. That's one month's worth from this command. I'm sure whoever offed Jonesy got whatever he needed at Euclid station. Our boy must have more copies and maybe more key items. So whatever Jonesy was onto, we'll be onto soon enough."

Kevin was reviewing all the paperwork Tony had just given him. He was a little puzzled as to why Tony was holding out, so he asked him.

"Why didn't you share this at the meeting today?"

Tony shrugged his shoulders.

"I didn't want to start on shit like that unless we eliminated everything else. I don't think a cop is capable of this...I mean, why? It just doesn't make sense."

Tony looked around again to make sure no one interrupted their conversation. He continued.

"You're right, I would have been doing the same thing Jonesy was doing–looking at everything and everyone. But you and me are going to follow his lead and not mention this to anyone. Nobody else is going in this direction; they've got their other assignments. Vinnie might catch on, but I doubt it. His job is tracking down all the witnesses Jonesy interviewed. Let's see if something else breaks first, and we'll tell Mike in a couple of days if nothing else turns up."

Tony noticed the concerned look on Kevin's face.

"Let's just see what happens...that's all I'm saying...Jonesy didn't tell anyone either ya' know," Tony continued. "He was playing it smart. If anything like that got out, it would screw up the whole investigation and put it in a different direction. And if that direction is wrong, we'll never figure out who did all this. Let's just wait a little while. That's all I'm saying."

Neither of them spoke for a few minutes. Tony re-directed the conversation.

"Are you going with Vinnie and re-do some more of Jonesy's interviews? Maybe something else will turn up."

"Yeah, sure. Vinnie asked me to visit the old lady and he ran it by Mike."

Tony got up and lit a Kent and stood in front of the muster board with his back to Kevin, looking at all the assignments.

"He was good, Jonesy was, a little misled that's all. Looks like he was on his way back into the game. It's a fuckin' shame."

Tony didn't turn around. Kevin got up and left the interview room, called Venera to set up an interview with Mrs. Addams for

175

tomorrow. He got in his car to go to his home in Woodhaven. He was very uneasy about this latest information, and the decision to hold onto it.

Chapter Twenty-Five

March 16, 2007

Kevin and Vinnie rode over to Mrs. Addams' house in St. Albans. On reviewing Jonesy's interview list, some of his notes appeared to be missing, but his appointments were still recorded on his E-mail in his computer. Kevin rang the bell. He also noted the difference between Mrs. Addams' porch and the one next to it. She opened the door and the usual smile with which she would greet people faded from her face. She spoke before they did, still polite though.

"Good afternoon officers. What can I do for you?"

Kevin smiled and Vinnie laughed and went into his *schtick*.

"I told you people recognize us as cops because of the way you dress. You and your white socks and penny-loafers."

Neither of which Kevin was wearing. A smile began to return to Mrs. Addams face and she responded.

"Actually it was you, Big Daddy. You look all pimped out and such, but the NYPD tie clasp is a dead giveaway..."

"Damn!" Vinnie exclaimed, feigning exasperation. "I never wear this thing. I couldn't find my silver one with the pearl in it!"

Twenty minutes later they were sitting in the living room, sipping tea and eating some of Mrs. Addams' pecan pie. Kevin began.

"This pie is unbelievable, Mrs Addams. Jonesy *did* tell us about your visit and what a good cook you are."

"That poor boy. He did have some manners though; he stayed with me for an hour and a half just talking about the South, my boy, and eating that pie."

She looked up at the picture of her son, which Kevin noticed was larger than all the other pictures in the house.

177

"Detective Jones loved that pie, too." The smile began fading from her face, as she realized yet another person she was fond of would not be tasting her pie again.

Kevin continued with the questions.

"Mrs Addams, we hate to be putting you through all this again, with your own loss and all, but we think it is a possibility that the same person who took your boy was responsible for Jonesy's death, too."

Kevin was good with people. He could talk with them, not at them. He continued.

"Jonesy was onto whoever killed your son. He was gonna' find him and arrest him. We're sure of it. That's why he was murdered. We'd like to make the same promise to you, Mrs. Addams. We're gonna' find the guy who did this to your son and to Detective Jones, but we need your help."

She looked into his eyes.

"Of course I'll help. I do need to be honest with you boys, though. I haven't had many experiences with white folk, except poor ones. As you might guess, I've seen a lot of ugliness in my lifetime, being from the South and all. Seen some ugliness up here too. Many a time some cops came up in here and put whuppins' on people. It has been a while, though, and I do get a good feeling from you boys, like you'all were brought up right. What do you want to know?"

Kevin and Vinnie knew she was going to cooperate, but they also knew not to make one comment about what she'd just said.

Vinnie asked, "Well, like we said, Jonesy was onto something, we just don't know what it was. We're going back talking to everyone he talked to. We talked to all the people near the area, and you're the last one that was on his interview list. Was there any particular line of thought you remember him talking about? Was there something Detective Jones kept coming back to, or asked a lot of questions about?"

She looked around the room, contemplating the question and trying to remember his visit.

"There was one thing that struck me as odd."

"What was that?" Kevin asked.

"He called the day after his visit and wanted some more details about it, too." She responded.

The two detectives just listened. She would get to it. She looked around the room again.

"The Marine insignia. My boy had a metal emblem he wore. It was the Marine insignia."

She was relieved that she remembered.

"He always wore it, and I remember Detective Jones finding it curious that it wasn't among the items returned from Kings County Hospital."

Chapter Twenty-Six

He sat in his living room, barely moving a muscle, for forty-five minutes. The room contained an old green-sculpted rug from the Seventies that had been well maintained for decades, except for the worn path from the living room to the kitchen. There was one bay window with yellowing sheer lace curtains, a coffee table, and two end tables with a few dated magazines on them. Between the end tables was an old couch with claw feet. It had two long seat cushions covered in a floral design. There were some poor copies of Norman Rockwell paintings, one on each wall in the room, to fill the void in what would be considered by most a sparsely decorated room. His grandmother had died ten years ago and left the Queens home to him. It was a Cape Cod style, brick house with a three-foot chain link fence in the front. The small back yard, barely big enough to accommodate a medium-sized car, was bordered by six-foot privacy fences put up by the neighbors. They didn't bother with him. He didn't bother with them, either. Not much had changed in the house since the old lady died. He didn't think about his surroundings that much, but he did keep it impeccably clean.

Hunter was getting tired. He knew he was taking too many risks. But he was also beginning to enjoy this. It was true. He had to admit it to himself. All the attention, headlines, and the news coverage made him swell with what? *Pride? Shame?* The only thing that was missing was his picture all over the papers and television.

That would come soon enough.

He was sitting on his leather recliner in front of the television. It was turned off. He was thinking how he needed to be careful not to make any more mistakes.

Number Seven would be the last. It would be the culminating piece to many months of effort and work. This last one would be different, though, and more complex than Jonesy's death. Number Six was originally supposed to be another homeless person, but Jonesy fucked that up. What's the difference? The outcome will be the same. Seven skells for seven years...

He began to go over the train information again. He would have preferred to go back to Manhattan. It was like a different country there. Different police precincts and districts, different detective squads; and there wouldn't have been the amount of heat there was due to the current investigation in the Rockaways. But he had no choice. He had his next victim already picked out. Jonesy had taken care of that decision. *Hunter* had the date. He just needed the right time and right set-up to get it done, and it would all be over. He was going over train schedules and roll calls and overtime. His mind started to drift.

...the day they took me out of mother's house. Cloudy. How could those dark, endless clouds, strung end-to-end, uninterrupted, embrace all that water, and not burst?

A Social Services worker had escorted him out of the home. She was a black lady named Mrs. Burns, who had visited his home half a dozen times, each visit documenting one abusive situation after another. As he was leaving, he hadn't shed a tear. He didn't have any left.

Why did they wait so long? Why did they wait so long before they did anything? Seven years. Why did they let her have another baby?

The Child Services Department finally removed *Hunter* when he was seven years old, and placed him with his Grandmother. But not until after *Hunter's* mother had abused and finally beaten to death her one year-old daughter, *Hunter's* half-sister. *Hunter* barely remembered the baby, only the constant crying and the equally disturbing shrills and shrieks from his mother. The father of the baby was never identified and the mother's long, pre-destined journey was moving like a train with no brakes. She had been abused as a child herself. She took on the role of an abuser, and finally a murderer. Her life played out as anyone who knew her would have predicted. She spent the next twelve years in jail. *Hunter* had had no desire to see her the entire time she was incarcerated.

Being in her custody for seven years was long enough.

He and his Grandmother had made no effort to contact her after she was sent away. *Hunter's* mother sent one letter during the first year in jail, but *Hunter* agreed with the old woman to just toss it in the garbage. Neither he nor his grandmother wanted to pry open old, painful wounds. They tossed it out without even opening it. Just prior to her release from prison, a letter was forwarded to *Hunter's* Grandmother's house. It was from a Department of Corrections Officer who wished to remain anonymous. The letter reported that his mother had served her full term. She never made eligibility for parole. They had denied her every time she went before the parole board. The letter also informed them when she would be released, and indicated she might come back and cause trouble for both of them. After twelve years, she had now been out of prison for one week.

At nineteen years of age, *Hunter* had recently enlisted in the Navy, and was fearful that his mother would come back into Grandma's life and make trouble while he was away. He was hoping she wouldn't show up at the house. He was hoping he wouldn't have to *do something* before he left. He thought about it often. It was only three weeks until he would depart for basic training. When they finally heard from her, it was three o'clock in the morning; a brick came crashing through the front bay window. It was no mystery to him or to his Grandmother where it came from.

The next morning, the Grandmother sat at the kitchen table, sobbing and smoking a cigarette with her coffee. *Hunter* sat next to the old woman, rubbing her back. In just twenty-four hours his

Grandmother, with her dyed red hair, appeared to be ten years older than her 71 years. She was babbling about how she'd never be safe, as she blew her nose intermittently. She was wearing a polyester sweat suit. One of a dozen she owned. This one was parakeet yellow with double white stripes down the arms and legs. It had a jacket with zippered pockets, where she always kept her Virginia Slims. She felt, as she was getting older, that she should be comfortable. He looked at her as she hung her head in despair, sitting in an ice cream parlor-style chair at the small, round dinette table in the kitchen.

Hunter's plan came together quickly. He couldn't leave her like this and he knew he couldn't stay here anymore, either. He wanted to start his own life. *Hunter* knew where to look.

It was a cool night in the middle of March. He drove out of his way and parked in Flushing, Queens. He could have taken the 'A' train close to home, but he drove across Queens, parked, and took the '7' line into the city. He wanted to play it safe and not encounter anyone he knew. He'd change trains once he arrived in Manhattan, and make his way over to the West Side. He would have to walk the last three avenues to get to the area in Manhattan known as Hell's Kitchen. She'd always hung out in the bars around that neighborhood when she was younger. He'd look around until he found her, and then finish this nightmare once and for all. As he floated over Queens on the elevated '7' line from Flushing into New York, he had what was the first of the periodic daydreams that occasionally would take him for minutes at a time for the rest of his life.

There is no other way. I can't let her hurt Grandma, and the cops and courts are useless. They were useless twelve years ago and they'd be useless today. If I don't do this now, she's gonna' hurt Grandma, and I'm not going to let that happen.

He switched trains and took the 'A' line down to 8th Avenue and 34th Street and walked up the stairs. He needed to walk over to 10th

Avenue and up ten blocks to be in the heart of Hell's Kitchen, a nickname that dated from the days of slaughterhouses, factories and railroad yards, when the Irish had fled their homeland during the Potato Famine. It used to be heavily populated by those Irish, but included a small German population as well. The area in Manhattan was approximately between 34th and 59th Street, and from 8th Avenue down to the Hudson River.

He walked the streets looking in different bars. In the spring he normally enjoyed New York, walking through different sections, taking in the architecture, the playgrounds, and the overflowing restaurants. But now he was on a mission, and without any luck for the last few days. *Hunter* went down to Hell's Kitchen every evening after the brick came through the living room window, with the intention of completing his plan before shipping off into the Navy. On the fourth night he began to doubt whether his mother would return to her old stomping grounds. It was just after midnight. He was on 49th Street and 11th Avenue, walking back towards the subway, about to call it another night. *Hunter* was walking east when he looked across the street. A figure stood with a bottle in one hand and a cigarette in the other. It was a woman with a familiar stance. She was talking to another homeless person. Her appearance was disheveled, but she had the arrogance of her own belief that she was still attractive. The homeless black man yelled at her.

"...that's too much! You're an old rag, get away from me..."

She responded to the angry black man with an unending river of profanity, combined with a raised middle finger on the same hand that held her bagged bottle. *Hunter* recognized the voice immediately. After an initial stab of fear, he remembered he was no longer an intimidated little boy. He crossed the street and headed straight for her, looking up and down the block first to see if any cars or people were coming. There was no one around except the black man, who had wandered off down the street. He wanted to get this over with.

She saw him approach out of the corner of her eye. She whirled around, still with the bottle in her hand, the cigarette now dangling out of the side of her mouth, which was smeared haphazardly with lipstick. She had recently colored her hair blonde, but it was flat and unkempt. Whatever beauty she'd possessed in her younger years was almost completely erased by time and the hard road she had chosen. She was wearing knee length black boots, a short skirt and a white, faux fur jacket that stopped abruptly at her hips. She looked like she'd slept in the streets since being released from prison, over a week ago.

She recognized him immediately. He stopped in the middle of the street and stared at her.

How did she know who I was? There's no way!

She spoke.

"Ya' got my message the other night, huh?"

Hunter remained silent, a steely reserve coming over him, as he slowly began walking towards her again.

She recognized me because she watched our house and saw me last week. Then she tossed the brick through the window!

"Whatsa' matter, you don't have a kiss for your dear old ma?"

He pulled his gloves out of his pocket and continued to walk closer. The left glove was lined with sand in the fist. A well placed blow would be devastating. He took another look around. His rigid face relaxed. He gave a reassuring grin to his mother as he stepped right in front of her.

"Yeah, I'll give you a kiss all right."

He grabbed her by the hair with his right hand and stood her straight up. She was light, like a rag doll. She was about to scream some additional profanity when he cocked his weighted, gloved hand and unloaded it squarely on her face. Her nose exploded with blood and there was a crunch as the sand-laden fist followed through and finished up somewhere behind where her head had been originally. The punch alone was near fatal, and would have put her in the hospital for weeks.

He still had her hair in his hand and was holding her dead weight up by it. He dropped her on the street, without care for any further injury. She was sprawled out, face down. *Hunter* was completely absorbed with what he had to do. Unflinchingly, he continued with the second part of his plan. He moved quickly, his movements fluid and almost graceful.

He took off the weighted glove and put it in his coat pocket, then reached inside the breast pocket of his coat and pulled out two surgical gloves. After putting them on, he pulled an eight inch long, flat black jewelry case from the opposite breast pocket. He opened the case. There was a glass syringe, encased in synthetic foam to prevent the vial from breaking. The syringe had already been filled with a green liquid, a combination of window cleaner and Naptha. He had read about the concoction in a Daily News story that ran for a week in the newspapers over a year ago. Someone had used it to torture dogs. He bent over without hesitation and plunged the needle into the base of his mothers neck, emptied its contents, then quickly placed the syringe back into its case and into his pocket as he calmly walked away. *Hunter* looked back and saw his mother's initial reaction to the lethal cocktail. She became just barely conscious and started to convulse with small tremors.

He turned the corner and never looked back. If he had looked back, he would have seen the full blown convulsions that rocked his mother's body, cracking her own skull on the sidewalk, her teeth severing her tongue. The extreme thrashing continued for an additional two minutes.

Chapter Twenty-Seven

March 19, 2006
5ᵗʰ Avenue
NY, NY

NYPD funerals for police officers are unparalleled. Even more memorable are funerals held in St. Patrick's Cathedral in New York City. With its three-hundred foot spires pointing to the sky, even though eclipsed by much larger buildings that surround it, the Gothic edifice remains a breathtaking sight, and is at the top of tourist's lists to visit while in New York.

This day, there were no fewer than five thousand uniformed officers lining the streets in blue. It was a moving, impressive sight. Sometimes police funerals reached as high as seven thousand officers in attendance, based on a variety of factors surrounding the life of the deceased officer: time on the job, number of commands the officer had worked at during his career, and whether he or she was an active member of a fraternal organization.

There are a number of organizations that an officer can join upon completion of police academy training. Almost all are based on ethnicity or race. The Emerald Society is for the Irish, Columbian for Italians, The *Shomrim* Society for Jewish and the Guardians or 100 Blacks in Law Enforcement for African-American police officers. Each group has some representation in the top ranks of the department. Depending on status, not as a productive police officer or based on quality of character, but the status of one's membership, there is always *one of your own* keeping an eye on things from the top.

The sea of blue had dispersed immediately after the services at the church. Jonesy was born and raised in East New York, Brooklyn.

His family was one of a handful of the nation's few black Catholics. He'd attended mass with his mother at St. Benedict's in Brooklyn, on the corner of Ralph Avenue and Fulton Street. The parish had closed its doors in 1973 and Jonesy hadn't been to mass since. However, Cardinal O'Shea, having heard about Detective Jones' untimely death, offered the services through the family and the Guardians organization. Both the family and fraternal group graciously accepted.

Jonesy hadn't been heavily into the Guardians, (nor was he heavily into Catholicism) and from time to time he had 'butted heads' with the leaders of that organization. This time, he would have no say in the matter. Although grateful to religious leaders for giving Jonesy a memorable sendoff, the Guardians were still upset and hitting the media hard. The President of the Guardians, Sean Smith, was outraged that there was no progress in the case. He also intimated that if it were a white officer, there would be more detectives assigned to the investigation rather than the dozen currently working the case. It was five days after Jonesy was killed and, according to the *Post* and purportedly to Smith, there was no solid direction for the investigation. The officer's funeral, usually a solemn, dignified event, was turning into a media circus in small spots outside the Cathedral, with sporadic interviews of black officers by local newscasters. Most officers, black or white, did not want their faces on TV. Those black officers who did give interviews responded with short, sincere condolences to the family. The camera crews didn't bother attempting to speak with any white officers. They were just trolling along Fifth Avenue looking for the right news bite. So far, they weren't having any luck. Sean Smith was temporarily removed from the spotlight and was in the Cathedral assisting with the end of the services, including escorting the family to the reception area at the Armory, a few blocks away.

Erica Wheeler had just left the church steps and was standing outside St. Patrick's with a few of the Guardians. She was in the middle of a conversation when a news cameraman and Mike Scott, a good-looking black reporter from Channel Four, approached the group. With microphone in hand he asked if anyone would like to give a statement about the lack of progress in the investigation.

Although Scott had grown up in Larchmont and gone to Catholic Schools all his life, followed by a BA in Journalism at Dartmouth, he walked right into one of the groups of officers and started slapping backs and clasping hands as if to say 'I'm one of you.' A couple of the officers in the group recognized him from TV, and were impressed by the star status. Wheeler wasn't one of them. She had learned early on from her family, and particularly from Jonesy, that there were a lot of brothers who '*went white.*' Wheeler looked him over.

It was bad enough when a black man 'made it,' became successful and then moved out of Brooklyn to Long Island or Westchester, but this turkey had never even lived here!

Wheeler didn't like him one bit. There were plenty of injustices to the black community in this town; Jonesy had always told her that. However, Wheeler knew Jonesy's biggest beef was the media and occasionally the Guardian's themselves, jumping into an event to cry injustice when there wasn't any. It took away from the real cases of mistreatment and racism. There wasn't any point in chasing something or setting something on fire to bring attention to an issue unless it was genuinely necessary. And with the Jonesy investigation, Wheeler didn't see it. Not yet, anyway. Wheeler knew who the best were, and Jonesy was one of them. He'd told Wheeler who the others were, too. White or not, O'Shea, Kevin and Vinnie would find whoever did this to her cousin.

They didn't need this TV faggot starting shit over nothin'.

Unlike Jonesy, however, Wheeler loved the Guardians and felt they watched over her and all the others like a family. But Wheeler also knew, as with a well-meaning parent, concern could cloud judgment

189

every now and then.

Scott spoke to the small group.

"Okay, my brothers. I know it's a tragedy when a young black man is struck down, and as I hear it, y'all got a real injustice here. If it were a white cop, they'd have a hundred people investigating this incident. Anybody wants to get their thoughts together and holler back at the Department, I'll make sure we do a brother right."

Wheeler spoke up.

"Why don't you peddle your sorry, nappy-headed ass back up to Westchester before one of us *"Brothers"* lights up your ass!"

Scott looked at Wheeler incredulously.

"Wow, my sister..."

"My sister, my ass..."

Wheeler yelled as she grabbed Scott by the right shoulder. Wheeler spun Scott completely around, put her foot squarely on his ass and shoved him with all her might.

"I said get out of here, motherfucker!"

Scott was propelled by Wheeler's foot through a gathering crowd. The other black officers grabbed Scott, laughed, and kept pushing him until he was out of their group and among other white cops. Expunged like an unwanted contaminant from a healthy cell. He didn't try to come back. The younger black cameraman didn't have a chance to film anything because Scott hadn't given him the go ahead. He just stood there grinning. Two other cops grabbed him and shoved him in the same direction as his predecessor, the grin quickly fading from his face.

Sergeant Mike O'Shea was on the top of the Cathedral steps in front of the ornate bronze doors that guarded the entrance to St. Patrick's, his medals covering the shoulder of his uniform. He observed Wheeler's interaction with Scott from a distance, with Sergeant Quinn and Inspector McHale standing right next to him. Mike liked Wheeler.

She showed promise.

A little hot-headed and somewhat militant, but she could be good.

Mike asked the head of Detectives,

"How are the numbers in the "brother" department, now that Jonesy's gone."

Mike knew what he was doing. If he asked for another officer to help out in the investigation, he might get a long list of regulations, red-tape and interviews. By the time he got the additional man, he'd already be retired. There was quite a process to becoming a detective. Worse yet, he might get some *schmuck* transferred from another command and be stuck with a pail of shit for ten years. No. Mike liked to handpick his people. He knew how to play this game. Demanding and ranting and raving didn't get you anything but negative attention. If he demonstrated a need, a political maneuver that made sense...

The Inspector looked at O'Shea. He was watching Wheeler and burst out laughing when he saw her put her foot up Scott's ass.

"I know I said *anything*, Mike, but that kid's a hot-head and you know it. Now that Jonesy's gone, who's gonna' slap her around when she needs it?" The Inspector asked.

Mike thought it over carefully. He didn't hurry with his answers if he didn't have one.

"Venera," Mike finally said plainly.

Inspector McHale looked at him. "I'm listening."

Mike knew what the Captain wanted to hear. The Captain was old school and gave people a fair shake, but he did have his own beliefs and prejudices like anyone else. But Mike was a chameleon, able to adapt to those beliefs, if necessary.

A means to an end.

Mike continued.

"Venera doesn't pull punches with anybody. If the *'righteous nigger'* crap comes out, he'll squash it. For us—she's black *and* a woman...we hit the affirmative action lottery."

McHale turned to Sergeant Quinn.

"What do you think Billy?"

Mike was burning. The last thing he was looking for was Quinn's opinion.

Quinn looked up at the Inspector, tears still fresh in his eyes. Not ready for business as usual like most of the cops here. Quinn had known Jonesy for 15 years. They occasionally hung out and drank together. He was always with Jonesy and not many others at Christmas parties or fishing trips. They got along well. Jonesy didn't piss off too many people. He was very easy going. You'd have to be easy like that to be a friend to Billy Quinn.

Billy slowly turned to McHale.

"Whatever, Inspector. Jonesy would be happy to hear that Mike was looking after one of his own."

Billy then walked away, down the church steps, a whiff of his beer breath wafting in the air. Quinn had started early today. He'd lost a friend and it wasn't easy on him. Mike was still a little surprised by his remark. Prior to Jonesy's death, Quinn had been making things difficult for the squad.

McHale finally agreed and told Mike to hold off until Monday, and then have a meeting with Wheeler. The Inspector wanted to throw this at Sean Smith, the Guardians President, first and make sure that the maneuver got some political mileage. Mike understood. Play the game; don't make any moves until the most impact in all arenas could be leveraged.

"Mike, let me do my dance with Smith first. This would ease up the media pressure and let the squad do what they gotta' do. You can break it down to Wheeler on Monday. Make sure you lay it down right."

The Inspector paused, rubbing his chin.

"I hope you got the right instincts about this kid. She could cause a lot of shit in the unit."

Mike nodded.

"I got it under control, Captain. Besides, Vinnie will have her on a short leash."

Chapter Twenty-Eight

After an NYPD funeral, there was usually a substantial gathering of a few hundred people, mostly those who were close to the officer, which took place in some hall immediately after the service at the cemetery. Plenty of officers were on hand prior to that, though. Like any good Irish wake, cop funerals were a celebration of sorts. Many officers were getting together with others they hadn't seen in years. Some were complete strangers to the deceased. They were habitual funeral attendees from different commands around the job, who were on duty and had a full paid shift to "represent the department" and eat food and drink beer.

Most of the officers in this ceremonial detail knew enough to lie low at these events and be respectful. However, there were a few who came to these funerals, were often the last to leave, and remained at the forefront of the festivities as if they were in a public pub with a free license to be a jackass.. At the end of the night, hopefully after the deceased's family had left, there was occasionally some trouble.

Today there were a couple of those officers present. Two of them were laughing and doing shots with Quinn at the small, makeshift bar in the Armory on Madison Avenue and 92nd Street. The rest of the hall was crowded with people, some rubbing elbows in the small bar area, while a substantial crowd filled the Veteran's room and spilled out into the hallway. There were three large, crystal chandeliers in the hall, hanging over the 100-foot long room with 25-foot ceilings. The walls were adorned with pictures of famous soldiers, hanging above decorative mahogany wainscoting. The far wall, opposite the main entrance to the Veteran's room, was lined with ten eight-foot long rectangular tables with white table clothes; they supported heated trays of aluminum foil pans filled with food. The Major Case Squad and the Guardians put out the spread. It was rare that any event of this magnitude had this variety and quality of food...from collard greens and macaroni and cheese to antipasto and lasagna.

Kevin had been there about an hour. He was one of the few from the squad who had actually gone to the cemetery services as well. He was hanging out with Pulaski and Malaro, drinking beer and enjoying their company. Unlike in public bars in New York, patrons here were allowed to smoke. It was a private facility. A cloud of cigarette smoke hovered high above the crowd of people. The officers and detectives were still in uniform, but jackets and medals were removed and hung up in the coat check room.

Tony was talking about some property he had scoped out in Sebastian, Florida. He looked forward to retiring in eight months, selling his house and moving down there with his wife. His two boys were in college at Florida State University, and he visited them whenever he could. Pulaski was near the end of his second marriage and hoped "the bitch would drop dead" before the divorce papers were final. His drinking habit extended long into his home hours, and had affected his first marriage the same way.

"My next one is either going to be Kevin's wife or a nice Puerto Rican girl..." Pulaski stated.

"...I'm tired of these *gringas*."

Kevin shook his head.

"Why does everyone want to marry my wife? She's a pain in the ass"

Malaro smiled and poked his chest. "You're full of shit!"

Vinnie walked up, out of uniform, wearing a gray, pinstriped suit with coordinating shirt and tie and his trademark expensive shoes.

"Who's full of shit?"

"Oh boy, here we go," Kevin said.

"Kevin is," Malaro continued. "He's says his wife's a pain in the ass."

"Yo, you *are* full of shit," Vinnie responded as he sipped his martini and continued to scope out the crowd. Vinnie never looked at anyone when he talked. He was always looking around.

Pulaski interrupted and pointed over to the bar.

"Hey check out Quinn, he's on his way to an ass-whippin' tonight."

They all looked over at the bar; there was no love lost for Quinn by any of them, but they did feel for him this past week. They knew he'd been close to Jonesy. He was hanging around with a couple of pails from Manhattan, who were getting louder as the day progressed. Inspector McHale had gone over to the bar earlier to give a friendly admonishment to the pair about this being a family event. They calmed down for a little while, but it looked like they were starting up again. There was some profanity flying, and the laughs were a little too loud, raising some eyebrows.

Kevin spoke.

"Maybe we better get Mike to get him out of here. Jonesy's daughters are still around and they don't need to see any of that crap."

Venera chimed in.

"Fuck that, I don't need Mike for that. Besides, Quinn's harmless. He'll finish up crying in his beer. It's those Manhattan assholes that need to go. Let's not start any shit, though. It would be disrespectful to Jonesy."

As Venera finished his last sentence, he strode over to the bar, still carrying his martini.

Quinn was still in full uniform, jacket and all, leaning on the bar. He was even wearing his hat, albeit crookedly on the back of his head. He hadn't left the bar area for a couple of hours, except to relieve himself. Despite all the food, he hadn't eaten anything, either. The two cops from Manhattan were patting Billy on the back, lining up another shooter and another bottle of beer for Billy, when Vinnie approached. He was all chest now, with a Kent in one hand and his martini glass in the other. He had an impressive frame, despite being forty pounds overweight.

"Hey Billy, what's up!"

He nudged past one of the Manhattan cops, who spilled his beer. Vinnie eclipsed him altogether with his back as he stepped up and put his arm around Billy's shoulder. The nudged Manhattan cop gave his buddy a *"what the fuck?"* look, but Pulaski interrupted the officer's gaze by striking up a conversation with him.

"Hey, buddy, where you guys from?" Pulaski asked.

The surprised and somewhat confused officer responded as he wiped the small amount of beer from his pants.

"Manhattan Task Force." He was of medium build with hair down to his neck, and an earring in his left ear.

He continued. "I'm Mike Powell and this is my partner Joe Franzione."

"No shit!" Pulaski exclaimed.

"Hey, Vinnie, these guys are from Manhattan Task Force. Don't we know anyone up there?"

Vinnie turned around.

"Yeah we know guys from up there. You guys know Louie Remy?"

"Yeah, he's our boss," Franzione said, obviously put off by the unexpected encounter.

He was much taller than his partner and had short black hair and a mustache.

"He is?" Vinnie asked.

He left Billy and walked over to the two Manhattan Task Force cops and put his arms around both of their necks at the same time. He was smiling but the force of his arms around their necks signaled something else. To everybody else, it would look like they knew each other from way back and were re-acquainting themselves.

Vinnie whispered. "My name is Lieutenant Venera," he lied.

"Now I noticed you two boys about an hour ago when the good Inspector McHale came over as a courtesy and asked you politely to shut the fuck up..."

Kevin looked around uncomfortably. He had been involved in a couple of Vinnie's *shows* before. Most of those incidents wound up being good stories. A couple wound up being all out brawls. The last one was in the win column, but not before Kevin got a pool cue over his elbow. Marie hadn't been happy about that.

The smaller officer, Powell, tried to unhook himself from Venera's arm, but Venera clenched a little more.

"Wait a minute, I'm making a point here. The good Inspector is old and maybe he didn't make his point. Ya' see, Jonesy was a friend of ours and his daughters are right over there."

He pointed to two pretty girls in their twenties.

"You haven't noticed, but every time you belt out a 'fuck you' or a belly laugh, the younger one, that's Olivia, she looks over wondering how someone could be having such good time at a time like this. And I was kinda' thinking the same thing."

Venera's message to Franzione was clear, but Powell was just getting angrier. Vinnie released both officers as he continued.

"Now the best course of action...that is before you get your asses whipped and then subsequently kicked out of the Ceremonial Unit...is to just leave."

Vinnie paused, then added. "What do you think?"

During this exchange, Pulaski had already grabbed their coats and jackets from the chairs near the bar. He handed them to the two Manhattan officers. Powell was boiling, while Franzione pleaded with his friend.

"We better go, it's getting late anyway."

Powell eye-balled Venera. If it weren't that he was a Lieutenant, they would have been on the ground as soon as the asshole touched him, but drunk as he was, Powell was not at the point to sock a boss at a cop's funeral. He was a little surprised though; he usually acted this way and had never been called on it before. He thought the people loved him at these things, and he went to two or three funerals a year. He decided maybe his partner was right. Powell then apologized, shook hands all around, and left. He and his partner would finish off the day at some local pub.

All in all, still a good tour of duty, Powell thought to himself.

After the two Manhattan cops left, Pulaski began.

"I thought you didn't want to start any shit? For about two seconds there, he was thinking about taking a pop at ya'."

"Fuck that asshole, he was soft. Besides that, he'd never hit a boss." Venera laughed.

Kevin added, "Maybe not, but he was sure thinking about it."

Venera responded.

"What's done is done. Two assholes down and one to go."

He returned to the bar. "Hey, Billy. Let's get something to eat."

Chapter Twenty-Nine

March 20, 2006
Woodhaven, Queens

Kevin woke up groggy, nursing a bruise over his right eye. Yesterday, at the funeral, had been a long day, and had lasted well into the night. Kevin had been away from home for over fifteen hours a day since Jonesy's murder.

He'd come home around 3:00 AM, after drinking a few beers at Mike's Pub on Jamaica Avenue. The official funeral activities had ended around midnight, and he'd left the hall with Tony, Vinnie, Mike and John Pulaski. They wanted to finish off the frenzied day without wall-to-wall cops.

They were belly-up to the bar, Vinnie on a chair and the others standing. The bar was a typical New York pub with a narrow passageway to the back pool table area. The twenty foot bar was dark oak with a six-inch brass step. Behind the bar the floor was worn from years of use, and had makeshift pallets as flooring, covered by a brown, indoor-outdoor carpet. A mirror ran the length of the back bar, which held all the booze. There were worn hardwood floors, a Skee-Ball machine in one corner, and a cigarette machine by the front door.

After Kevin and his crew had been there for over an hour, Franzione and Powell, the Manhattan cops from the funeral, stumbled in the doorway. In the span of four hours since they'd been asked to leave by Venera, they had discovered that Vinnie wasn't a Lieutenant after all. Powell, the shorter one, approached the corner of the bar. He didn't notice the others at first. Franzione did, but didn't say anything. In fact, he immediately began to suggest other bars with more "action" to his partner. Powell looked down the bar and noticed the group he'd met at

200

the hall. At this point, Venera and the others had already been drinking for a long time as well. Vinnie shouted over to Powell to get his attention.

"Hey, Powell. Good news."

"They demoted me back to Detective since the last time I saw you."

Pulaski and Tony burst out laughing. Mike and Kevin looked uncomfortable. They were tired and both thought they were getting to the point in their lives where this stuff wasn't fun anymore. Powell's face turned from unpleasant to maniacal. He'd had a bad taste in his mouth the whole night after the episode at the hall. His mood got even worse when the cops they'd run into at the last joint told them Vinnie wasn't a boss. Powell regained some composure and walked up to Vinnie, who was chewing on a stirrer, not bothering to turn around as Powell approached him from behind.

"I don't appreciate you lying to me and making me look like an asshole," Powell said bluntly to Vinnie.

Vinnie responded to the mirror without turning around.

"Who gives a fuck what you appreciate...Are you just gonna' talk, or what? I heard enough of your bullshit at the hall...and your dirty looks are beginning to frighten me now."

Powell was beet red.

As Vinnie turned around on his swivel chair, about to get up, the barkeep came over. He was about six feet tall, sixty years old, with white hair. He said one thing.

"Take it outside, boys."

Vinnie started to stand as Powell took a large, round, swing at him. Vinnie saw it coming, faded back in his seat, and the punch hit Kevin, who was standing next to him, in the head. Kevin snapped. He grabbed Vinnie by the back of his jacket and yanked him back against the chairs. Vinnie fell on the floor laughing, as three chairs tumbled over him. Kevin was stronger than he looked, and Vinnie knew enough not to provoke him any further. He stayed on the floor laughing, as he watched Kevin turn and light up Powell's face with three quick shots. Powell dropped to his knees, and then Kevin kneed him in the face. Kevin could be as brutal as anyone, and those who knew him were wary enough to stand clear when he clenched his fists and his lip began to tremble. He was still puffing, his fists up, when Franzione approached him and grabbed him by the shoulder. Wrong move.

"Hey dude, calm dow..."

Kevin whirled on him and dropped him with one punch. He hit the floor hard and cold. He was out.

Vinnie was still laughing when Kevin went up to him and grabbed him by the collar with both hands, pulling him off the ground like he weighed fifty pounds. Vinnie stopped laughing as Kevin berated him.

"This ain't funny, *schmuck*. I've got a wife and kids, and I don't need to get hurt or lose my job over your macho bullshit!"

"Hey Kevin , I hear ya', but I didn't throw one punch!" Vinnie exclaimed, his hands open in a surrender position.

Kevin continued yelling at him.

"Yeah, but you made him feel like an asshole. What else was he gonna' do? Huh? Ya' treated him like a bitch twice today. Whattya' expect?"

"I expected to beat the crap out of him, but you beat me to it!"

Mike called two cabs after retrieving the Task Force cops wallets for their addresses. Pulaski grabbed some water from the barkeep and threw it in their faces. They both groaned and became semi-conscious. Mike and Pulaski helped the cops to their cabs, paid for the rides, and sent them off.

The next morning was Sunday. Kevin hadn't had a regular day off in a week. He was planning on staying home today. Marie was downstairs with the girls. He smelled the bacon all the way upstairs in the bedroom. He touched the bruise above his eye and winced.

Kevin and Marie had two girls, Rose Elizabeth, four years old, and Francine, eight years old. Marie had been an emergency room nurse until the first baby was born. She was itching to get back to work, but they both agreed that if they could swing it, it would be best if she stayed home. The girls went to elementary school at St. Thomas the Apostle, in Woodhaven. The whole family tried to make it to Mass every Sunday, but if Daddy wasn't around, a vote would be cast and they'd stay home and hang out in their pajamas.

Kevin got up, hit the bathroom, and went downstairs. He had on his boxer shorts and a robe and slippers. At the bottom of the stairs was a makeshift memorial for his brother, Jackie. John McCaffrey, a twenty-nine year old New York City Firefighter, had died at the World Trade Center on 9/11. The wall held thirty photographs of his brother Jackie. The pictures spanned from when he was a child all the way up through his seven years with the Fire Department. Kevin passed the largest portrait of his brother in his dress uniform and patted it as he did every morning when he went downstairs. It had been four years since the attack, and there weren't many days passed that he didn't think about his baby brother. The girls heard him coming and hid behind the stairway wall. As he hit the last step and touched the picture, they both jumped out at him to scare him. This time he *was* a little startled.

"Oh, shit," he slipped.

"Ha ha! Daddy said the "S" word!"

They both squealed with delight, as it was usually Kevin who snuck up on them. The girls ran into the kitchen as Kevin followed. They immediately turned him in to Mommy for swearing.

"Nice," he said as he came in.

Kevin continued, "I taught them well...never take any shit from any man—unfortunately that would include me."

The girls ran off to another room to play, after they were reminded to kiss their father good morning. His wife gave him her big smile, like she always did when he woke up or when he came home. They loved each other and they were best friends. Kevin couldn't remember when he didn't enjoy her company. They weren't without problems, but as they always agreed, compared to most, their problems weren't even worth mentioning. She walked over and gave him a kiss. Marie was a small woman, with a plump rear end; her hair in a pony tail. She hadn't seen too much of him in the last week.

"Your mother and father called this morning. They'll be up from Florida in two weeks, and they want to stay here." Marie said.

"Great...why don't you just shoot me in the head and get it over with," he replied.

"Come on, it's not gonna' be that bad. They only want to stay for three or four days."

"Whatever," Kevin gave in.

He had his coffee and ate breakfast with the girls. They would attend mass and be back at the house by 1:00 PM. They had been going to church regularly since his brother died.

They lived on 79th Street in Woodhaven, Queens, in a fairly large house. Kevin and Marie had put a great deal of effort and money into restoring the Victorian beauty. There were a lot of compartmentalized rooms; the living room, sun parlor, dining room, sewing room, etc., and four bedrooms upstairs. Each room was freshly painted with matching curtains and area rugs. Periodically they would talk about selling it and either moving out to Long Island or to Upstate New York or Connecticut. There were some recent, serious crimes and break-ins in the neighborhood, and hanging around was to Kevin just playing Russian roulette with his family.

He was drinking his coffee, looking out the back bay window into his small yard. There was a house directly behind him, and houses eight feet to the right and eight feet to the left. He had bought a huge swing set for the backyard that looked out of place on the tiny property. He also had a mini-log cabin shed with a flower box with flowers in it. He kept his large tools and lawnmower in the little cabin.

He thought about what he could do around the house today and what needed mending, but his thoughts drifted back to his conversation with Tony about the police roll calls and overtime schedule. It didn't make sense not to tell Mike and Vinnie about the additional items Jonesy had in his locker. Surely those guys were clams. They wouldn't repeat it to anyone. But Tony did have a point about not going in that direction until other avenues were explored. If it ever did get out, they would be locked in one direction. It had been a couple more days now, though, and it was time to at least let the tight crew in on some of this information. He was going back and forth in his mind over this issue when the telephone rang. Francine answered it and gave it to him with a frown on her face without saying anything. She knew where Daddy was going when he got a phone call.

Sergeant O'Shea was on the line.

"Hey, Kevin, sorry to bother you at home."

"Sure Mike, what's up?"

"When I spoke with Wheeler the other morning, she had some interesting information that Jonesy shared with her."

Kevin squirmed in his chair.

Mike couldn't see he was squirming...could he?

What Kevin didn't know was that Mike was squirming too, wondering if he should share this information with anyone.

"Yeah?" Kevin asked.

"Well, I've been sitting on this for a day now and...it ain't sitting good," Mike said uncomfortably.

"Spit it out, Sarge" Kevin said.

"Jonesy thought there was a good chance it was a cop from District 23."

Kevin knew it was coming, but he couldn't reply.

"Kevin, you still there?"

"Yeah. That crossed my mind, but I didn't want to think about it too much. I mean, Jonesy had all the data on every angle except that one, and I can't see him not taking in that possibility, after all the information we gathered."

Mike was a little surprised. This scenario had crossed his mind, also, but it was dismissed quickly. He'd have to go over the re-cap sheets and see where Kevin would get that inclination. Mike continued.

"The possibility of it being a cop might have been part of the shit Jonesy uncovered that was stolen from Euclid the night he was killed. I think I'd like to meet with the team, just us, for a little while, maybe an hour or so. We can all put in for the four hours of overtime, anyway. How about we meet at the Empire Diner by you? Maybe we can call Tony and Vinnie, too. We might be off in a whole new direction and a lot of time has gone by..."

Kevin agreed.

"Okay. I'll call Tony and Vinnie and meet you there at three."

An hour later, Kevin was sitting on his porch in his rocker, smoking a cigarette, when Vinnie drove up, beeped twice and parked the newer-model, red Mustang across the street. He loved to stop by and say "Hi" to the girls. Rose Elizabeth was playing with her make-up case on the other side of the porch when she looked up.

"*Ciao*, Binnie," Rose said as she got up, flattened out her pleated skirt with two hands and ran over to kiss Vinnie hello.

"*Ciao Principessa*," Vinnie responded. She got closer and he bent over to give the four-year-old a kiss. She then asked him,

"*Como Esti?*"

"*Beni Beni*," Vinnie answered.

He got more than a big kick out of this. It was the only Italian she knew, but he had been teaching her for years. You would think she was an immigrant how well she had the accent and those two phrases down. Kevin interrupted.

"Stop with that *Guinea* crap, will ya'; next she'll be trying to turn stupid, just to fit in with the Dagos."

Vinnie looked at him sternly and shook his finger at Kevin.

"Nice...Ya' know, you never acknowledge that those kids are half Italian. You shoudn't be givin' them whatcha call-it, *misrep...misinterp...presentations.*

"Yeah right, ya' got that, genius?" as he flicked an ash over the porch railing.

"Shut up," Vinnie finally said.

Rose interrupted.

"Daddy, when are you gonna' stop smoking? You promised you were going to quit."

"I know, honey," Kevin sighed.

Vinnie bent over, put his hands on his knees and told Rose.

"I told him, Rose, if he doesn't quit he's gonna' die and then I'm gonna' marry your Mama."

Rose put on a fake frown. She knew Uncle Vinnie kidded like this.

"You're mean, Uncle Binnie. and my Momma said she'd never marry you!"

Vinnie and Kevin laughed.

Kevin got up and yelled into the house to tell Marie that he was leaving. He walked with Vinnie to the car. Kevin grinned at Vinnie on the way to the Mustang.

"You know she loves you, Uncle Binnie, but blood is thicker than water...there, you see? I do teach her some Italian things!"

Mike and Tony were already sitting at a booth in the back of the Diner, sitting opposite each other. Kevin and Vinnie nodded to the two and squeezed in across from each other. Vinnie laughed at Tony and spoke first.

"Hey you, that piece of shit out there is going to be towed as an abandoned vehicle."

Vinnie was referring to Tony's 73 Dodge Dart Swinger. Vinnie had kidded Tony about it ever since he'd bought his souped-up Mustang. Vinnie went on.

"Stop leaving your key under your seat and put it in the ignition already, maybe some mutt couldn't resist taking it."

Tony added. "Hey, as soon as they steal it, I can buy a new one!"

He had been saying that for ten years now, except no one ever took the bait. Not much demand in chop-shops for 73' Swingers.

Mike then added,

"No shit. He picked me up this morning in that piece of crap, and when he made a turn on Jamaica Avenue, the door flew open. If it wasn't for Tony grabbing my arm, I woulda' spilled onto the sidewalk."

Tony laughed out loud.

"He almost pissed himself! I can't lock the passenger door anymore, because it won't ever open again. It's been like that for a year."

Mike began and got right to the point.

"All right, here's the deal. I'm just gonna' get right to it and throw it out there...Jonesy told his cousin, just before he was killed, that the mutt we're looking for might be a cop from District 23."

Tony and Kevin knew about this information, but Vinnie, taken aback, slapped both hands on the table and threw his head back.

"Holy Shit" he yelled.

"Keep it down, knucklehead!" Mike rebuked.

Vinnie lowered his voice.

"That's a pretty big jump. Got anything to back it up?"

Kevin was stealing looks at Tony as Mike went on, wondering when Tony was going to share what he'd found in Jonesy's locker.

Mike continued.

"After gathering the re-cap sheets and running of roll call and overtime stuff, and assuming the *skells* killed were done by the same person, which I'm willing to stick with, it all points to the command. All of this stuff can be retrieved from different databases all over the city, some of the information can also be obtained in different parts of Brooklyn and Manhattan. You have the trainmaster using their own operating system, the Operations Unit using their program, and other data that can be obtained from Jay Street or at One Police Plaza. If you follow on that train of thought..."

Vinnie then finished his sentence for him.

"But, the only way to get all that information in one place is at District 23."

"That's right," Mike said. "One stop shopping. Who the fuck else, besides a cop, would know that Jonesy was in a room at Euclid Avenue at one o'clock in the morning?

O'Shea didn't wait for an answer. He continued.

"And another thing. I don't believe in coincidences. Both those broads were pregnant. All right, I can see somebody noticing the Prodski girl and a nut gettin' a bug up his ass about that and knockin' her off. But the Jane Doe wasn't showing. If our guy knows she's pregnant...How would he know?"

The rest of the detetctives at the table didn't have an answer. O'Shea filled in the blanks.

"It was on an ejection report. In fact, both these *skells* reported their condition to two separate uniformed cops. Jane Doe was kicked off a train in District 33 a month ago for panhandling, and the Prodski girl was thrown off a train in District 1, in Manhattan, two weeks ago."

Tony finally interjected, "Our boy being a cop is making more sense to me." He reluctantly took a stack of papers out of his inside jacket pocket.

Kevin saw Tony getting the papers out, breathed a controlled, silent sigh of relief, and lit up a Kent.

Tony spoke.

"I found these in Jonesy's locker on Day Two. I didn't want to stir up any shit, because I thought we might break something else before we started spreading rumors or going into a direction we didn't need to."

Mike took the papers, quickly went through the roll calls, overtime and the TPF runs. He looked disappointed. He riffled through everything quickly. Mike wasn't going to hammer Malaro, not now anyway. Not in front of everyone else. Everyone at the table knew Tony should have shared this information right away, but Mike knew Tony was a solo guy and didn't do things the same way he did. He moved on.

"All right. Tony's got a point here. Let's look at this. If we go beyond this table, we might spook our scumbag. We need to tread lightly till we nail this mutt. The thought that it might be somebody from that command scares the shit out of me. The fact it might be a cop is just fuckin' mind-blowing! We'll keep this off the re-cap sheets and start a clandestine operation amongst ourselves."

Vinnie looked at him with a puzzled expression.

Mike answered. "That means it's a secret, stupid."

Vinnie nodded and pointed his finger like a gun.

"Gotcha."

Chapter Thirty

March 21, 2006
Ozone Park, Queens

One of Vinnie's tasks on the team was to retrace Jonesy's steps in the investigation. He was to re-interview known contacts to determine if there was anything of merit that Jonesy might have picked up before he was killed. Since Jonesy's death, the investigation mirrored the work he'd done, but with over a dozen cops working the case, the amount of time to arrive at the same conclusions was considerably shorter. Vinnie stumbled onto some additional information while interviewing shop owners. The Korean liquor store guy, Mr. Mazowa, reported that there was another regular in the neighborhood that he'd noticed on a number occasions around the 80th Street station. He described this individual as a young black kid who went by the nickname of Little Pippa. According to Mr. Mazowa, Little Pippa sold weed and apparently had a nice little market going for himself, mostly from white kids driving in from neighboring towns or Long Island. Mr. Mazowa said that Little Pippa had been around for about eight months and was picked up once by the cops, but managed to get rid of whatever he was holding during a long foot chase through backyards and alleys.

Little Pippa was a small-time drug dealer, who'd dropped out of 10th grade four years ago to sell marijuana. At that time he'd made about $750.00 a week and school, jobs, or the future didn't mean that much to him. His mother had raised him mostly alone. She'd had her own problems, including a long-standing methadone problem, which had been precipitated by a long-standing heroin problem. She'd been clean when Little Pippa was born, but was an on-again, off-again, junkie until Little Pippa was twelve years old. By then Little Pippa, whose given name was Tremaine Pippins, was taking care of himself pretty well, so she sank back into her old habits. Big Pippa, the boy's father, had been shot to death when Little Pippa was seven years old.

Little Pippa had been walking up and down 83rd Street for a mile or so, switching to the opposite side of the street when he changed directions. He was about 5'11, had a small afro with a giant, grey, hoodie pulled over his head. He had the hang down jeans, but not loose enough that he had to pull them up all the time. He was also wearing a modest pair of Nike sneakers. He wasn't looking to stand out.

After two runs up and down Liberty Avenue, he switched his routine and walked up to Rockaway Blvd. Vinnie had been watching him for forty-five minutes and determined, correctly, that if this was the way Little Pippa operated, he wouldn't be on the same street for more than an hour. It would be easy for him to go relatively unnoticed for the three hours a day he pursued this activity. Vinnie noticed the non-descript attire and thought that was uncharacteristic for a *brother* in this neighborhood. Vinnie would later find out that this routine also involved a rotating location a few miles down Woodhaven Blvd. in Richmond Hill, Queens. Little Pippa had quite a business going for himself.

Vinnie laughed. No wonder it had taken him a few days to track the kid down. Vinnie had watched him long enough and observed three buys take place. He called the 113th Precinct on his cell and spoke to the Desk Officer, whom he knew from his uniformed days. He arranged for four units to come and pick up Little Pippa with lights and sirens and the whole nine yards.

"Okay, slick," Vinnie said to himself. "Let's see how cool you are now."

Vinnie was sipping his coffee, smoking a Newport that he'd bummed off an officer at the squad, when two marked cars came from one end of the street, and two more came from the other. Little Pippa was in the middle. The drug dealer saw two of the cars as they turned down the block and hit the lights and sirens. Vinnie observed that whatever evidence Little Pippa had on him was down the sewer before the cops could even see where he'd tossed it. He then moved quickly about twenty yards past the street sewer grate. By the time the cops jumped the curbs with their vehicles, and threw him up on the wall against the movie theater, he was clean. He didn't offer any resistance, much to the officer's disappointment. Vinnie wouldn't be squeezing him for any information now that all the leverage was floating under the street.

"Shit!" Vinnie cursed as he watched the whole scene unfold.

He got out of his car and hurried across the street, putting up his hand to keep from getting run over by a bus. The bus horn blared, Vinnie's hand gesture turned into the middle finger, as he quickly got to the cops and Little Pippa. As Vinnie saw it, he needed to do two things. The first was to get the drug dealer out of there before the uniformed officers beat the shit out of him. The second item was to figure out a way to get this mope to cooperate. Vinnie already surmised that if anybody had an eye for things that went on in this neighborhood, Little Pippa was that guy.

Vinnie took out his badge and had it on a chain around his neck, as plainclothes officers are required to do at any scene. The Desk Officer had told the uniforms that Little Pippa would have something on him, and Detective Venera wouldn't be visible until they took him back to the command. They were a little disappointed when the search turned up nothing. They were about to antagonize the alleged offender into a disorderly conduct beef if they couldn't take him in on any other charge. Vinnie got there just as the fun was about to begin. Two cops had started shoving Little Pippa around.

"Thanks boys. I'll take it from here."

Little Pippa was already hand-cuffed from behind. When the cops turned around to acknowledge Vinnie, in what appeared to be one fluid motion, Little Pippa jumped up in the air and swung his arms under his legs so his handcuffed hands were now in front of him, and bolted. Before anyone had a chance to react, Little Pippa shot out from between the cops and was fifteen yards down the street. Vinnie was already halfway back to his car when the others started running after him. Two cops ran back to their Patrol car, but by the time all the cars turned the first corner, Little Pippa was gone.

The handcuffs were dropped off later that night in a box on the precinct steps with a note that read:

I didn't want a larceny charge, so I brought these back. Have a nice day!

Chapter Thirty-One

March 22, 2006
370 Jay Street
Downtown Brooklyn

    Sergeant O'Shea asked Vinnie to meet him in the supervisor's office. Vinnie was wearing a tan velour sweat suit with matching top and pants, and a zipped up jacket with a bulge in the right pocket where he carried his wallet and cigarettes. His gun was in his ankle holster. He came in, pulled up a chair and put his feet on Mike's desk. Mike was sitting at his desk riffling through some papers when he noticed Vinnie's sneakers.

    "Get your feet off my desk, you fat fuck!" Mike screamed.

    Vinnie complied, laughing.

    "Ya' know all this talk about my weight is gonna' ruin my self-esteem."

    "You couldn't hurt your self-esteem with a brick, dumb-ass."

    "What's up?" Vinnie asked. "I gotta' go get breakfast, then hit the *gook* who owns the liquor store and see if our friend Little Pippa's been around. Those cops at the 113th are pissed off. They blamed me for distracting them when this kid bolted... the assholes."

    "I have a favor." Mike said bluntly.

    Vinnie responded. "I'm listening"

    "I'm not gonna' give you the party-line shit. Straight up. Since Jonesy died, we're down one guy in the unit..."

    Vinnie interrupted, a bit disturbed. "You guys don't waste time, do you?"

    "Whatever." Mike dismissed Vinnie and continued.

"I like the Wheeler kid. She's made some good collars and I think she's got a future. I want you to train her."

Vinnie shot back a response as he stood up abruptly.

"Oh, what the fuck! That broad's like a Black Panther or something! I don't have no time to break in another rookie... Kevin was easy, he came practically built for this shit, but Erica is going to be trouble. Besides, what's she got, three months on the job?"

"Two years, but whose counting?"

"I am!" Vinnie said with a whine. He sat back down.

"It took me *ten* years to get in this unit and if it wasn't for McHale sticking up for me, I wouldn't even be here."

Mike laughed. The reasons nobody wanted Venera in the unit were legendary.

"Well your shooting record wasn't great."

Vinnie rolled his eyes. Mike continued.

"Let's see...Hmmm...there was the gun going off in the locker room when you were a rookie. There was that booth clerk on the 'L' line. You shot her in the ass..."

Vinnie interrupted.

"Oh no. Don't bring up *that* shit. That fat-assed clerk shouldn't have been retrievin' tokens in the middle of a robbery." Vinnie went on.

"And when I fired at that scumbag in Coney Island..."

Mike interrupted. "I forgot about *that* one!"

Vinnie continued.

"Well, like I always said, that was just a bad shot. I'll admit that..."

A long pause followed as Vinnie gazed out of the window, suddenly melancholy.

"I felt bad for that dog. To this day I can't see a German Shepard without shedding a tear...and that Canine cop spits on the ground every time I run into him."

Vinnie's thoughtful look faded quickly.

"Hey! I know what you're trying to do. I wasn't half the problem this kid could be. If Jonesy were around maybe he could tame her wild, black-ass, but—"

Mike cut him off. Sometimes Vinnie could just keep going on and on.

"Look. Here's the deal. If we get a shuffled deck from Police Plaza, we could wind up with anybody. The way I figure it is this. This kid's got talent and you know it. She's smart. She's made some good collars and most of them weren't just luck. She anticipated things. She looked at the incident post cards in the muster room. Nobody does that. She's checked the pin board for patterns and made collars, except for one thing."

"What's that?" Vinnie asked.

"There *are* no pin boards out at District 23. Erica made her own miniature pin board in her locker. She's *that* good and it's *this* simple. We need her. You're gonna' be the one who shows her right. She respects you and she knows you ain't all racist and shit. Besides, I don't want a *schmuck* in here. If we don't snatch her up while we can, we could get anybody. If she's got talent, we can work with anything else, right?"

Vinnie looked at him, exasperated. He knew when he was beat. More importantly, Mike *was* right. They could get stuck with a pail of shit for ten years if someone else made the decision. There was a limited window of power with the Inspector's offer to help out in the investigation. The offer would be off the table once this was over. Vinnie knew he could straighten out Wheeler when she needed it.

"All right, but I don't want to hear it if I tune-up some motherfucker and this kid goes straight to the ACLU."

Two days later Vinnie was driving a silver Caprice with Erica Wheeler sitting next to him. The tour had started at 7:00 AM. It was 8:30 AM and neither had said much during their short time together.

Vinnie lit up a Kool.

Wheeler spoke matter-of-factly, as she stared out his passenger window.

"That's your third one in an hour."

Vinnie didn't reply. Ten more minutes elapsed.

Wheeler tried a different tactic.

"You know, I didn't ask for this." She paused.

"Sergeant O'Shea asked me to be in the unit. What was I gonna' say?"

No reply.

Wheeler then spoke in a stereotypical, white-nerd voice.

"Golly gee, thanks Sarge, but no way, I got plenty of ass kissin' and a decade to go before I prefer to enter the Detective Bureau."

Wheeler then changed her voice back to normal.

"No. I don't think so. If they want to throw a bone to a nigger, then that's fine with me...I'm not going to turn that opportunity down."

Vinnie interrupted with an exasperated sigh of frustration.

"You talk too much. Shut the fuck up for five minutes, will ya'?"

Vinnie continued. The long silent treatment was done.

"Did you know Jonesy was the third black guy in this unit? The two before him sucked. They weren't worth their weight in shit. So if you want some advice, take care of business, do good work, and be successful."

Vinnie was speaking calmly now. He had Wheeler's attention.

"But above all else, if you want *more* brothers to make it into the squad, don't be spoutin' off '*hungry nigger*' speeches and such. It'll give everyone a damn good reason for keepin' the spooks out."

Vinnie looked over at Erica and he winked.

"... if you get my drift."

Wheeler just stared at Venera. She couldn't identify what she was feeling. She was angry that a white man used the words 'nigger' and 'spook', but Vinnie didn't say them in an offensive manner. She *did* like the way Vinnie spoke his mind. She would like to be able to do the same thing.

Wheeler then responded.

"Look, I know I got a reputation for being a little verbal. I'm gonna' be workin' on that. I was just trying let you know is all. I'm gonna' bust my ass here to show that I belong."

Vinnie relaxed a little more.

"To tell you the truth, I didn't know what to expect from you. What you're looking for is respect. Well, so is everybody else. You got a little because O'Shea vouched for your ass. But in here, results gets you respect and we watch out for each other... always."

Vinnie and Erica talked more and more as the day went on. They talked about the squad, the bosses, Jonesy, and then the case to which they were assigned. Erica doubted there would be any other caper that would mean as much to her as catching the guy who'd killed her cousin. Vinnie was telling her about Little Pippa, and how he was like a rabbit, getting away from all those cops the other day. Vinnie and Erica were on the way over to the 80th Street area to see if they could get lucky and find Little Pippa.

"This kid..." Vinnie continued. "...the way I figure it, this kid sees everything around the neighborhood. If our guy scopes out victims way in advance and plans things in a meticulous way, like we think he does, maybe this Pippa kid saw him a couple of times."

Vinnie made a turn onto Rockaway Blvd.

"By the way, Sergeant O'Shea told us about what Jonesy shared with you. That's pretty fucked up, someone being from the command and all. And talking about that, the first thing you should always do when you're looking into something is never come to a quick judgment. If you do, you're more interested in directing the investigation into proving to yourself or others that you're right, rather than trying to find out what actually happened. It's human nature. Everyone wants to be right. Just pay attention to your own agenda. Thinking about being right that way, though, clouds your judgment. Everything you initially do might point in a certain direction, then in the middle or at the end, it's the opposite of what you first thought. Take your time, get all the facts, talk to all witnesses and don't leave anything unanswered, if you can. For instance, tell me your first guess about what we'd look for in the command.

Wheeler hesitated, then spoke.

"Well, like Jonesy already had a copy of roll calls, overtime assignments, shit like that."

"Okay. Sounds good. What else?" Vinnie asked.

Wheeler continued.

"I guess the TPF stuff, Task Force assignments that cross over into the district."

"Anything else?"

Wheeler knew she had good answers, but she got the feeling they weren't all the ones Vinnie was looking for. Wheeler shrugged her shoulders, as if to say "*I don't know.*"

Vinnie spoke again.

"So, you'd be on your way, plenty to do and a lot of stuff to cover to start off with, right? Right." He answered his own question. "But, because of what I just told you, quick judgments remember? You already made one and don't realize it."

"What's that?" Wheeler asked.

"Cops. You're looking at just cops. Who else works there that aren't cops?"

He answered his own question again.

"...porters, Transit Authority maintenance people, secretaries, auxiliary buffs. Think about it. There are about twenty–thirty people that are around that command all the time. At first, you don't think they'd have access to anything, but someone who's been there a while could pick up all kinds of information and no one would even know it. Now, I'm not trying to break your balls here, ya' gotta' keep an open mind. Ninety percent of the people who work in the command are cops, so odds are, that's who we're looking for, that is if O'Shea's theory is right, but it is something that should be in the back of your head. He may be wrong. Plenty of that information can be obtained from other sources."

Wheeler interrupted. "So where do you start?"

"Well," Vinnie went on. "We already did. You go with the odds, see what turns up, like Jonesy was doing. He was on his own so he would have got to this kid sooner or later. With all the other guys working on this, it won't take as long: Kevin running down Tactical Patrol Force runs, Malaro's doing overtime assignments and Mike running the show. Normally, you'd just be on your own or partnered up with one other detective. Anyway, if the initial run turns out to be a dead end, you try something else. Right now, we're going back to the scene. I gotta' feeling that this Little Pippa saw something before that Addams kid bought it at 80th Street. It's not much, but it's something that's been gnawing at me. But like I said, run it down, you never know what you'll get just for asking a simple question."

Chapter Thirty-Two

March 23, 2006
District 23
Rockaway Park, Queens

Sergeant Quinn was sitting as the Desk Officer in District 23. He was hung over and had been in the same condition each of the three days since Jonesy's funeral. There wasn't anybody in the command who talked to him when he was hung over, not even the Captain. Tonight he was a little mellower than the previous three nights, but no one would notice, because they were all simply avoiding him. Quinn was busying himself at the desk, recording the required parking lot and command inspections, which was required of every Desk Officer, but no desk officer actually performed.

The first two nights he'd helped out with the investigation with the squad, but tonight someone from the command called in sick and he'd offered to cover the Desk. He'd go back to the investigation team tomorrow night.

Sergeant Mike O'Shea walked into the command with Tony Malaro. They both signed in and stood by the desk until Billy looked up. Quinn and Mike really didn't get along that well, but since Jonesy's murder, Quinn knew if there was one person who could catch this mutt it was going to be Mike and his team. However, Quinn wasn't thrilled that Malaro had been hand-picked from the command to go back to the Detective Division. He'd never liked Malaro and made no bones about it. The feeling was reciprocated, but Tony never confronted Quinn since he'd made boss. However, the underlying animosity was always palpable when both were in the room. It was the same now. Tony just walked away to let the two Sergeants talk.

Mike began. "What's the good word, Billy?"

Quinn replied, more off guard and relaxed then usual.

"Nothing much." He continued the rest in a whisper.

"Rumor has it you guys are looking at the command for this mutt."

Mike looked like he'd been hit with a sack of nickels.

"Where'd you hear *that?*"

"The Captain," Quinn replied.

Mike looked puzzled, but didn't confirm or deny what Quinn had said.

Quinn changed the subject.

"That was a good thing, takin' Wheeler with you. You should keep her after all this. She doesn't belong here with these pails of shit. Jonesy would've liked that you took her under your wing."

Quinn's eyes looked as if they were watering a little.

"Huh?...oh, yeah...right Billy." Mike was still wondering why the dumb-ass Captain would say anything and how he got his information.

"Let me know if you need anything." Billy said. "I'm pretty good with the nuts and bolts of this command. Just say it and you got it."

Mike took a long look at Billy. He was genuinely offering help. Not the usual tough guy act.

"Thanks Billy. I'll keep you posted."

Mike wasn't sure if he should mention his next thought, but he did anyway.

"Ya' know, Billy...this possibility of it being someone from the command is supposed to be low key and a bit of a long shot..."

Quinn interrupted and put up his hand.

"Enough said. I don't know why that *schmuck* told me in the first place. I didn't want to hear that shit."

"Good enough, Billy. Is the Captain around by the way?"

"Yeah," Billy said. "That squirrel is in here somewhere."

Mike walked back into the muster room. Tony was sitting there finishing up a cigarette. There were two uniformed cops writing down their assignments from the roll call posted on the bulletin board. Mike walked in.

Tony spoke.

"What'd that asshole have to say?"

"What's with you two anyway? And how long has this been going on?"

Before he answered, Tony had his own question.

"Was he mellow tonight?"

"As a matter of fact he was. I kinda' feel sorry for him."

Tony continued.

"Oh don't do that. He's got a buzz on. That's why he's mellow. I've known him for years and I was always sick of people keeping his dirty little secret of being a drunk."

Mike was taken aback. He didn't know how to respond. He'd smelled it on Quinn occasionally in the past, but never acknowledged it to anyone except his wife. Billy was going to get jammed up one day, but it wasn't going to be by a fellow Sergeant. There were plenty of bosses who were aware of his condition and did nothing about it, including the supervising Captain in the command. Mike wouldn't have tolerated it from anyone he supervised. It was one item he wrestled with himself about. It wasn't right and he was one of the few who should do something, but wouldn't.

We all have our skeletons.

Tony interrupted his thoughts.

"You never heard the story between me and Billy-boy?"

"No, I didn't."

"Okay. I guess you should get the dirt, right? You *are* my boss again."

Tony took a long drag of his cigarette.

"About fifteen years ago, we were cops together. I never really got along with him that good but that all got worse. We had a dual post at Myrtle and Broadway on the 'J' line."

He stubbed out his cigarette and continued with his story.

Tony Malaro had been on the job four years. He had uniformed post assignments, and lately he'd been substituting in the district Anti-Crime Unit. He was a rising star, with good street sense and a reputation for being tough. One Saturday night, he was assigned to Myrtle and Broadway on the 'J' line on a dual post assignment, four to twelve shift. His partner was a rookie, with 10 months under his belt, named Billy Quinn. Billy's reputation as a police officer was also solidly forming...he was a prick.

Mopes hated him, and cops didn't care for him that much, either. Other officers within the command at District 33 in East New York dreaded working with him, but Tony didn't care. It would be a short tour. If he could collar up, he'd be in central booking for the majority of the night, anyway, and be rid of Quinn for the entire shift.

They were both hiding in a porter's cleaning closet. Cops from the command used a little hole in the closet they could see through to catch farebeats. It was a favorite spot. Cops would wait until mopes hopped the turnstiles or went through the gate without paying. Billy liked to give farebeat summonses. To him it was like fishing. He wrote about sixty a month, where the command average was ten to fifteen per officer. Tony had heard that Billy was the type of cop who would get other cops punched out over bullshit summonses, primarily by escalating a situation intentionally to the point of violence. It never occurred to Billy that even petty criminals of the lowest level responded to being treated respectfully. Most mopes would comply and do what cops requested no matter how poorly they were treated. However, cops like Billy who escalated incidents and pushed hard enough, would always be wrestling on the ground sooner or later.

There were a few cops like Billy. Not a lot of them, but they existed. They were the ones who made the papers. Some of them were the ones black people see in their nightmares after they've been pulled over for no reason.

Billy was sitting on a high stool peeking out of the hole. On the other side was the Myrtle Avenue subway station. He had an unobstructed view of the elevated mezzanine area. The turnstiles and emergency yellow gates were right in front of him. Beyond the turnstiles was the token booth. Two clerks were on duty because it was a busy station. There were two separate staircases to the street, one on each side of the booth. One potential summons with corn rows was waiting by the turnstile, talking to two of his buddies standing by the northbound exit stairs.

Back in the closet, Tony yelled over to Quinn.

"Take it easy, rookie, we need to sit here for a while, finish our coffee and wait until the mopes don't think we're in here. Did you put the lock back?"

Billy turned on the stool and looked at Malaro. "Shit! I forgot."

Some cops in the command rigged the lock outside the door so when you clasped it shut and closed the door from the inside, it appeared to be locked from the outside. Farebeaters would normally look around for cops, verify the room was locked, and jump the turnstile. Some were aware of the fake lock trick, having been caught before. They would wait and let other unsuspecting violators go through, followed by the cops bursting out the door to catch them. If there was a crowd, it made for plenty of amusement for people who had nothing better to do on a Saturday night, and more importantly no money to get on the train anyway.

Billy walked out of the room. He and Tony had been in the room for fifteen minutes already. They'd have to wait until the remaining, would-be farebeaters, left the station. Billy was aggravated now because he knew these mopes would give him and Malaro up to anyone who came in the station. The two cops wouldn't get any summonses with a crowd telling everybody that the cops were hiding behind the door.

The kid with the corn rows was a young seventeen-year-old black man, with a Lakers tank top and high top Nike sneakers. He was hanging out on the other side of the turnstiles ready to jump, when he saw Quinn come out of the room. "Corn Rows" had received a summons here three weeks ago, falling for the locked-door routine. Billy was setting up the lock with his back to the turnstile area. He needed to figure out a way to kick the kids out of the station or wait for them to leave. He hadn't decided yet. He would decide in about two seconds.

"Corn Rows" shouted to Billy, as he was working on the fake lock.

"Hey, you forget something?"

There were howls of laughter from the two friends of "Corn Rows," magnified by the desire to be heard by the officer. They were still standing to the right of the booth by the exit of the northbound elevated platform. There were a few working people who came through as this exchange began. Most of the passengers had tokens, put them in the slots and went on their way. Others heard the makings of a good scene, and thought they'd hang around to see what the red-faced cop was going to do. Billy walked over to "Corn Rows."

"You talkin' to me, asshole?"

"Corn Rows" stood up, the smile quickly disappearing from his face.

"Ya' know, officer, there's no need to be disrespectin' people like that. Who do you think you are with your pink-assed face, coming up in here disrespectin' a brother. I didn't do anything wrong."

"Corn Rows" was getting louder and angrier as he finished.

Tony heard some of the exchange and could predict where it was going, but didn't foresee the speed at which it would arrive. He walked to the door mumbling to himself.

"This is the last time working with this fuckin' guy!"

When he opened the door, Billy was already coming down on "Corn Row's" head with a rain of blows with his slapper; a flat, heavy metal weapon covered in leather. It was less obvious than a nightstick and cops who used them did so sparingly, and more often than not, as a one shot "wake-up" call rather than an all-out beating. Slappers could be deadly if swung hard enough, and they were illegal. "Corn Rows" was knocked unconscious with the first shot and didn't see the first direct hit or the several that followed. Billy continued to beat him about the bloody head, even though "Corn Rows" was far from a threat, slumped out cold, his face forward over the turnstile.

Just as Tony was running to stop Billy, the two friends of "Corn Rows" jumped over the turnstile to help their friend. The tall one with a doo-rag punched Billy in the face three times, as the shorter one with a sideways Yankees cap reached for Billy's gun. Billy's face was bloody and he could hardly see. As Tony was running over, Billy grabbed the tall one's head and pulled it down under his armpit with a hammer-lock grip. The tall one was frantically trying to escape Billy's grip. Billy was clamping harder on his neck with one hand, while clutching the hand of the shorter mope, whose hand was on Billy's holster, with the other. The shorter one who'd tried for Billy's gun didn't see Tony fly from the room with a nightstick in one hand and a can of mace in the other.

Tony let a full-blast of mace hit all three of them. Billy screamed the loudest because the pepper spray stung the open wounds on his bloody face and eyes. Later, Billy told others that he thought Tony had sprayed him on purpose. It was true, but Tony never admitted it to anyone.

The shorter mope let go of Billy's holster and clasped his face with one hand and began blindly charging at Tony. Tony stepped back and to the side and nailed him with his night stick, one hard shot to the back of the head as he ran past. He collapsed in a heap and was handcuffed immediately. The taller mope's head was released by Billy when they were all maced, and he was now holding Billy around his waist. He was temporarily blinded and did not want to let go of the officer, for fear of a worse beating than his buddy had received.

Tony called a 10-13; a request for emergency assistance, put his gloves on, and walked calmly over to Billy, who was still being bear-hugged by the taller mope. Billy was applying lame blows to the mope's back with his slapper, which had never hit the floor because it was still attached to his wrist by a leather loop. Billy was exhausted from the brief but all-out brawl. Tony reached from behind the mope and, with a two-fisted maneuver similar to the Heimlich for choking victims, applied pressure to the tall one's nose. Eventually he let go of Billy, and had his legs swept out from under him. He hit the ground face first and was subsequently handcuffed.

Everyone but Tony went to the hospital. The response was tremendous, as there always was for a 10-13 called by a police officer. The patrol supervisor was Lieutenant McHale. He asked if Tony wanted to accompany "his partner" Billy to the hospital in the ambulance, to which Tony replied,

"Fuck him, Lieu, I feel worse for the two mopes I had to jack because of that idiot."

The initial charges for disorderly conduct on the three suspects were dropped. However, the three were convicted on assault charges on Billy, including the one Billy jacked-up for no reason except the unfortunate remark he made about Billy's "pink-assed face." There were also civilian complaint charges on both Quinn and Malaro, filed by all three of the arrestees. Billy reported that the first kid, "Corn Rows," punched him first, followed by the others. The booth clerks corroborated what Billy reported about the two jumping the turnstile. They hadn't seen what "Corn Rows" did because they were working and didn't look up until the melee was in full swing. Tony hadn't seen anything until after the two were already assaulting Billy. It was Billy's word against the mopes on how the altercation began. There were two additional witnesses who never showed up at the hearing.

Four weeks later, Billy was in the locker room getting changed. Tony was one aisle over, also getting ready for his tour. Billy still had a yellow bruise around his right eye from the fading black eye he'd received at Myrtle Avenue weeks ago. The rumor that got back to Billy was that he got his ass kicked, and if it wasn't for Tony, they would have shot him dead. Billy's perception was that Tony was a little slow getting out of the room, and it could have cost him his life. He didn't repeat how he felt about Tony, because Tony was so well-liked that no one would believe him. Billy and Tony hadn't talked about anything since the day after the incident, when Billy had called Tony at home from the hospital to ask what he was going to say to the bosses, and to the Civilian Complaint Review Board. Tony had responded to the question.

"Billy, you're a fuckin' asshole. The fact of the matter is, I woulda' jacked you myself, if those two mopes didn't!"

Tony had slammed the phone down after that. They hadn't spoken since.

One of the clerical cops came into the locker room holding a letter addressed to Billy from the Civilian Complaint Review Board. He gave it to Billy, saying,

"Thought you might want this right away, so I didn't put it in your mailbox."

The officer, knowing the impact of this notification, walked away. He didn't care too much for Quinn, either. Billy frantically opened the letter and scanned it as a smile grew on his face. Billy laughed out loud. Loud enough for Tony to hear, because he knew Tony was in the next aisle getting dressed.

"Unsubstantiated," Billy said. He paused for a moment.

"...No thanks to you, Tony."

Tony had heard the laugh and was going to ignore it. He knew what the letter was. He did not ignore the comment, though. Tony walked around the aisle, his uniform pants unbuckled and wearing his white tee shirt, socks, and no shoes.

"What'd you say?" Tony asked.

Quinn looked up. He was in his striped boxer shorts and white tube socks that covered his two skinny white legs. His uniform shirt and tie were complete and buttoned. His face was turning red, beginning with his neck and traveling past his chin. It was like watching a thermometer rapidly reach boiling point. He replied with a little more conviction than the first statement he'd made, which had been said more to be thrown out there to hang in the air, rather than start a fight. Deep down he was scared shitless of Tony, and most everyone else for that matter. But now it was too late, and he knew it.

"You heard me." Billy said unconvincingly.

Tony walked closer to Billy. Close but not threatening–yet. Tony spoke to Billy for the first time since he'd hung up on him weeks ago.

"Billy, what kind of reaction do you think you get with mopes when you begin by calling them an asshole?"

Billy stood there not saying anything, attempting, with no luck, to stare Tony down. Tony continued about that night six weeks ago.

"Yeah, *asshole*, I heard your whole interaction and I had selective amnesia when the CCRB asked me if I saw or heard anything about how that entire situation began. You didn't know that, did you? You also didn't know that the few witnesses they had didn't show up for the hearing. You were lucky." Tony was getting angrier as he spoke. He continued.

"You're gonna' get someone killed some day and you almost got me hurt at Myrtle Avenue. I could give a fuck about you, but I got little kids and a wife at home. You deserved every inch of the beatin' that mutt gave you."

Billy responded finally, his face at near peak on the redness meter. Not being very good at these interactions among peers or people he couldn't mace or hit with his slapper, he said the one thing he shouldn't have.

"Fuck your wife and ki...."

Billy didn't finish his sentence. At this point, Tony was just looking for a reason. He hit Billy a solid shot right in the same eye that was healing from the injury he'd received at Myrtle Avenue six weeks ago. Billy fell back and landed on the bench and rolled onto the floor, moaning. He was knocked unconscious.

Tony went back to his locker and finished getting dressed. John Pulaski was standing two aisle's down during the entire incident with three other cops, listening and giggling. Pulaski had bet the other two that Tony was gonna' pop Billy one. The other two officers didn't think anyone would ever do something like that and risk getting suspended. He'd bet them ten bucks each. Pulaski collected his money, walked by Tony's aisle and said plainly,

"Nice shot."

He then went down the aisle past Billy lying on the floor, moaning, semi-conscious. Pulaski stepped right over him.

"Excuse me, Billy" he said, and continued down the aisle to his locker.

He'd never liked Billy, either, and ignored him completely while he recounted his money and put it in his pocket. Later it was reported that Billy had "slipped" in the aisle, and he was out sick another week, tending to his eye. Billy went to Lieutenant McHale to file a complaint, but McHale put him off, reminding him that disparaging another member of the force's wife with profanity could result in some discipline for him as well as Tony.

Billy decided not to file a complaint.

Chapter Thirty-Three

March 24, 2006
District 23
Rockaway Park, Queens

Kevin was in District 23's locker room finishing getting dressed when the Captain walked by the supervisor's area. The Captain almost passed the aisle and Kevin saw him out of the corner of his eye. He was hoping he'd keep right on going. The Captain stopped in mid-stride and came back to the aisle where Kevin was tying his tie in front of the small mirror on the back of his locker door.

"I always liked those suits in the DD," the Captain said.

There was an uncomfortable pause. It was not an unusual occurrence when speaking with Captain Reitman. Kevin continued politely.

"What can I do for you Captain?"

The Captain went on, the purpose of his conversation somewhat vague. That *was* unusual for the Captain.

"I need to go over some things with you...sort of bounce things off you, if you will."

Another pause.

Kevin waited, becoming impatient. Soon he'd have to think of some way to bow out of this moment with an important interview, meeting, or something. The Captain continued.

"There was something Jonesy gave me just before he was killed and I want to talk to you about it."

Kevin just looked at the Captain with his mouth open. The Captain missed Kevin's gaze. Like everything else, Kevin's look went right over his head. Kevin stood there, stunned. His hands were still on his tie, but they weren't moving. His mind was racing.

Over two weeks went by in this investigation and this boob holds onto information given by the victim just before he was killed? What an asshole!

The Captain was still talking, oblivious to Kevin's look of dismay.

"You *do* need to be discreet, though. I don't want you saying anything to anyone for now. Come see me after you get some coffee. Shall we say nine o'clock?"

The Captain walked away. Kevin had not responded. He was still holding his tie. He snapped out of it and finished dressing. He'd be there at nine all right.

Kevin already had a full day planned. He was to review autopsy records, hospital records and vouchered property. Vinnie was to ride with Wheeler and try to track down Little Pippa. According to Mike and Vinnie, it was looking more and more like Jonesy was onto something, and he was close; that's why he was killed. Kevin had gone to Far Rockaway and interviewed Malcolm Sturbidge, the conductor who found the first dead *skell* that rode the train for hours. He'd asked him about the dead girl's clothing, and if he'd noticed anything else before the cops arrived on the scene. The conductor had only noticed one thing. She had some marks on her neck. Kevin would have to review the pictures and the autopsy report again to follow up on that information. Since the other *skell* was missing that Marine insignia, it was not going to be a surprise that something would be missing from each of the DOA's. But it would be a benefit to discover what the missing item was on each victim.

Kevin knocked on the Captain's door at two minutes to nine.

"Come in, Kevin," said the Captain.

He was standing in his white uniform shirt, looking out the window at the parking lot as if it were his kingdom. He rarely got involved in the day-to-day functions of the command, even though he was in charge of it. He found it easier to delegate nearly all the tasks to underlings. This way if a mistake was made, he could always blame it on someone below him. Kevin walked in and sat down in the chair in front of the Captain's desk. The Captain continued to look out the window.

"Have a seat, Kevin." The Captain said.

Kevin rolled his eyes behind the Captain's back.

Jesus. That's what I like about you Captain, that keen sixth sense that exudes from you.

"Kevin," the Captain began tentatively, "...I have some information that Jonesy shared with me. I just want to run this by someone and get an opinion..."

Kevin interrupted.

"Why me? Why don't you run this by Sergeant O'Shea. He's running the show and he's top dog around here."

The Captain responded with his back to Kevin.

"Don't sell yourself short, Kevin, and I appreciate loyalty, but the fact of the matter is, before I put my dick on the line with a supervisor, I want to run this by *you*. I trust you and you pretty much keep to yourself. Some of those guys in the squad are too tight. They remind me of the popular boys in high school."

Kevin couldn't figure out where that remark came from. The Captain was still staring into the parking lot. Kevin was beginning to squirm in his seat. This guy was always borderline uncomfortable. The Captain broke away from the window and looked at Kevin. He was walking slowly and had his hands clasped behind his back.

"Anyway, like I said, I trust you won't share this information with anyone until I give you the go ahead. It's pretty sensitive shit and I need your word on that, Kevin."

Now it was Kevin's turn to be a little tentative. He was not going to make any promises on keeping quiet about something he hadn't even *heard* yet.

"Captain, I can't make that promise. If you tell me something illegal, I can't make that promise."

The Captain snapped back.

"For God's sake Kevin, what do you think I am? My integrity since I've been on this job is impeccable!"

He regained himself quickly.

"Of course I won't tell you anything inappropriate. I wouldn't want to put you in any position to impact your future. I'm just confused with what Jonesy gave me. It's a potential mess and we need to proceed carefully is all."

Kevin responded.

"Spit it out Captain. Let's see what ya' got."

The Captain went to his mahogany desk, opened up the top middle drawer and pulled out a green folder. He handed it to Kevin. Kevin opened the folder and leafed through the contents. Most of it was similar to what Mike and Tony had already recovered; overtime assignments, roll calls, TPF runs, etc. There was one piece of data that was not part of all the information Mike, Vinnie, and Kevin had already gathered. It was a list of everyone in the command. Stapled to that list was another list. It contained all the regular days off for every person in the command as well. A thought dawned on Kevin as he was reviewing the lists. Immersed in his own revelation, forgetting the Captain was in the same room, Kevin murmured to himself.

"Jonesy was not just looking at people who were on duty the night of the murders. He was also looking at the list of all the people who were *not* working on the night of each homicide."

The Captain grinned.

"I was thinking the same thing. I mean it stands to reason; someone would have to be available to do these things. They might have been off duty to plan all those murders. Do you think you can run that down for me? I mean cross-check that list and see who comes up consistently being off duty and all. I can't get wallowed down in the details. Besides, my computer skills are lacking, to say the least. And Kevin, I *do* need you to be discreet. I don't want you reporting back what you find to anyone but me. This information could blow this wide open and I don't want anyone else in on it. You understand don't you?"

Kevin looked up at him. His mind was racing. *What did he just say?*

"Does it have to be an official order?" The Captain asked again.

"No sir," Kevin replied. "I understand."

Chapter Thirty-Four

March 25, 2006
80th Street and Liberty Avenue
Ozone Park, NY

Vincent Venera and Erica Wheeler had been together for four days now. Vinnie liked Erica. She *was* a little militant for Vinnie, but she did have some valid points. Wheeler was comfortable with Vinnie, too. Virtually any conversation she had with Vinnie would wind up entertaining. Erica had a hunch about "Little Pippa" returning to the 80th Street area after a few days of cooling off, and she wanted to check it out again. Except this time, Wheeler suggested they go and park early and wait, not drive around and be noticed when they turned a corner. They used a maroon unmarked van, also at Wheeler's suggestion. It was 2:00 PM, and they had been sitting in the car since 11:00 that morning. Wheeler was on a rant after Vinnie had made a remark about a large percentage of arrests for black people using crack cocaine. Wheeler was talking about the futility of chasing small fry when all that was necessary was to follow the food chain to the top. She hypothesized to Vinnie about the man at the top.

"…I bet he wouldn't be no skinny nigger either, with a name like Little Pippa."

Vinnie interrupted.

"Hold on a minute. We're not tailing him for drugs. Mike and I think he's a sharp character, doesn't miss much. Ya' know what I'm saying? We figure if our mutt plans things out, then a reasonable assumption would be he was here a lot before he killed that Addams kid."

Wheeler nodded.

"Okay, I get it. But take a kid like this. We got a whole unit to cover these small-time shits. Every once in a while they nab someone with a trunk-load of dope. They take a picture of all the drugs and a few guns and put it on the front page of the *Daily News* and *New York Post*. They also show a picture of the dozen gangsters who are taken away in cuffs, as they try and cover their dark faces with their coats or shirts."

"Yeah?" Vinnie answered plainly, clearly not knowing where this was going.

"So what?" he added

Wheeler looked at him, puzzled. She continued, incredulously.

"What do you mean, so what? Who hired those dozen dark faces? Where did they get the guns from?"

Wheeler paused, as if Vinnie might have a response to the question, which he did not.

"I'll tell you what..."

Erica continued as she observed Little Pippa walk down the platform stairs from the 80th Street station. Erica didn't miss a beat, though. If she was excited about her hunch being correct that Little Pippa would be here, she didn't show it. She just nodded her head and pointed him out to Vinnie.

"Take that little shit there," as she pointed at Little Pippa.

"I bet there are no more than four links directly up the chain to somebody who runs it all. And, like I said before, I bet it ain't no coon either."

That got Vinnie's attention. He turned his head sharply and looked at Wheeler, smiling. Vinnie laughed out loud.

"*Coon?* Ha! Do me a favor...don't ever use that word again. It offends me."

Vinnie continued laughing and mumbling the word to himself.

"Coon...I haven't heard that one in a long time."

Vinnie was redirected back to business. He couldn't keep up with this conversation and watch Pippa at the same time. He started to open the door.

"Slow down, big fella." Wheeler said, grabbing Vinnie's shoulder as he was about to get out of the car.

"You told me this guy's like a bunny rabbit. Let's wait and see."

Vinnie wasn't offended. A good instinct was a good instinct, even from a rookie. Most of the squad worked that way. That's the way they got things done and that's why the unit had such a high clearance rate. It was part of O'Shea's training and education. They listened to each other, rather than try to out-do each other.

Vinnie agreed with Erica's input, and then spoke.

"When you're right, you're right. Hey listen..." Vinnie continued. "...I know this neighborhood pretty good. If he gets up to that automotive store, we can spook him. He'll run right down that alley. That's what I would do. Normally he'd get away anyway because he's that fast."

Wheeler caught on. "Except?" She asked.

Vinnie continued with his plan.

"Except when he bolts down there, you'll be waiting for him just inside the CVS drugstore doors. When he gets there, you'll come out like a customer out the back, with bags and shit...then nail his skinny ass."

"Man, you're beautiful!" Wheeler said laughing.

Wheeler hopped out of the van and made it over to the front of the CVS store.

Little Pippa looked up at Wheeler briefly, but took no real notice. Wheeler did not even glance in that direction, although tempted to do so. She went into the store and identified herself as a police officer to the manager, and asked for help in filling two large paper bags with

241

some light items. She went to the back and called Vinnie on his cell phone.

"I'm ready. Let me know when he's around, and then let me know again when he's near the store and you're about to make him run."

Vinnie responded. "10-4."

Little Pippa walked around the same spot for about ten minutes. Then he decided to walk up the block. He was hyper-aware of any cops who might be around. He knew he'd spot cops early and, depending where he was on the block, there were a variety of routes to take to disappear. He was fast.

They forgot me by now. I'm small time. He laughed to himself.

Little Pippa was about five yards in front of the alley when, from across the street, Vinnie pulled out from the curb abruptly, making as much noise with his rotating tires as possible, heading straight for Little Pippa. Vinnie didn't hit the lights, but gave a few whelps from the siren as he rapidly pulled from the parking spot up the block from where Little Pippa was standing. The whelps weren't necessary. As soon as Vinnie pulled from the curb, Little Pippa was in the alley sprinting down towards the rear entrance of the CVS store.

Vinnie gave Wheeler the signal just before he screeched out of his spot in the front. Wheeler grabbed her bags off the counter and peeked out the back. Little Pippa was more than half-way there already. Wheeler walked out of the store pretending to look for her keys in her pockets with both hands full of two paper bags.

Pippa rapidly approached and saw Wheeler coming out of the store.

What's that girl doing coming out the back? Damn! She got out of that busted up van that took off! Pippa stopped running immediately. He was ten yards away from Wheeler. He knew if he kept running, the cop would just tackle him and it would be over.

Wheeler still had the bags in her hands when she saw Pippa come to a dead stop and then begin walking. Wheeler was surprised. Pippa must've thought he shook the fat guy chasing him and decided to stop.

No need to jack him now. Let me just play it cool, put him on the wall and bust him.

Pippa was almost five feet way when he looked past Wheeler's shoulder, stopped and shouted.

"Okay officer, I ain't going nowhere."

He began to put his two hands over his head, as if to surrender.

Wheeler turned around briefly, surprised that Vinnie had made it to the opposite end of the alley so fast. When she turned to see who it was Pippa was talking to, Little Pippa breezed by at top speed. Wheeler dropped both bags and tore off after him. She thought she heard Little Pippa whisper something as he flew by her.

Did that motherfucker call me a "punk-ass-bitch"?

Little Pippa turned the corner at the next street and doubled back towards the train station at 80th Street. But unlike the last time he was chased, when he turned the second corner, someone was fifteen yards behind him and closing. Little Pippa looked over his shoulder after he rounded the corner and was shocked that the sharply dressed sister was keeping up with him. Little Pippa's usually cool demeanor was slowly eroding. He was getting panicky.

I shoulda' never left that note with the cuffs! He thought to himself as he heard a northbound train in front of him over his head, just stopping at the station. The stairs were directly in front of him. He took the 80th Street elevated subway steps three at a time and was determined to make the train, hopefully with the black cop long behind in the station. He flew through the mezzanine area and vaulted over the turnstiles at which the booth clerk yelled emphatically over the microphone,

"Pay your fare!"

Little Pippa was brushing past discharged passengers coming down off the train on the stairway between the mezzanine area and the platform. They had just come off the train he wanted to catch. He was near the top of the platform as he heard the conductor over the train PA system announce:

"Watch the closing doors."

Wheeler was right behind Little Pippa, but lost some ground when the rabbit in front of her took the stairs three at a time. Wheeler was flying over the turnstiles, when she landed in the hands of two white District 23 uniform cops who came out of the bathroom door, hoping to catch the farebeat that the booth clerk had just yelled and warned them about. They grabbed Wheeler and threw her on the wall opposite the turnstiles. They were about to cuff her when Faisano, a large Italian man with red hair, an Irish face, and BO that reminded people of warm milk, recognized Wheeler.

"Erica, what the fuck are you doing?!"

They let her go instantly. Wheeler never answered; she bolted up the stairs as if she were on a mission. She heard Faisano yell up the stairs as they followed behind.

"Wear the color of the day next time, Superstar!"

Little Pippa made the train just before the doors closed, walked quickly to the middle of the eight cars and peeked out the doors before they shut. He looked down the platform. Whoever it was didn't make it. He had made up his mind.

Time to pack up and find two new places to sell merchandise.

That was easy to do. New York was a big place and going back to 80th Street meant going to jail and he wasn't going to do that. He just couldn't figure out why they wanted *him* so bad.

As the train was pulling out of the station, Wheeler hit the top of the platform. She wasn't thinking. She was just reacting. She knew if this kid disappeared now, she'd never see him again. Vinnie and Sergeant O'Shea were right. So far, this kid was their only shot, even though a slim one. Wheeler never missed her stride running to the middle of the platform, where she leapt onto the chained door area of the last car of the moving train as it pulled out of the station. She grabbed onto both handles of the door and landed with her right foot on the ledge in front of the sliding door. Her left foot slipped and dropped two feet. The train was picking up speed now, and she pulled herself straight up onto the door ledge using only her arm strength. She removed the chains and hooked them to one side, then pulled her train key out and entered the last car on the northbound 'A' train.

Faisano and his partner, a young rookie-in-training with a crew cut and a hat that looked one size too big, were at the top of the stairs when they saw Wheeler leap onto the moving train. The rookie exclaimed, "Holy Shit!"

They watched and held their breath when Wheeler made the misstep, then saw that she had entered the car safely. Faisano pulled his radio from his holster as he spoke casually to the rookie police officer, Ruiz.

"Now that is a perfect example of what never to do. I don't know what she's after that guy for, but number one, if you are ever in plainclothes and your cover is blown anyway, you need to wear the color of the day. Her being a spook and all, running all over the place with a gun can get her killed."

He paused.

"2307 to Operations." He continued speaking to the rookie.

"Number two, the only way I'd be jumping onto a moving train like that is if the lives of my wife and kids depended on it, and I'm bettin' that wasn't the case."

Faisano then continued with his radio call to the Operations Unit.

"2307 to Operations." He waited.

A crackle and broken transmission came over the radio.

"Go ahead, 2307."

Faisano transmitted.

"Operations, be advised, we have a female, black detective in pursuit of a suspect on a northbound 'A' train that just left 80th Street. The next stop will be Grant Avenue."

The Operations Unit responded.

"10-4, 2307. Attention all units in the vicinity of Grant Avenue on the 'A'...."

Wheeler walked through the cars. The train was at top speed and would not be stopping until Grant Avenue. She needed to go through the cars quickly before the doors opened at the next station. She didn't want to make that run again. Wheeler was in pretty decent shape, and was a high school and college track athlete, but was not prepared for, nor accustomed to, that type of exercise. She was physically whipped. Erica briefly thought about how dangerous and ill-advised her last maneuver had been—jumping onto a moving train—then cleared it from her mind.

She walked through the last three cars and was headed for the conductor area when she saw Little Pippa with his back to her, just inside the next car. Little Pippa was holding the silver bar over his head to steady himself. He appeared relaxed, after "losing" whoever was chasing him. Wheeler hurried up to an end seat right next to the door between cars, across from the conductor. Little Pippa wouldn't see her unless he walked back a car. Grant Avenue was approaching.

"Grant Avenue, next stop." came over the PA system. Wheeler was directly across from the conductor's booth and got the conductor's attention. The conductor was a tall black man with a mustache and glasses. He smiled at Wheeler when he saw the badge. Black cops were a welcome relief from the sea of white cops he always ran into. A female in that category was extra special.

"What can I do for you, officer?"

Wheeler told him briefly.

"No problem." The conductor answered.

The train arrived at Grant Avenue. Little Pippa was ready to bolt off the train and up the stairs. Once he made it up top, he'd be gone. They wouldn't be able to get responding police cars to this station that quickly. The train came to a slow stop. Pippa had one hand on the bar and was standing in front of the doors. The doors didn't open. He saw passengers pass his door. The rear doors opened first and passengers from the back were being discharged from the train. Pippa and other passengers in the front half of the train were growing impatient. An announcement came over the PA system.

"Last stop, Little Pippa."

He looked up to the speaker. Pippa's heart rushed up to his throat and nearly choked him. Immediately after the announcement, the doors in front of him opened. While he was staring at the speaker as the doors opened, Detective Wheeler's arm came crashing in from the recently opened door with one cuff cocked in a speed cuff position. Wheeler slammed down on Pippa's left wrist. Pippa looked down from the speaker when his cuffed wrist was pulled down sharply and the other end of the handcuffs was snapped onto the bar of the seat.

Little Pippa had his right hand free. He brought it up to protect himself, which Wheeler had expected, but she would later explain that it appeared the perpetrator wanted to fight back. It would also appear that way to any witnesses. Wheeler blocked Pippa's arm from coming up and landed a solid blow with her right forearm to Pippa's face. Pippa's lip opened up like a ripe orange. He then covered his face with his one free arm.

"You're under arrest," Wheeler said.

She then came close and whispered softly in Little Pippa's ear.
"Who's the punk ass-bitch now!"

Chapter Thirty-Five

March 26, 2006
Woodhaven, Queens

Kevin was sitting in the kitchen, drinking a cup of coffee. He was wearing an open robe, T-shirt, and long, green and white basketball shorts. He was quite a sight, he had thought to himself earlier this morning when he caught a glimpse in the full length mirror they had opposite the front door.

All the girls were still asleep. It was 7:30 in the morning, and he had been up for two hours. He had gone over all the assignments that Jonesy had given Captain Reitman. He brought them home and went over them again, just before going to bed at eleven o'clock. Last evening he'd also decided to start making highlight marks on all the names that came up for each homicide after the first one. For this first query, he wanted to begin in chronological order. If there was a match for someone on an regular day off or sick day, and he or she came up the second murder too, he'd highlight that name.

By the time he got to number five, there were only four cops who had been off duty every time someone got killed. One of those names was the reason he couldn't sleep. He was taking a long draw on his Kent when Marie slipped downstairs quietly. She walked up behind him and slid her warm hands and arms around his neck and gave him a wet kiss on his neck. After fourteen years, she still enjoyed waking up to him in the morning, and he felt the same way.

Marie whispered. "Did you make coffee, dumb-ass?"

He laughed.

"Yeah, I did. And I'll be making breakfast too, or do you want to start pulling your share around here?"

Marie grinned and shook her head no.

"I pulled my share Thursday night, and if I'm not mistaken, you almost missed a day of work because of it. You better start takin' some vitamins or something."

"Nice," he said plainly.

She poured her coffee, added her creamer and sweetener, and sat down with one leg folded underneath.

"I thought you were gonna' quit?" she said as she disgustedly waved the smoke out of her face.

"I will soon as I'm done with Jonesy's case."

She finished waving her hands and said,

"All right, out with it. I see that far away look in your face, like someone kicked your dog or something..."

He tried to change the subject.

"Maybe I should study for the Sergeant's test."

There was a long pause. She looked at him with a puzzled face. She knew that wasn't it, but she let him continue. He took another long draw off his cigarette and was staring into his coffee.

"I mean, I don't get much overtime anymore. This last thing with Jonesy got me thinkin' about you and the girls. Maybe I should start looking long-term and get my shit together, instead of wallowing around in a cesspool all day."

He finally looked up at Marie and her eyes locked his.

"Cut the crap, Kevin; you'd shoot yourself after a month of shuffling papers and what-not."

He responded.

"Maybe at first, but after a year or two, I could get hooked up at Police Headquarters and One Police Plaza and ride the rest of the years out in comfort."

He trailed off as he finished. It didn't even sound sincere to him, never mind his best friend of nearly fifteen years.

"What's the problem, Kevin? What is it? Spit it out already," Marie pleaded.

He took a sip of his coffee and stubbed out his cigarette.

"It's this list. This list Jonesy gave the Captain before he died."

"What list?" Marie asked.

Kevin continued.

"We gathered all this information. Mike has each one of us looking up specific items, some items are things that Jonesy pieced together before he was killed and some things are what we came up with since Jonesy was murdered: re-tracing Jonesy's witnesses, going over statements, crime scene notes, and so on."

"Yeah?" Marie asked.

"Jonesy was looking at suspects in the command," Kevin said.

"Get the fuck outta' here!"

"No shit," he said evenly.

Kevin went on talking about the investigation, all the assignments, the missing items and the data that the team had gathered.

"...the fact that two of the first victims were both pregnant is no coincidence. It was information some cops jotted down on an ejection report weeks ago when each of the patrol officers kicked these *skells* off the trains. Jonesy found it. Someone else did, too. We don't know how the marine fits into this yet."

Kevin continued.

"Then that dickhead Captain calls me into his office yesterday and drops this bomb on me...says that Jonesy came to see him just before he was killed and tells the Captain he thinks it might be someone from the command."

There was a long pause.

"Why did he wait so long?" Marie asked.

"Good question. I get the feeling the good Captain's holding out on me, like he knows more but wants me to come to him with it, like he's my mentor or something, and he wants to give me a chance to figure it out on my own."

"*And?*" Marie asked.

"The problem is, he's a fruitcake. He looks at this like it's all a big game."

Marie added. "Don't you?"

"Not this time...I mean, I know we do the same shit... treat it like a game, but in our hearts and minds, we know it could be for keeps. It could be dangerous. Ya' know, Mike always reminds us, don't take things too lightly. The final mopes we *do* grab are going away for a long time and there aren't many who wouldn't fight to the death not to get caught or go to jail. But this Captain is a moron, he'd take this too lightly and get himself, or more importantly someone else killed. In his mind, this might be his big chance. He's just a fuckin' boob, though, and I don't trust him."

"So now what?" Marie asked.

"Now I got four names of people from the command that were off duty every time one of these homeless people got offed."

"Yeah?"

"And I gotta' go look at them like I would look at any other suspect in any other case, except I'm not too comfortable with that," Kevin said.

"And why is that?"

Kevin picked up a note pad and folded over a page of the spiral notebook to reveal an otherwise blank page with four names on it. He showed it to Marie.

Marie looked at the names, and a combination of disappointment and sadness took over her face like a large wave.

"Oh," She said. "I think I understand now."

Chapter Thirty-Six

Hunter was starting to fall apart. He found himself drifting for minutes at a time. Most of those times he was home or in his car, but lately, he was drifting off at work. He'd have to catch himself during conversations with others. *Hunter* would have to consider going to a doctor instead of self-medicating all the time. He had gone to the family physician for an AIDS test. It was negative. He was relieved about that, and now suspected it was a ploy to draw him out. That mistake made him more anxious. He needed more pills. He got prescriptions filled online and had them mailed from Canada to his house. He had stolen a variety of prescription pads from different doctors over the years and filled them out randomly; he had no problem getting whatever he wanted, based on his own diagnosis. He'd read about his symptoms and researched possible ailments online. He'd read that his "problem" probably stemmed from the negative relationship with his mother.

No shit. I cured that, though.

However, the unresolved nightmares and the "drifting" might have been symptomatic of all the killings, including his mother. One of the ailments from which he believed he suffered was called *conduct disorder*. It was all over the internet and he couldn't read enough about the topic. It seemed to fit him perfectly; had he no objective to his madness. Or so he thought.

These are violent acts. There is no reason to think that these practices wouldn't manifest some thinking errors in my own mind as inherently wrong and devastating. I need to keep my eye on the original plan. What was it? Oh yeah, that's right. The women. The women can't have any more babies. They couldn't take care of them. They were hard to find, though. Soon it would be all over, and the nightmares and drifting would stop. Who wouldn't have nightmares? One to go. That should do it. Mom's boyfriend wasn't in the original plan...that was bizarre. That marine couldn't have been her boyfriend. It was a long time ago. He would be much older now. Shit, he'd be dead by now! Fuckin' skells. One dies, another takes his place. Jonesy was a necessity. He wasn't a skell but he was on to me. He said it himself. I had no choice. Just like this last one. Not a skell either. Number Seven wouldn't be a skell either. But it finishes it all up nicely...

Hunter chuckled softly to himself. He was sitting in his kitchen, staring at the coffee pot. He looked up at the clock. His coffee was cold. He had been gone for about forty minutes this time. He drifted again. He had no plans for today. He'd do his last one tomorrow. Tomorrow will be Number Seven. Tomorrow it will be over.

There will be no need to continue with this, after my goal is accomplished. I won't have to kill anyone anymore. But, so what if I did continue? That's why I chose them to begin with. Nobody cared. I was right. No one looked into their deaths too much at first...These poor slobs, living on the streets in seven degrees during the winter and ninety-seven degrees in the summer... Everybody ignored them anyway. They were sub-human...vermin. I watched those commuters coming in from Connecticut on their trains step over the skells *after arriving at Grand Central Station. Not one of them would even throw the homeless a measly buck for a cup of coffee or a sandwich. It would be easier on everyone if the Connecticut people, and others like them, didn't have to see those* skells *on their path to an obscenely expensive and entertaining day.*

He continued to bounce around in his scattered thoughts.

This last one is necessary. This last one isn't a skell, *but it's necessary. Just like Jonesy. No grand-standing. Simple. Straight in and straight out. Finish this off and wrap it all up.*

Chapter Thirty-Seven

March 27, 2006
District 23
Rockaway Park, Queens

     Roll call on the midnight tour was more relaxed than on the rest of the tours. The day shift and four to twelve shifts were hot. Midnight shifts were dead. Every once in a while a heavy caper would befall the midnight crew, but even bad guys needed to sleep, and traditionally midnights were slow, especially in the Rockaways. In Manhattan or certain spots in Brooklyn, NYPD was out in full force for bar fights or shootings, especially on Friday and Saturday nights. Bars in New York were open until four o'clock in the morning. The Rockaways, by and large, was a ghost town by 2:00 AM.

     John Pulaski was in the District 23 locker room, getting dressed next to Tony Malaro. Both had signed up for overtime beginning at midnight, and were about to put in four hours beyond their nine-hour shift. Pulaski would hit all his assigned post stations, make sure he had small talk with the booth clerks for the first hour, then go to his own apartment off Liberty Avenue on the 'A' line. He'd met a cute Puerto Rican girl earlier in the week and made arrangements for her to pick up a twelve pack and meet him at the bottom of the stairs at his home station. He'd then walk two blocks and hang out in his apartment with a DVD movie, a twelve pack of Miller High Life, and a beautiful girl. Pulaski was whistling while he was getting dressed.

     Not bad for time and half. He thought to himself as he pulled up his pants.

     "You sure you don't want to join me? Evelyn has a friend that's just as hot as she is." Pulaski asked Tony.

"No thanks, lover. I don't want to interfere with your big plans."
Tony laughed.

Pulaski responded.

"This is my first date with this broad. I don't know if my big
plans are gonna' pan out or not. The beer should help, though. Anyway,
give me a call if you want to stop by on your meal. I'm makin' pork chops
and she's gonna help me make rice and beans."

"Okay. Thanks," Tony said. "I might take you up on that. I have
to do a booth relief at 88th Street at 2:15, and that's about it. But if I call,
tell it to me straight. I don't want to interfere with you gettin' laid. I
wouldn't be able to take the uncomfortable silence."

Pulaski shook his head as he was tying his shoe on the bench.

"Oh, don't worry about that. If I even get an inkling in my pants,
I'll let you know. Wouldn't matter, I'd be done in two minutes anyway.
Sex exhausts me and it's painful."

Malaro laughed.

"It's painful cause you're Polish...Try unzipping your pants next
time."

Pulaski brushed past.

"Thanks. Now you tell me. Why don't you let me get married
two *more* times before you tell me all the secrets to successful love-
making."

Malaro gathered his crossword puzzles, pack of cigarettes, and
picked out his coffee places. He didn't stray too much from his assigned
patrol posts. Every once in a while he'd stop by a cop's apartment for
meal or a break. He rarely stayed longer than his allotted hour meal time
or fifteen-minute break. Nobody ever caught him dirty on duty. He
finished getting dressed and walked to the radio room. Tripper was in
the clerical 124 area again. He stood out among the younger cops with
his short silver afro and a tooth pick in his mouth. He saw Tony and
walked slowly to the radio room window. He smiled.

"The Italian Stallion!" the older cop exclaimed. "Whatcha' doin' Tony? How've you been?"

Tony returned the smile.

"Hey, Tripp. What's happenin'?"

"Nothin' much, just waitin' to die, I guess." He laughed.

Tony asked. "What's Quinn doing tonight?"

Tripp told him.

"You don't have to worry about him tonight. Looks like he had a long one before he came in. He's on special detail to track down this mad-dog killer. I'll bet he'll be sleeping in his van by 1:30. He won't be giving scratches tonight."

"Sounds good." Tony replied, and added, "He hasn't been bothering anybody since Jonesy bought it."

"Yeah..." Tripp said, smiling when he thought of Jonesy.

"...Jonesy was Quinn's boy all right. Although I don't know what Jonesy saw in that pile of milk shit."

Tripp didn't talk to too many people in the command. He was an older black cop who came on the job as a Transit officer when there weren't many black cops at all. He'd kept to himself and laid low for twenty-five years. He didn't participate in too much of the precinct gossip. In fact, he discouraged it among the young brothers, but he felt he needed to share this latest information with Tony.

"Hey listen man, you know me a long time..."

Tripp whispered and leaned his chin on his two hands, elbows resting on the radio counter. Tony was signing out his radio.

"That shit-for-brains Captain has been making copies of roll calls and shit. I already heard you guys might be looking at a mope from this command."

Tony knew Tripp was a salty old bastard, and he'd thrown that statement out there for confirmation more than intending to share anything. He stared at Tony's expression as he said it. If he was looking for any clue to confirm or deny his information about a suspect being from this command, he'd never get it. Tony looked up and tried to change direction.

"What was he copying, anyway?"

Disappointed, Tripp stood straight up again and went on.

"Well, let's see, there were some roll calls, overtime and all the squad assignments for all the shifts and RDO's in the command."

Tony looked up at Tripp, his mind racing. Tripp was going on about how the Captain was making copies at the machine, when he noticed Tony staring off into the radio room. Tripp stopped in mid-sentence.

"Hey Tony, are you all right?" He waved a hand in front of Tony's face to get his attention.

Tony snapped out of it.

"Listen, Tripp. All this talk about someone from here. Where'd you get that shit?"

Tripp answered. "I first heard some of it before Jonesy got killed."

Chapter Thirty-Eight

Hunter was upset. He was getting increasingly anxious as it came closer to the final one. The critical part of this last killing, as with all the others, was timing. It was 1:30 AM. He was in the abandoned part of the 88th Street station. The booth clerk and open mezzanine were at the opposite end of the station. The *skell* was unconscious on the bench in front of the closed turnstile area. The booth and turnstile areas were empty; closed over a decade ago because of lack of passengers. The tops of the platform on the closed ends of the station were typically gated and locked, as were the entrance stairs from the street.

Thirty minutes before, he had grabbed the *skell* at East New York, in the second to last car of the southbound 'A' train going towards Queens. *Hunter* had approached the already unconscious man on the moving train and injected a needle with a moderate sedative into his thigh. The middle-aged, white, homeless person had jumped with fright and begun to react to the injection until *Hunter* jacked him over the head with a slapper. The blow didn't knock him out, but it had immobilized him until the sedative kicked in.

Four stops later, when the train pulled into 88th Street, the doors opened and *Hunter* removed the homeless man by dragging him out of the train backwards, his gloved hands under the *skell's* armpits. The Conductor looked down at *Hunter* as he was removing the *skell*. *Hunter* waved him to go on. The conductor, Malcolm Sturbridge, the man who had found the dead girl at Rockaway, looked down and observed the uniformed officer conducting yet another ejection of a homeless person from the subway system. He was thinking of the girl again, when he noticed something about the officer. He couldn't pinpoint it at that moment, but was to recall it later with remarkable

259

clarity.   As he was looking down the platform, another passenger interrupted his thoughts by asking what the next station was.   He answered and was thrown back into his routine, announcing the next stop and his standard speech about the approaching terminal-end station at Lefferts Blvd. and the need to remove all property and belongings.

Hunter dragged the *skell* and propped him up against the wall at the end of the platform as the train left the station. He quickly unlocked the gate down to the closed up mezzanine area of 88th Street. Prior to proceeding to the abandoned area below, he looked up and down the platform on both sides. There was no one. He left the platform gate open and dragged the *skell* down the stairs, giving little thought to the leg injuries he might be causing as the unconscious man's knees banged off the stair railings. He stumbled as he dragged him down and almost fell with the victim, until he realized he didn't care.

What the fuck is the matter with me? What do I care about this piece of shit?

Hunter let the *skell* tumble down the last twelve steps, then followed after him.

I still need him alive. Okay, buddy boy.

Hunter dragged him through the doors and onto the benches in front of the closed turnstile and booth area and sat down next to him for a few minutes to regain his thoughts and plan for the next part. *Hunter* sniffed around as he came back to reality. He had been drifting again for about five minutes. The homeless man smelled horrendous. In addition to his long-term funk, he'd wet himself when he was tossed down the stairs.

Son of a bitch! I've had it with this shit!

He pulled out his Glock and put it to the man's forehead.

Wait a minute. Wait a minute! What was the plan again? What was the plan? Wait for it. Wait for it. All right. Take a deep breath.

Not yet. Number Seven. Number Seven. What do I have to do next? Damn this skell stinks!

Hunter slowly lowered the gun from the unconscious man's forehead.

"Number Seven." he said out loud.

"Number Seven."

A slight grin grew on *Hunter's* face as the plan rushed back into his head like a bucket of fresh water. He remembered it all now. It wasn't that complicated and the toughest part was over. He'd have to make the call first, and everything would come together. He used a cell phone with a calling card. It could never be traced back to him. He'd even boosted that from a store. The plan was a good one. He spoke briefly and hung up the phone.

Number Seven was coming...

Chapter Thirty-Nine

The phone rang downstairs. Kevin and Marie were long asleep. Kevin slept with a fan on all year round. He defended this habit to his wife explaining that he had done it since childhood.

"It drowns out all the background noise."

Marie responded on several occasions.

"It would drown out calls for help, too! Not to mention the dog barking to warn us about a fire, and..."

The argument popped up from time to time. When the phone rang for the fourth time, Marie woke up.

"Answer the phone, *schmuck*!" She elbowed him, hard.

"Kevin. You turned off the phone up here again. Answer the phone!"

Kevin woke up with a start.

"What the fuck is the matter with you....Did you just punch me?" He asked incredulously.

Marie laughed. "Answer the phone!"

Kevin fumbled around for the phone on the end table next to his bed. He picked it up. A familiar voice was on the other end. He listened.

"Who is it?" Marie asked.

Kevin, still sitting on the bed, swung his feet over and put them on the floor. "Okay." he said in a muffled voice.

Marie continued to listen with interest.

"It can't wait until tomorrow?" He paused.

"No, no, you're right; I wouldn't be able to sleep for a while if that happened. Where do you want me to meet you?" Kevin asked.

Chapter Forty

Hunter was waiting. He was feeling better than he had all week. The end was near.

Kevin pulled up two blocks from the 88th Street subway station. He parked the car and looked up and down the avenue. There were a few cars parked on one side of the street on Liberty Avenue. The 88th Street station was one stop away from where Bryan Addams had been killed. He sat in his car for a few minutes, looking out of his windows, using his mirrors looking for something, anything. He had that bottom of the pit feeling in his stomach.

Something is not right here. I can smell it.

Kevin had been on the job long enough to know not to ignore these feelings. He got out of his car and looked at his watch. It was 2:10 in the morning. It was a little chilly and he put his hands in his overcoat pockets. He pulled his right hand out again and checked the 9mm Glock in his shoulder holster. He pulled the butt of the weapon and checked the flap, to make sure the snap-on button didn't stick. He also had his .38 caliber Smith and Wesson snub nose revolver in his coat pocket. His right hand gently rested on it as he walked slowly to the 88th Street station.

Kevin reached the closed-end stairs at 88th Street. The gate at the bottom of the stairs was closed but left unlocked. At the other end of the station, over a block and half away, was the full time booth and clerk. He looked up the stairs and could see all the way to the top. There was some light coming from the mezzanine area. He knew this station well, as he did most of the others in the borough. It was supposed to be abandoned. This end of the station had been put out of service years ago due to lack of passengers.

He walked up the stairs slowly, toward the middle level mezzanine area between the street and the train platforms. A northbound 'A' train had passed about four minutes earlier. He had watched it rattle by, sparks arcing down two or three feet. He looked around, stopping every few steps as he walked up. He heard somebody yelling from above. He stopped again in the middle of the stairs and listened attentively as he watched his breath float in front of his face. The temperature felt as if it had dropped ten degrees since he'd left his car. Then he heard two voices. He recognized one of them instantly. It was the voice of one of the people on the list he'd shown Marie.

He ran up the stairs and stopped at the door, looking in. There was a *skell* on the bench, hands and feet tied with duck tape. There was a uniformed officer bent over the *skell* with a switchblade knife in his hand. Kevin put his hand back in his pocket on the snub nose Smith and Wesson. He looked at the mezzanine door. The chain lock was removed and hanging over one of the door handles. He quietly opened the door and slipped into the booth area.

Hunter knew Kevin was on the stairs. He waited patiently for the scenario to unfold.

Kevin was watching the *skell* and the uniformed officer as he crept slowly into the open area. He heard the homeless man scream at the uniformed officer.

"What are you doing?" He slurred and continued.

"What did you stick me with? Why am I bleeding? Somebody help me!"

"*Louder,*" *Hunter* whispered.

The homeless man's subsequent shriek was deafening, but would not be heard beyond the mezzanine area, except by the final players who were all present now.

Kevin was standing in the mezzanine area on the other side of the turnstile. He heard the uniformed officer yell.

"Shut the fuck up and let me do this!"

Kevin observed that the homeless man had already wet himself from fear.

Kevin stated calmly.

"Tony, what are you doing?"

Tony Malaro jumped back with the switchblade opened in his hand and turned to face Kevin.

"Kevin, you scared the shit out of me."

Tony initially appeared startled, then said cooly, "What are you doing sneaking up on me like that. You could get yourself killed."

"Drop the knife, Tony."

"What?" Tony said, laughing.

"Drop the knife, Tony. Do it now!"

The second command was stronger than the first.

Tony's smile slowly left his face. His expression turned from surprise to rage in an instant. In one fluid motion, he brought his arm down, seemingly to drop the knife. He let go of the blade and went for his holstered pistol at the same time. Kevin wasn't expecting that. He had already removed his hand from the pocket where it had been resting on his back-up revolver. Kevin had misjudged the situation, thinking Tony would give up without a fight. He was in straight panic mode as he reached for the 9mm Glock in his shoulder holster. Tony had cleared his weapon from its holster already, and was in a combat stance, facing Kevin, yelling.

"No, N-"

A deafening crack resounded through the mezzanine, then two more. The third shot was from Tony's weapon, after he'd been hit twice. Tony was already dead before he fell to the ground. As he was falling, his hand squeezed off a round and it caught Kevin in the arm. Kevin dropped his Glock and crouched down. He turned around slowly to look at who had fired the first two shots from behind him and saved his life.

Hunter was finished.

Chapter Forty-One

March 28, 2006
Rockaway Parkway, Queens

Inspector McHale was standing in front of a group of microphones on the train platform at Rockaway Parkway. The department was experienced on how to stage press conferences to have the most impact. There was one train in the ground-level island station with passengers milling about in the background to give a subtle indication that it was once again safe to ride subways in New York City. The Inspector had begun giving information to the twenty reporters. Some had their hand-held recorders for the radio, and the rest were television reporters. This was one of the biggest stories of the year, and would be on the front page of the *Post* and *Daily News* for more than a week. It was three o'clock in the afternoon after the 88th Street showdown, just in time to make the six o'clock news on every major station in the city.

"Captain Alan Reitman and Detective Kevin McCaffrey were following up on some information regarding the homeless murders and found the suspect at the 88th Street elevated subway station. At this point, in the beginning stages of the investigation, we have one homeless man, and the two members of the force who are still being interviewed. It is believed that Mr. Malaro was allegedly in the process of carrying out this criminal endeavor and did not want to be taken alive. When he drew his weapon, Captain Reitman had no choice but to defend himself and Detective McCaffrey, who was already wounded by Mr. Malaro..."

The department had already begun its spin to distance itself from Tony, by calling him "Mr." and reporting that he had fired the first shot.

McHale went on.

"...the preliminary fact-finding team has cleared Captain Reitman and deemed the shooting to be justifiable."

Mike Scott, from Channel Four, was around again and a flurry of questions flew at Inspector McHale from all of the reporters whenever he paused. Scott got the Chief's attention.

"Excuse me, Inspector; was there any other evidence that pointed to *Officer* Malaro?"

Scott emphasized *Officer,* not quite ready to dismiss the police officer/serial killer angle yet. This story was going to run for a long time.

McHale answered.

"Mr. Malaro's car was seized at the command and his car and locker were searched. There was additional evidence recovered in both the locker and his vehicle. It's too early to comment on that, though," the Inspector said, ignoring the fact that he had just made a clear comment.

The news conference went on another 20 minutes. The film pieces put on the air that evening didn't add up to two minutes.

Two days passed. Vicki Malaro had Tony buried quickly, with no services. Mike O'Shea was the only person to visit her house. He had done so on three occasions after the incident at 88th Street. The newspapers and camera crews were relentless. At Mike's suggestion, she had Tony buried without fanfare in an unmarked grave in Queen's Cemetery on Woodhaven Blvd. She then took a plane down south to stay with her sons. She had forbidden them to come to New York. She wanted to spare the boys the circus that was her husband's death.

Later on in the evening, after Vicki Malaro had arrived in Florida, and after the six o'clock news had already aired, Inspector McHale was sitting in a chair at Jamaica Hospital, in a private room with

Kevin McCaffrey. The Inspector had been sitting in a chair at the end of Kevin's bed for ten minutes, facing the TV, without saying a word. Kevin had just finished clicking back and forth through four of the local channels, getting bits and pieces on the third day of the news reports on the "Killer Cop." There was no sign that this story was getting any weaker. Many of the stations had pictures of Malaro from when he was at the academy. Each night since the shooting there had been more photos of Tony: in uniform, when he was in high school, etc. There were additional clips of Captain Reitman, as the hero of the story who had saved Kevin's life. There were several interviews with the Captain on different local stations.

It was all true. Kevin thought to himself.

The Captain did save my ass. Tony was going to blow me away. The Captain wanted to put himself in a place to catch the bad guy and he did it.

"Unbelievable," Kevin muttered.

The Inspector responded as he continued to look at the screen.

"Ya' better believe it. They found shit locked in his car in a big green folder under the passenger seat. Roll calls, assignments, train schedules, you name it, it was in there and his prints were all over it. I can't believe they found anything in that piece of shit he drove. They said they had a hard time unlocking the doors and there was garbage all over that car."

Kevin kept on clicking through the stations as the Inspector continued.

"At 88th Street, the Crime Scene Unit found a couple of trinkets he took from each of the dead *skells,* too. They found them in a bag on the bench next to the *skell.* Tony's prints were on the bag too. It was all there, the Marine pin from the Addams kid and the leather necklace from the Polish girl."

There was a long pause. McHale continued as he looked from the TV to Kevin.

"He wanted back in the squad, Kevin. He wanted it bad. The Captain says he met informally with Tony five times in the last six months. In each conversation, Tony asked Reitman what he could do in the command to get back to the Detective Bureau. The Captain said he counseled him about this and made some suggestions about making some good collars and increasing activity. The other guys in the squad have been piecing together some scenarios, too. One of them is that Tony was going to plant all the shit on this last *skell* and either kill him or arrest him. It looks like he was going to get in some sort of scuffle with the *skell*, then shoot him in self defense. He was going to put the evidence from the other dead *skells* on this last body and then get rid of the bag with the prints."

Kevin listened to all this about the cop who had taught him everything. Someone he'd known for over a decade. He looked like he was about to cry. Kevin finally spoke, a touch of aggravation climbing in his voice.

"Hey, I've been in a fog for a few days, but I don't see Tony talking to that Captain for anything. I know that much."

Inspector McHale replied.

"Ya' got a point there."

Kevin clutched his broken arm. His right arm was in a cast and there was an IV tube in the other. The bullet had grazed the ulna on his right arm, just enough to make a clean break. He was lucky. The painkillers and the inactivity were starting to take their toll, though. He'd had a brief fever after the second day in the hospital, and the doctors wanted to keep him in for a couple more days. McHale interrupted his thoughts and tried to change the subject.

"So, how're ya' doin' Kevin?"

The Inspector pulled his chair closer to the bed. They talked some small talk for a short time before Kevin stopped talking and began running things back over in his mind again, something he had been doing for two days now. He decided to share some of those doubts with the Inspector. McHale tried to be reassuring, and put this thing to bed, but something was still missing for Kevin. McHale explained the scenario and the evidence again. Malaro wanted to be back on top because he was tossed aside and railroaded for shooting that woman. Most of it made sense, but it was clear something wasn't right.

"Kevin, you saw him there yourself. *You* heard the *skell* ask Tony why he stabbed him with that needle. *You* heard the *skell* yelling at him, asking him why he was doing this. *And,* he was also standing over him with a knife."

"I know," Kevin replied sullenly, and went on.

"It all fits together, Inspector. Except it don't. It's like a puzzle in my mind, almost complete, but not quite. The last pieces feel to me like they're crammed together to make sense, to make the puzzle look whole. But to me it doesn't look whole. It looks just like what I said, like it was made to fit. I don't care what I heard or what I saw. The more I think about it..."

He paused.

"...the more I look at his face as he was drawing down on me...It just doesn't fit, that's all."

He looked at the Inspector for some acknowledgement. The Inspector just stared at him.

"I gotta' get the fuck outta' here," Kevin said.

McHale got up.

"I'll talk to one of those witch doctors they got around here, see if they could wave some old bones over you and get you out. I'll see ya' later, Kevin. Take it easy. And Kevin..."

The Inspector looked uncomfortable as he rose from his chair.

"...he did it, Kevin. If you want to find out why, I don't see anything wrong with that. I know he was your friend and all...it's understandable...but I don't think there should be any doubt, only as to the 'why.' I'm sorry, Kevin."

Marie came later in the evening. They talked about the girls and how he would either be out of the hospital tomorrow or the next day. Kevin didn't want the girls to see him like this. He hadn't been much for conversation these last few days. Marie understood. She brought him food and he had just finished a Whopper and was washing it down with a Coke. It was one of the first solid meals he'd had in days.

Marie looked at him and finally said what she had waited to say for days. She had put it off until now. She did feel for him. Marie ached that Kevin was in this much pain, physically and emotionally. He had been on medication, had a fever, and was enduring an emotional tug of war that he wrestled with each day in addition to the physical trauma. He'd lost a friend; more than that, a mentor. He was starting to come out of it now, and she was ready to talk.

Marie knew him well.

"Kevin...Kevin, there's no way Tony could have done all this shit. It wasn't in him. It wasn't in his eyes."

Kevin looked up at her and smiled and then snapped, full of sarcasm.

"Yeah, okay Marie. That's just great! Let me see how this goes...Well, ya' see your honor, despite all the evidence and fingerprints that point to our suspect here, *and* the fact that he actually attempted to shoot me..."

He stopped short. The smile was completely gone.

"So what the fuck are you saying, Marie?"

Her eyes instantly welled with tears, as they did whenever he cut her like that, which wasn't often.

Kevin continued.

"He did it Marie. Get over it. I am."

Marie gathered her things quickly and told him that she'd see him tomorrow and left with tears streaming down her face.

Kevin felt terrible about what he'd said, but he needed to start making this final, get some closure and move on. He didn't want to talk about this anymore with Marie, or anybody else. The Inspector was right.

Kevin slept solidly for a few hours, but awoke periodically throughout the rest of the night. He dreamt about the police academy and that he was running and swimming with the other recruits. He then saw himself running after the Puerto Rican suspect he'd shot at Bushwick and Aberdeen over a decade ago. His eyes opened and he sat up in his bed. He looked at the red digital numbers. It was 5:30 AM. His brow was wet and so was his night shirt.

Kevin looked around. There was someone else in the dark hospital room with him. His heart beat faster. Kevin couldn't see who it was at first. He cleared his vision, rubbed his eyes. He was still groggy from the medication every time he woke. Kevin noticed the shadow, not moving as it sat in a chair by the window. The curtains were pulled closed and there was no light, just a barely discernible figure. The shadowy figure reached over and pulled the chain on the floor lamp next to the yellow leather chair. It clicked on. It was Billy Quinn. He was drinking a Budweiser and the remains of half a six pack were in a paper bag by his foot. He was wearing a NY Jets sweatshirt and a pair of jeans.

"What the fuck are *you* doing?" Kevin asked.

"Keeping an eye on ya' sport." Billy replied.

"What the fuck are you talking about?"

Chapter Forty-Two

Billy got up from his chair and opened the blinds. Kevin squinted and Billy came into focus a little better.

Why would he want to watch me?

Billy interrupted his thoughts.

"Something's not right," Billy said as he sat back down and took a long draw on his beer. He continued.

"Like I was saying to Mike earlier...I couldn't stand Malaro. He was a hot shit Detective, I'll give him that. We all know that. But he always treated me like crap."

It was Kevin's turn to interrupt.

"What's not right, Billy?" Trying to get him off the subject of why he and Tony never got along. Kevin had heard most of it before.

Billy snapped out of it. He was prepared to go into his and Malaro's long history, but he didn't. Billy continued.

"Tony...Tony couldn't have done this. Vinnie and Mike agree."

Kevin's mind was spinning. He was getting a little nauseous. This was the first morning he'd wanted to stay off the medication. It was affecting his judgment. It also made him cranky. He slowly reached over and grabbed the glass by his bed and drank some warm water left over from last evening. Billy went on.

"Part of my assignment this last couple of days while you were in the hospital was to help wrap this shit up. When I got my detail after he shot you, it was pretty plain to everyone...Tony did it. On paper he fits everything, and the evidence is there: the fingerprints, the shit in his car, and he's got nobody to put him somewhere else when all the killings went down. What got me thinking was the shit about his car. After CSU processed 88th Street, they came back to the command. Ya' should have seen the place. It was upside down. Once they knew it was a cop, they needed to work fast for damage control. They knew they shoulda' got a warrant, but they also knew it would never go to trial, because the defendant was dead. So they scampered to get as much evidence as possible. They got stuff from the station, from his locker, and his car. It was the car..."

Billy took another long swig of beer.

"What about the car?" Kevin asked impatiently.

"Tony's car. That piece of shit. They had a hard time getting it open. It was all locked up and nobody found his keys."

Billy finished the last sip and went to throw out his can while Kevin digested some of the information.

Kevin looked out the window into the dark morning. His mind was working quicker than it had in days. It hurt. He rubbed his forehead.

His keys. His keys. He didn't have keys. He had one key. What did the Inspector say earlier, how they had trouble with Tony's car when they gathered more evidence?

Kevin didn't remember until now.

"His keys were in the ignition," Kevin said plainly as he stared, trying to get back some sense of consciousness.

He'd been drugged up and sedentary for so long, it was affecting everything. Billy answered, smiling as he sat back down and cracked open another beer.

"That's right. His keys were in the ignition. He always left them there. He could care less if someone stole that car. As a matter of fact, he was hoping they would."

Kevin added. "He always thought if someone wanted that piece of shit...go ahead. He was waiting for it to happen for years. It was going to be his good excuse to go buy a new one."

Billy continued.

"Except... nobody wanted that piece of shit Dodge Dart Swinger. It was a District and squad joke. Everyone knew about it. Everyone but one."

Kevin said, more excitedly now.

"He never locked that car, either, for the same reason. I remember he'd get pissed if you were driving with him and you forgot. He left both doors unlocked in case he accidentally locked his. He could always get in from the passenger side. The knob was missing, too. If you locked it, the rod would go below the door line and he'd be screwed."

Billy concluded.

"That's the problem. Look, I don't know what happened at 88th Street, Kevin. Mike and Vinnie don't get it either. But the other stuff doesn't add up. Tony would never have locked his car, and besides, he would never have left all this shit to be found if he got caught. He was too smart. Even if it was him, we'd never know about it. And that's what's not right."

Chapter Forty-Three

April 2, 2006

In the days following the shooting, it wasn't difficult to convince anyone that Tony was the killer. The evidence was overwhelming. Mike admitted to Vinnie that it "didn't look good" for Tony, especially after he shot Kevin. Regardless, Mike and Vinnie had instructed Wheeler to put together a photo array of everyone in the command. The detectives were going to poke around on their own to see what was what. If it was Tony who did all the others, the detectives were going to be professionals and wrap it up right.

However, after a couple of days investigating, they knew that the Tony theory was full of holes and unanswered questions; but they also knew the department would distance itself from Tony and the murders. The squad members were on their own. The *skell* that was tossed down the stairs at 88th Street was still in the hospital and pretty much incoherent. He was experiencing DT's and currently useless as the only witness to the shooting besides Kevin and the Captain. The brass had no choice about naming Tony as the obvious suspect. The evidence against him was strong, and no other evidence had been found to prove otherwise. Anything from the department that was hesitant about sticking with Tony as the killer would reek of impropriety and a cover-up.

Little Pippa was angry. Vinnie had charged him with a whole host of things the night of Tony's death, including the theft of the handcuffs, even though he had returned them. When Erica and Vinnie initially brought Little Pippa back to the command, they planned to let him sit in the holding cell for a few hours. Then all hell broke loose, with Kevin and Tony and the Captain at 88th Street. Vinnie left the command to go to the 10-13 emercency call at 88th Street and let Wheeler process the arrest. Vinnie called later and directed Wheeler to add as many charges as possible, so that Little Pippa couldn't make bail. Vinnie knew he needed to talk to him sometime, and putting the small-timer on ice at Riker's was a good way to ensure that he would be able to interview Little Pippa without having to track him down again. So, off Little Pippa went the night of the shooting at 88th Street, and hadn't been seen or thought about for four days.

On day five, Vinnie went to get him with a special writ from the courts to release him into his custody. As Vinnie signed him out at the gate, Little Pippa verified that Vinnie's instincts were right. If they had ever let Little Pippa loose, they never would have seen him again. They were driving back to the command in the maroon van. Vinnie was driving and the witness was cuffed to the bench seat in the back. Little Pippa was silent the first half of the trip, and then began his Riker's story from hour one.

Kevin was getting out of the hospital. He'd been directed by the doctors to take it easy, but he told Vinnie and Mike he'd like to meet the team at District 23 to go over some things before he went home to rest up. Kevin was designated "out sick," and would continue to be out for several weeks until he fully recuperated. Mike O'Shea would be Kevin's driver, and take him from the hospital to District 23, then back to his house for a get-together with friends and family.

Kevin was packed and ready to go. He was dressed in a shirt with no tie, and his brown tweed sports coat was draped over his good arm. His right arm was in a sling and hanging just below his chest. He'd already made up with Marie for his outburst the other night, and he was eager to get home. It was easier for Mike to take him than have Marie come with the girls. Besides, it gave him an opportunity to hit the command before his long break from work and see if anything more had developed since he'd talked with Billy Quinn. He sat on the edge of the bed with the television off, staring at his reflection in the television screen, waiting for Mike. He was looking into the screen as if his reflection was about to tell him something profound and answer all his questions and fears. His reflection didn't move, but appeared to communicate to him anyway.

Malaro was one of the best. And the best don't leave evidence if they don't want to get caught. They know how investigations run and what direction investigators take. No. If it was Tony, no one would ever have known.

He remembered what the Inspector had said about Malaro.

"He did it Kevin, get over it."

He turned the TV back on and was going through the channels rapidly when he saw Tony's Police Academy picture on one of the stations with yet another report.

Chapter Forty-Four

District 23
Rockaway Park, Queens

Kevin was sitting in the muster room smoking a Kent. He was now wearing his tweed sports coat. Except for his right arm being in a cast, he looked like he was ready for a tour of duty. He had his injured limb resting on the table as he took long, thoughtful drags of his cigarette. It was 5:30 PM, and it was between shifts. He was alone in the roll call room. Mike had picked him up from the hospital, dropped him off at the command and gone to get coffee. Vinnie was on his way back from Rikers to have his witness look at the photo array that Wheeler was working on. The cigarette smoke wafted up through the air, creating a thick cloud that hovered about seven feet off the floor, unmoving, unbroken, and silent.

Kevin's head was swimming. Since Quinn's visit, it was becoming more difficult to remain focused, and he was frustrated that he was not part of the discussions within his own tight-knit group. Three days ago, he had been willing to digest the fact that Tony had done it. All the evidence pointed to him. It was pretty clear. The shooting was justified. Kevin had been about to shoot Tony himself. Then Billy gave him the latest information about the car being locked.

But I saw him draw on me! Why?

Kevin went over every other crime scene involving the homeless victims in his mind. Tony had been there at each homicide location, supposedly, as some detectives surmised, to see who knew what, and to keep an eye on things.

Surely he wouldn't be worried about Feuss and Jonesy. He was ten times the detective they were...Oh fuck! There's no way this clambake would go to trial. Not criminal court anyway. Some of the dead victims families would probably file a lawsuit against the City of New York, claiming someone should have known about Malaro's dirty little secret. The city would settle. The newspapers would fan the flames...They gave him a gun, trained him to be a killer and an abuser of rights.. the city did that with every cop, right?

There were a lot of New Yorkers who thought that way.

Yeah, right. All for a starting salary of $28,000 dollars a year!

Kevin was drifting in and out of his own thoughts, the pain ebbing and flowing in his arm. He'd have to ask for more Percosets. Although still a bit confused, his mind *was* the clearest it had been since Quinn had visited him in the hospital. The doctor said he was lucky the bullet Malaro fired hadn't done too much damage. It had broken the bone cleanly and passed into the wall on the platform.

As Kevin was daydreaming, Captain Reitman came into the muster room. He sat down across from Kevin, before Kevin even noticed that he'd entered.

"How ya' doin,' Kevin?"

Kevin looked up at him as if he'd just appeared in the seat like an apparition.

He answered.

"Not too bad, I think."

Neither spoke for a few minutes. The air was saturated with discomfiture, which the Captain had been spreading among others around him for years.

The Captain broke the silence.

"It's done with, Kevin. You did a great job."

He patted Kevin on the back.

"I know you would have gotten it within days of me. I'm not that bright. I just got lucky and put together a couple of things, that's all."

Kevin stared straight ahead.

"Okay, Captain."

He just wanted him to go away, but the Captain was apparently a little full of himself lately, due to all the publicity. He continued with some small talk about an administrative position in the Detective Bureau, and other unimportant items. Kevin continued the verbal exchange with Reitman, but was thinking about something else.

Reitman was a prototypical loser and probably had been for decades. Most likely, he was the last to be picked for dodge ball in gym, the kid who always ate his lunch alone, all the way up through high school. With one fateful act, the shooting of Tony Malaro, he'd become captain of the football team, homecoming king and had nothing but green lights ahead, all the way to balling the homecoming queen. All nice and neat, wrapped into this one caper that he'd solved... Bullshit. He was lucky. Reitman wasn't hiding any innate intelligence that had gone unrecognized for twenty-five years. He was what he was. What was it Malaro once told him? "He couldn't find his balls with a flashlight and a map."

The Captain was talking about an invitation to a dinner with the Mayor at Gracie Mansion.

Kevin interrupted.

"I need to go check with the clerk at 80th Street. Jonesy never did get a chance to get her statement the night they found that Addams kid shot dead."

It was a necessary task, but not important. He just wanted to get away from this guy.

"Oh, I'll drive you over, Kevin. It's not that far from my house in Howard Beach."

Kevin caught the tone of a *new friendship* trying to be bridged here.

Great.

He didn't want any new friends, especially not this guy. But he didn't want to be disrespectful, either. After all, he had saved his life.

"Okay, Captain," Kevin answered unenthusiastically.

The Captain interrupted.

"Come now, Kevin, after all we've been through together, call me Alan."

Oh shit...

Chapter Forty-Five

Erica Wheeler was waiting for Vinnie to bring Little Pippa back from Riker's Island. She was in the interview room. There was a neat book with employee photos that Wheeler had arranged from the computer network, which contained the entire data file of picture ID's for everyone in the command. Wheeler had worked on this for days, and was able to access all the photos for porters, secretaries, and even the auxiliary cops. She also retrieved all the pictures of anyone who worked the overtime, TPF runs, and any other assignments that involved the command.

After he'd brought Kevin back to the command, Mike O'Shea had stopped in the squad room to check out the progress. He'd been impressed with Wheeler these last few weeks. Erica was thorough. Anyone who worked or stepped into District 23 over the last few months, even if it was for one day, had their picture in the book that Wheeler had created. Mike hadn't believed the Tony scenario from the get-go, but had only shared his thoughts with Vinnie, Billy, and finally Kevin. Erica was still too new to bring into the loop, and there was too much pointing in Tony's direction. Mike knew it was still too early to float something different out there to Erica or anyone else outside his circle. He couldn't convince the bosses, never mind the public that he had a "hunch."

Mike still hadn't figured why Malaro would draw down on Kevin, though. Mike had directed Vinnie to pick up Little Pippa from Riker's Island and give the photo array a shot. If that didn't pan out, they'd look to other things. The next item would be the blood they recovered between Grant and Euclid. A comparison test was due back within a couple of days, and Mike was betting it wouldn't be a match to Malaro. In addition to that, Mike was in the process of following up on all the medical claims from all the officers from the command over the past two weeks. He wanted to see if anyone had had a recent AIDS test. It was illegal to track down that information, but he had his methods, and friends at the Health and Welfare Fund, who maintained the insurance records for all.

Mike examined the photo array that Erica had put together. It was printed out in black and white, and placed in a notebook with twenty pictures per laminated page. There were twelve pages. It was professional, neat, and would definitely hold up in court.

"Nice job, Erica" Mike said.

"Thanks Sarge." Erica answered proudly.

Erica was cleaning up her area where she'd finished cutting out pictures and organizing the photo array. She knew it was a lot of work for one witness, Little Pippa. It was a long shot, but Vinnie was right. Taking care of business and going from one lead to another was what worked best. If this didn't lock it up tight, they'd move on to the next piece of evidence. Erica believed that Mike and Vinnie were still working this case as if they'd never got the killer. She hadn't known Tony well enough to be convinced that he wasn't the one. She also wasn't naïve. She hadn't been here long enough for members of the squad to share their thoughts on one of their buddies, especially one who'd been plastered all over the papers and tubes as a vicious murderer.

However, she knew by their actions and the continued assignments that they didn't believe Tony to be the one for the other killings. Erica just didn't know why they wouldn't share that information by now. She hoped they weren't just operating on emotion. It looked pretty clear to her that Tony did all of it. Erica thought back over the last three weeks. Her cousin being murdered was horrendous, one of the biggest tragedies she had ever experienced. But she knew she fit in the squad with these other Detectives. She felt a little pang as she realized the price Jonesy had paid to get her here.

Erica's thoughts were interrupted when she heard Vinnie bounding into the command. He was yelling at Little Pippa as he signed in the blotter and walked past the Desk Officer.

"Shut the fuck up!" Vinnie ordered, although he had a slight grin on his face.

Pippa walked alongside Vinnie, with his hands cuffed in front of him. He was fairly animated when he responded. The kid had a high pitched voice and was unintentionally cracking Vinnie up.

"There's no need for language like that officer. You left me to rot on that island. That wasn't right."

Vinnie laughed and let him continue, as he had for the last half of the ride to the Rockaways.

"You laugh officer, but when you got some bald, three hundred pound nigga' comin' after you in the shower talkin' about 'tossin' salad,' you lose your sense of humor. I think I lost ten pounds in four days runnin' away from that motherfucker."

He paused, and then continued.

"I don't even know what a 'tossed salad' is... And I don't want to know! So don't bother tellin' me officer."

Little Pippa continued to shake his head.

"No. No sir. That wasn't right leavin' me up there like that...almost was converted to be a bitch for life!"

Pippa had been carrying on like that following thirty minutes of a brooding silence in the van. He hadn't stopped talking for the *last* thirty minutes, and was becoming increasingly more agitated. Vinnie stopped in the hallway halfway to the interview room. Little Pippa stopped in mid-sentence after he'd begun talking about how bad the food was at Riker's.

"Look," Vinnie pointed his finger at Little Pippa's face. Vinnie was serious now.

"I liked it better when you didn't say shit when I picked you up."

Vinnie had been escalating into a menacing demeanor, but then he relaxed and put his finger down.

"Look, I'm sorry. Okay? You happy? A friend of mine got killed the night we pulled you in, and we got, excuse me, *I* got caught up and forgot your sorry ass. We couldn't let you go. You woulda' bounced."

Vinnie just looked at Pippa waiting for a response.

"You forgot!"

"YOU FORGOT?" Little Pippa squeaked louder the second time.

Vinnie uncuffed one hand and escorted him into the interview room. Vinnie started laughing again as he took the free cuff and attached it to the heavy steel chair in front of the table. Little Pippa kept ranting all the way into the room where Erica was waiting with the photo array.

After Vinnie attached Little Pippa to the chair, he turned around, said "Hey" to Erica and grabbed the book. He directed Pippa to sit down at the table. Vinnie leafed through it quickly.

"Man this looks great," Vinnie said to Wheeler, as Little Pippa mumbled and ranted to himself, satisfied that anything he said would fall on deaf ears. Vinnie interrupted Pippa's mumbling.

"Hey, listen, Pippa my man, I'm gonna' give you this book and I want you to take your time. There are a lot of pictures in it and we think one of them might be the guy who has been killing all the homeless people. Either way, I'm telling you now, we're gonna' cut you loose when you're done."

Pippa raised his eyebrows.

"It's about motherfuckin' time...DAMN!"

He was starting to go on another rant when Vinnie put up his hand, this time not laughing. Little Pippa stopped abruptly.

"You can skip right over the guy and leave. We wouldn't know the difference, but you would know. You can stop this guy from killing someone else, or you can decide to keep your mouth shut. I don't know if you could sleep too good anymore, but deep down you look like a decent sort."

Little Pippa looked at him with a puzzled expression.

Vinnie paused and went on.

"Oh, whatever...point him out if you see him. Detective Wheeler and myself know you're a sharp kid and don't miss much."

Vinnie put the book down on the table, sat down next to Little Pippa, and opened it to the first page.

"These are all the people who work in the area."

Vinnie was careful not to mention some were in the police department. Little Pippa began to settle down. He now took his role seriously, and was listening attentively.

Erica spoke.

"Our guess is that this nut was around 80th Street plenty of times. And if he was around, you woulda' seen him."

Pippa spoke as he turned the first page.

"You're looking at cops too, huh?"

Erica and Vinnie looked at each other. Erica spoke.

"We knew you didn't miss much."

Pippa looked at the book for three more minutes, turned to page six, and with his free, left hand, slammed his index finger on a picture.

"That's him. He was hanging around there three or four times before you guys tried to catch me the first time...mostly by those back-end stairs, the one that's closed up all the time."

Vinnie and Erica looked down at the picture. They both looked up at each other, shaking their heads.

Vinnie said "Holy Shit."

Wheeler retorted. "Huh...never woulda' guessed that."

Then she remembered that this was the man who'd killed her

cousin.

"That motherfucker is toast!" The anger was rising in her voice as she stood up sharply, knocking her chair down behind her.

Pippa interrupted their gaze.

"What? WHAT?" Pippa repeated, the level of anxiety in his voice slowly rising.

Vinnie answered by getting out of his chair and heading for the door.

Vinnie and Erica walked out of the room, leaving Pippa with his chin nearly hitting the table.

"YOU MOTHERFUCKERS SHOULDA' LET ME SEE THIS FIVE DAYS AGO..."

Vinnie was walking down the hall looking for Mike. He heard Little Pippa squeaking louder now. Vinnie wasn't laughing this time. Little Pippa had followed them into the hall, dragging his chair, to which he was still handcuffed. He was yelling after them.

"WHY DIDN'T YOU SHOW ME THIS WHEN I WAS IN HERE LAST TIME?...ALL YA' HAD TO DO WAS ASK!" He paused. "YOU BITCHES!"

Vinnie and Erica checked in with the desk officer. Kevin had told the DO where he and the Captain were headed. The two detectives bolted out of the command.

Three uniformed officers came out of the locker room when they heard the commotion. Pippa turned around and began calming down immediately.

"Let's take it easy now, officers. That nice Detective said I can go now," he said as he was backing out of the hallway into the command, dragging the chair in front of him, the steel squeaking against the tiled floor.

One of the officers answered. It was Faisano, the big red-headed Italian.

"Yeah? Who would that be?"

Pippa turned around, looking down the hallway. Vinnie and Erica had disappeared. Pippa cursed.

"Aw Shit! This ain't right!," as Faisano approached.

Chapter Forty-Six

They flew over Jamaica Bay on the Cross Bay Bridge from the Rockaway peninsula to Cross Bay Blvd. The Captain was driving at a good clip.

Probably wants to show me how good a driver he is in a high-speed chase. Kevin thought.

They made a left at the light under the elevated station at Rockaway Blvd. Eightieth Street was up ahead, past the movie theater on Liberty Avenue. The street lay directly beneath the train tracks. Kevin wasn't paying attention when the Captain drove by the first set of stairs at the 80th Street station, where the open mezzanine area and clerk were located. Reitman drove to the second set of stairs at the end of both platforms.

The Captain jumped out of the car, droning on about some other familiar caper *back in the day* which Kevin remembered clearly as some other cop's story that the Captain had taken as his own. He was caught up in his own tale when he insisted on getting the door for Kevin as they stopped. He ran to the side and opened it like a chauffeur would have done. Kevin thought the Captain must be under the mistaken belief that he'd found a new friend, because he was fawning all over him like he was royalty. It made Kevin cringe.

Kevin held up his right arm in the cast, got out, and followed the Captain up the stairs, trying to figure out what had made him accept a ride with this uncomfortable prick in the first place. He had been fumbling in his own thoughts all afternoon, trying to get things straight after being confused for several days, and now was no different. The Captain approached the top of the stairs and pulled out his keys. He continued to talk as he opened the lock and held the gate.

"Oh shit, we're at the closed end of the station, aren't we? Oh well. Kevin do you mind walking the platform, or shall we drive back?"

What? WHAT THE FUCK? This idiot's got me at the wrong end. Thank god I'm not in trouble and needing him to respond. He doesn't know his ass from his elbow!

Kevin's words did not betray his thoughts.

"No, no...it's okay, Captain, we can use the platform," Kevin answered politely. "We're halfway there anyway."

The Captain let the open lock dangle on the chain behind them. They were in front of the multiple doors on the mezzanine area in front of the booth. Captain Reitman took out his keys and popped the second gate lock on the first try. They walked by the abandoned booth, pulled open the yellow gates next to the turnstiles, and walked through the doors, up the northbound platform stairs. The last locked gate was at the top of the platform at the closed end of the station. Reitman stopped five steps before the top. Kevin wasn't paying attention and bumped into him.

"Oh, I'm sorry, Kevin, old habits are hard to break. I always stop and take a peek to make sure I'm not walking into a bazooka or something," he finished with a snicker.

Kevin just grinned, retracing the last two minutes in his head...

First lock—the right key. Second lock, pop. Third lock...

Kevin watched the Captain carefully this time, as he opened the third and last lock to the gate on the platform.

The third lock had a bright green dot on it, next to the key hole.

They both exited the top of the stair area and were walking on the northbound platform to the other end of the station, where the open mezzanine and booth clerk were located.

The Captain was walking down the platform, not realizing he was having a conversation with himself.

Kevin was running through his own personal history lessons quickly in his head. He slowed down almost to a stop.

The Captain was now five feet ahead of him, still talking.

Kevin was still in retrieval mode from sometime, long ago...years in the past.

Who was it?... "*Most cops carry all those keys...you only really need four...*"

Kevin was getting panicky now.

Nobody popped locks like that. Everyone fumbled with one or two keys before they got the right one. Unless they'd been there before... this clown had never worked these stations. Even when he was a cop, he was never on patrol here.

Kevin's mind was racing.

Green dots! Green Dots!

Reitman stopped talking, realizing he was walking by himself. He turned around.

"What's the matter, Kevin? Are you all right?"

Kevin was at a standstill when he looked up. He realized he was now ten feet behind Reitman, who had just finished babbling on about something. The Captain had stopped and turned around. Kevin knew that Reitman had just asked him a question, but he had no idea what it was.

Green folders, red folders, matching file systems, his meticulous office. He'd been here plenty of times, and got in and out quickly, with no one seeing him. He'd used the color dot on the lock to match a color dot on his key to the locks. He'd been in and out quick.

Goosebumps went up his arms to the back of his neck. He'd have to try and play this off. He was helpless to act, as he tried to put the rest of it together quickly. Jonesy had been putting it together, and now

Kevin was trying to do the same thing. Kevin stood frozen on the platform.

The Captain asked Kevin again. "Are you all right?"

As Kevin looked at the Captain, Reitman's face changed from friendly concern to full knowledge. The Captain saw it in Kevin's face. He put his right hand in his overcoat pocket.

"They were just *skells*, Kevin." *Hunter* said plainly, with a chill in his voice. The Captain disappeared into the recesses of *Hunter's* mind. He was shaking his head, with his right hand still in his overcoat pocket, walking slowly back toward Kevin.

"I knew I blew it when I opened the second lock, but I was hoping you wouldn't notice. I mean, how the fuck would I have the keys for here of all places, never mind knowing what key to use, right?" He was smiling now.

Kevin was nearly in a state of shock, caught unawares. His off-duty weapon was shoulder-holstered on the left side.

Force of habit.

In order to reach it normally, he'd have to reach over his chest with his right hand and draw it out. With the cast on his right arm, it would be difficult to access the weapon with his left hand. With recent events apparently having been wrapped up, he hadn't thought about needing it. Kevin needed to think fast. *Hunter* wasn't going to hesitate. He was going to kill him right here. He was going to do it, just like he'd done Jonesy. But Jonesy's murder had been planned.

This shithead is playing it cool, like he's an old hair bag...but deep down he's just dickhead Alan. He's scared. I can see it in his eyes...maybe I'll get lucky.

Kevin spoke.

"Yeah, they were just *skells*, Alan. You probably did society a favor...especially the pregnant ones."

He said it cringing inside, to think that people actually believed that bullshit, not just this psychopath.

"But Jonesy and Malaro weren't *skells*, Alan."

Hunter frowned.

"Jonesy was a lazy nigger, and you know it. As for Malaro, he treated me like shit for decades, making nasty remarks about me at crime scenes, dismissing my input, even though I was ranking officer at a lot of those scenes. Blaming me for fucking up that little girl's case in 1989. I heard him myself. I'll shed no tear for him. God only knows what else he said about me."

He spoke matter-of-factly as he stepped closer.

Kevin's mind was racing. He decided to get him angry, to what purpose he hadn't figured out yet, a distracted shot...maybe he could make it to his gun with his free left hand. It would be some trick to get it out.

"Oh, I know what he said, Alan."

Kevin continued, attempting to provoke *Hunter*.

"What was that favorite expression of Malaro's concerning you?... Oh yeah, he said you couldn't find your own balls with a flashlight and a map."

Hunter's confident grin shifted to a frown. He slowly began closing in. He didn't want to miss.

Kevin backed up a few steps.

He could see the barrel of the gun, its outline protruding from the pocket.

Kevin continued.

"Mike, Vinnie and Erica talked about you, too. They talked about matching blood samples they found on the tracks to you. They all know now, you do-nothing piece of shit. Are you gonna' kill them, too? I think you better just get the fuck out of here, maybe go hang yourself or blow your own brains out."

Kevin continued rambling and backing up slowly on the platform.

"Yep, Alan, you'll be your own self soon. There won't be any more dinners with the mayor or the District Attorney. Hey, as a matter of fact, your picture will replace Tony's on the cover of the *Post*!"

Hunter's face was twisted. Kevin was working on all cylinders now, getting the upper hand...

"Too bad you had to shoot Tony, though, huh? It was a shame. If I'd shot him, we probably wouldn't even be here. But then again, it worked out for you, right?"

Kevin was backing up further as *Hunter* tried to get closer. He was gaining ground.

Kevin went on.

"You even got the added bonus of getting the bad guy. You solved it all, called me that night to get me to the station..."

"Well, Kevin" *Hunter* said, regaining some of his composure, the smile slowly returning to his face. "He would have killed *you*. You saw it yourself."

"No, I had that wrong... didn't I?" Kevin answered.

"You're smart, Kevin, I'm sure you can figure that out."

Kevin continued.

"I know Tony figured it out. He was ten times the cop you'd ever be, ten times the man..."

Just then there was some commotion from the open booth area, down the platform where they were originally headed.

Hunter heard it, too. He pushed the gun further into the coat towards Kevin, now about four feet away from his target.

Kevin sucked his teeth.

"Tsk, tsk, Alan, that's what happened to me when I tried to shoot Tony; my gun got caught in my pocket. You can't shoot anyway, you pussy!"

The Captain took another step and the gun went off in his pocket. The round missed Kevin by two feet. Kevin was on the right track. *Hunter* was rattled.

Kevin backed up and went for his Glock, his left hand tucking under itself and reaching under his left armpit, searching for the handle. He fell backwards on his butt. At the same time, *Hunter* was frantically struggling to get his gun out of his coat pocket. It was caught in the silky lining, and he was ripping at it, pulling it away from his jacket. A frustrated whine was coming from the bottom of *Hunter's* throat. Kevin heard the groan and wanted the Captain distracted even further as he grasped his Glock and pulled it from the holster.

"Temper, temper, *'Hunter'*. Those *niggas* up in Attica don't like their bitches with an attitude!"

The barely audible whine erupted in a high pitched scream as *Hunter* ripped the pocket cleanly off his coat, with the silk still clinging to the hammer. Kevin had his Glock firmly in his grasp and was raising his left arm when a shot rang out. It hit Kevin in his bad shoulder, knocking him back onto the platform. Kevin landed on his back, still holding the Glock, but dazed. Venera and Wheeler were rapidly approaching from the other mezzanine area with guns drawn.

Hunter turned around. He let off a shot that went toward the running Venera, with Wheeler behind him. Wheeler and Venera both ducked behind a large garbage dumpster in the middle of the platform. When *Hunter* turned back around to finish Kevin, he was gone. *Hunter* looked around. Kevin couldn't have made it to the back stairs. The gate was still closed. He looked again. All *Hunter* saw to his lower left was a 9 mm Glock with an arm attached to it, protruding from the track area, four feet in front of him. Kevin's body was eclipsed by the platform. He'd climbed down onto the tracks for cover when the Captain turned and fired at Venera and Wheeler. Kevin was five feet under *Hunter*, with good cover and a point-blank shot.

Kevin yelled. "Drop it, Alan!"

Hunter didn't hesitate and shot at what little target he had, missing wildly.

Kevin fired seven times with his left hand, hitting *Hunter* center mass with five of the seven shots.

Epilogue

Kevin heard voices whispering somewhere in the room when he woke up in Jamaica Hospital. He'd initially forgotten where he was. He was frustrated when he remembered that he was back in the hospital again. He looked around the room to find the direction of the voices. Wheeler, O'Shea, and Venera were by the door, drinking coffee, when Kevin reached over with his left hand and put on the light. He moved his bed upright with the electronic clicker and sat up.

"You can stop whispering now, you assholes. I'm up."

The members of the squad walked over to the bed, smiling. Kevin's cast was positioned in an 'L' shape, posted in the air by a support under his torso. His elbow was bent, and looked like he had it propped on an imaginary counter top. He'd had the bullet removed from his shoulder in surgery yesterday. Again, he was lucky to only have some minor ligament damage and rotator cuff issues. However, the awkward cast was necessary for full recovery and use of his arm. The doctor said he'd have 100% use of his arm in six to eight weeks.

Mike spoke first.

"Well, Kevin. It looks like this clambake is over. After you did Reitman, we went back and looked over the 88th Street shooting of Malaro."

"*And?*" Kevin interrupted. He was a little annoyed.

Mike continued.

"When that *skell* came out of his drunken stupor and DT's, he turned out to be useful. He said he saw Reitman pointing the gun at the back of your head, about two feet behind you. That's why Tony drew down. Reitman got you to come, and then he planned on Tony finding the *skell* in the mezzanine He even went to the roll call and switched the assignment for Tony to make an inspection of that area at that time. He hid in the room behind you until you were fully engaged in catching Tony in the act....so to speak. He suckered Malaro into going for his weapon and then blew him away."

Kevin looked away and closed his eyes. The anguish was plain to see on his face.

Mike went on.

"You couldn't have prevented it, Kevin. If it hadn't worked out the way he wanted, I'm sure he had a back-up plan. He would have shot both of you. Oh, and that conductor, Sturbridge, he ID'd Reitmann, too. He saw the Captain pulling the *skell* off the back of the train. Sturbridge recognized him from the station, even with the dark glasses and cop's uniform. The Captain never paid any notice to TA workers, so he probably never considered the possibility that anybody would recognize him.

He was an industrious little prick, too. His house was covered with the *Post* and *Daily News* with his picture cut out and placed in neat little files all over his kitchen. He had train schedules, roll calls, and overtime assignments. He was methodical. But he was stupid, too. He took the bait and went for an AIDS test. We were tracking down that shit. Eventually we would have got to him. Anyway, the theory is that he would've stopped killing, him being a hero an' all. That's all he wanted. That and the fact that he was fuckin' crazy.

From what we can piece together, he had a bug up his ass either from childhood or some other shit. He certainly didn't want any of those women to give birth. He found out their condition from the ejection reports. We'll never know why he did the marine. The bottom line is that he wanted the notoriety without putting in the time to get it the hard way. They're also gonna' go back to his service time in the Navy. There were some rumors of dead *skells* in the Philippines at the same time he was stationed there as a radio operator."

Vinnie then spoke, obviously something weighing heavily on his mind.

"Ya' know it wasn't my fault. That prick moved at the last second. I had him clean. I don't know how I missed."

"Yeah, it's not like something like *that* ever happened before!" Sergeant O'Shea added.

They all laughed except Wheeler. She wasn't aware of Vinnie's marksmanship history.

Mike continued.

"Vinnie's going up to Rodman's Neck again for re-training. Joe Anderson from up at the shooting range called me two days ago and said they can't wait to see him again. He's the only cop in the department to have his own locker up there and they all know him by his first name. It won't be too bad."

Kevin wasn't angry.

"Don't worry about it, Vinnie...fact is, if you two didn't show, I was toast."

He paused as Vinnie hung his head.

"I probably deserved it. I mean I did see you with the gun out. I should have shot myself and gotten it over with...it was inevitable anyway."

"You're an Irish prick, Kevin. I do feel bad, though. I'm sorry I shot ya'."

Kevin answered again.

"Like I said, he woulda' killed me if it wasn't for you and Wheeler showing up like you did. Thanks"

Mike interrupted.

"I think I'm gonna' be sick..."

The morning was a bit brisk and bleak, like the subway stations of East New York. At the top of the 'J' line at Broadway Junction, there was a grand view of the neighborhood. There were abandoned buildings everywhere below the tracks. Time stopped here. Buildings were torn down or about to be demolished. In the morning, nothing moved except above the ground on the elevated stations, with miles of 'J' line and 'L' line tracks that appeared woven together like a rollercoaster.

He stood above it all, looking down, smoking his Kent. He'd been out of the hospital three weeks and still had a full cast from his shoulder down to his hand. Yesterday, the doctors removed the post that had his arm awkwardly positioned up and in front of him. He was now in a regular sling, with a new cast to just above his bicep. He was standing at the highest point on the top of the station, the upper level 'J' platforms, trying to get some air and finish off his last cigarette at the same time. He'd promised Marie and the girls he'd quit. This case was finished and he was trying to keep his word. He'd come early into the command to clean out Tony's locker for Vicki and the boys. Tony's family wasn't too keen on cops recently. They'd had a full Ceremonial funeral for Tony two weeks ago. They used a giant portrait in lieu of the actual body for the services. It was a great send-off, everyone nearly forgetting how he was painted initially by the department and the media when he was killed. Vicki even came back from Florida with her sons to attempt to polish up Tony's tarnished memory. She gave the local news stations and papers something to chew on after the services when she blasted the city, the media, and the department for maligning the good name of Tony Malaro. She'd receive full pension and health benefits, and there was talk of a lawsuit.

Kevin finished off his cigarette and walked back to the escalators towards the command. When he turned from the rail he banged his hand on a steel column, cursed Vinnie Venera, and winced in pain.

Later that same morning, Vinnie and Erica arrived at District 33 in East New York, Brooklyn. They were investigating a string of booth clerk robberies that were occurring on the upper 'J" line elevated stations at Marcy Avenue, Hewes Street and Lorimer stations. They both arrived at the same time and parked in the Fulton Street lot. Vinnie was dressed neatly in a sharp brown jacket and matching pants with a white turtleneck. Erica had her hair up in a pony tail with a new, expensive pants suit and heels. They were walking to the command together. Vinnie was asking Erica where she wanted to eat lunch today. Wheeler was yelling at him.

"Damn it, Vinnie! It's 6:50 in the morning. I don't want to talk about lunch."

"How bout we go to the Diner for breakfast then?" Vinnie asked.

They crossed the street and were entering the East New York subway station in Brooklyn. There were a number of trains one could catch at the station: the 'A', 'L', and the 'J' lines all connected at East New York. District 33 was located just inside the station to the left, directly behind the booth clerk. It was a short five steps up the stairs and into the command. Both Erica and Vinnie passed the booth and waved to a couple of uniformed post cops by the turnstiles when they entered the station.

"Okay Vinnie, eggs sound good, the Diner it is..." Erica acquiesced after a long walk from the parking lot. As they were approaching the stairs, a canine cop came out of the District with his German Shepherd on a leash. The cop walked a few steps and noticed the pair of Detectives. He shortened the grip on his dog, and abruptly pulled the canine to the other side of his body. The officer put himself between the pair and his dog. Wheeler noticed the maneuver and also noticed the angry, twisted expression on the canine cop's face. Wheeler knew from the past, for whatever reason, some of these dogs went crazy when they saw a black officer that wasn't in uniform, or any black people in civilian clothes, for that matter. This time, however, the dog didn't react at all. It was the canine officer who had a menacing look and appeared agitated. When the duo passed by Vinnie, the human half of the team spat on the ground at their feet.

Erica would tolerate the dog being out of line, but not the cop. She went after him.

"What the fuck is your problem?"

Erica started to get in the canine officer's face. The dog went wild, and was restrained by the canine officer immediately, and the man and dog team quickly exited the building.

Vinnie grabbed Wheeler and stopped her from following the canine cop outside.

"That wasn't for you. It was for me," Vinnie said.

Wheeler looked at him like he was crazy.

"What the fuck? Why would a guy spit at you like that?"

Wheeler looked closer at Vinnie.

Are his eyes welling up?

Vinnie took a deep breath and blew it out slowly as he turned towards the command.

"It's a long story. I'm not sure if I'm ready to tell you yet."

He paused.

"It's still early in our relationship."

He walked up the stairs leaving Wheeler at the bottom, with her mouth wide open and a dumbfounded look on her face. Wheeler snapped out of it and yelled after him as she followed Vinnie into the command.

MAN UNDER

"You better tell me, motherfucker, or you can forget the Diner and it will be hot dogs for lunch again..."

Glossary of Terms

10-13- Police officer code request for emergency assistance

10-63- Police code for gone to meal/lunch

124 Room- Clerical locations within the command responsible for precinct/district paperwork

4 x 12- Shift of duty that begins at 4 p.m. and ends at midnight

ADO- Assistant desk officer; a police officer who rarely goes out on patrol, sometimes referred to as a "*House Mouse*"

Booth relief- Assignment for Transit Police to escort a booth clerk with money out of the booth

Ceremonial Unit- A unit in the Police Department consisting of police officers from each command assigned to a funeral detail when a member of the force is killed in the line of duty

COMSTAT- Command Statistics meeting; upper echelon NYPD administrators review data among the individual precincts and transit districts

Civilian- Any non-member of the police department

CSU- Crime Scene Unit; assigned detectives process crime scenes upon request for fingerprints, blood and trace or physical evidence

DO- Desk officer; district or precinct supervisor responsible for the shift and command operations during the tour; arrests, assignments, roll call, etc. usually a Sergeant or Lieutenant

DOA- Dead on arrival; cops refer to *all* dead bodies as DOA's

Farebeat- Someone who avoids paying the subway fare, usually by jumping over a turnstile

FTO- Field Training Officer- assigned to train new police officers

Guardians- A fraternal organization in the police department for officers of African American descent

Major Case Squad- A Transit Police unit assigned high profile cases within the subway system

Man Under- Transit Police slang for a victim hit by a train

ME- Medical examiner; works in the morgue

MISD- Management Information Systems Division; responsible for computer and communications data throughout the department

Mope- Criminal/bad guy, occasionally called a *mutt*

Pails- Derogatory term for substandard police officers; as in *pails of shit,* sometimes also referred to as *buckets*

PBA- Police Benevolent Association; the police union

RDO- Regular day off

RMP- Radio motor patrol car

Skell- Police slang/derogatory term for a homeless person.

TA- Transit Authority

TPF- Tactical Patrol Force; a uniformed unit with primary responsibilities to ride trains between districts and boroughs, the shift is usually from 8 p.m. through 4 a.m.

Vegetable- Transit District 33 slang (circa 1986) for a rookie police officer

MAN UNDER

Brian Shaughnessy

Out From Under

A new novel by Brian Shaughnessy

Introduction

September 11th, 2001
World Trade Center
10:50 a.m.

He was barely conscious and gathering his thoughts. There was beeping everywhere. Most of the noises he remembered from the training sessions...the Pak-Tracker transponder system. When firefighters went down, an automatic signal was activated on the Scott Pak in order for responding emergency personnel to track the disabled rescue worker. The device let out a loud, high-pitched wail to locate firefighters in the event smoke was overwhelming and visibility was low. Although this time there was not just one alarm going off. There were several alarms of different pitches, creating a cacophony of screams, none of which were human.

Car alarms? How could there be car alarms? Didn't I just pass the third floor stairwell sign? Where the fuck am I?

His breathing instantly increased in conjunction with his anxiety. He was the type of man who was usually cool under pressure; those who knew him thought he actually thrived on it. But the fact that he was totally disoriented initiated a feeling in him that he rarely had; fear. His eyes were still closed as his recent memory was coming back, slowly. His body was not prepared, nor willing to engage yet. He tried to relax.

MAN UNDER

His name was Tommy Bowen, a 27-year veteran of the New York City Fire Department. He was a tall man at 6'3 with a chiseled, dimpled chin and a dirty blonde, flat top crew cut. The last thing he remembered was that he'd completed three round trips on foot into the North Tower of the World Trade Center. The last trip, he'd made it to up to the 52nd floor. There were some gaps in his thinking. He continued to piece things together while his memory gradually came back. The last thing he remembered was a loud roar...

Seventy minutes earlier, he and other emergency responders were busily moving civilians from both of the two disabled buildings. The rescuers speculated, nonstop, about what the worst case damage would be from two commercial jets plowing through each tower of the World Trade Center buildings at top speed. They were about to find out.

The Fire Department practiced high-rise emergencies once a year, usually with a civilian emergency manager designated for each floor in the WTC. The plane impact was just above the 93rd floor in the North Tower and was too high to drag any equipment that would be effective. Within fifteen minutes of the first crash, the NYFD chiefs had already made the correct decision. The mission was to be a rescue operation rather than go in a firefighting direction. Over a thousand responders were dispatched by various agencies in just seventeen minutes after the first plane hit the North Tower; then the second plane struck.

When Tommy Bowen initially arrived at the World Trade Center, he was about to run into one of the North Tower's West Street entrances when a Battalion Chief grabbed his arm. He stopped and looked at the Chief as the Chief looked up. Tommy then looked in the same direction to see a vast number of victims high in the first tower who chose to plunge to their own deaths rather than burn in the flames. He'd never forget the sickening sounds of those choices. As the Chief continued to hold his arm, Tommy was an eyewitness to the first Fire

311

Department fatality; a civilian landing on a firefighter as he was running into the Tower. They both gasped. During that instant, Tommy got hold of himself quickly. He was a man who could dismiss disturbing images as fast as he encountered them and still tackle the job that needed to be done. The Battalion Chief ordered a spotter to call out when it was clear to enter the building. Bowen ran in when directed and became engrossed with the evacuation, and he took it upon himself to get up the tower and help as many people as possible.

The first trip the firefighter made up the #1, WTC North Tower was unprecedented, but routine. Tommy Bowen was at a check point on the 12th floor, making sure people didn't panic as he kept them moving down the stairwells. He helped one group get all the way down to the first floor because they had a difficult time pacing themselves and random, anxious civilians knocked a few people over. Anyone going too fast or slow could cause a serious back-up with further injuries or clog the stairwells with bodies. Much to his surprise, it was manageable. People were orderly and calm. It wouldn't have been had there not been a cadre of authority figures present to allay peoples fears enough to prevent a full-scale panic situation. On his second trip up the North Tower, Bowen was part of a group of firefighters he didn't recognize and four Port Authority Police Officers. They assisted a middle-aged man in a wheelchair down from the eighth floor. Because of smoke and crowded conditions, they had to switch staircases twice. The firefighters were told by one of the Port Authority cops that none of the 99 elevators in the building were working.

The third time up, Tommy and the other firefighters passed some Emergency Service, NYPD cops coming down the stairs who were escorting a handful of civilians. Tommy thought they were moving a little too quick to trot down over fifty floors safely. He remarked to one of the passing police officers.

"It's a long way to be sprinting down there…"

One of the officers responded without slowing down.

"We got the order to get out...I suggest you do the same."

The officer finished his sentence as he disappeared down the next stairwell. He never broke stride. The police had received the order over their radios directly from a Police Chief for all police personnel to evacuate the building immediately.

What did they know that the Fire Department didn't?

Tommy wasn't paying much attention to anything other than evacuating people from the tower. After the cops passed, he did notice there were hardly any clear transmissions since he'd entered the building. He switched his radio to Tactical Channel One, a channel dedicated to the complex. There was a repeater radio system installed specifically for the World Trade Center after the 1993 bombing. Once he changed to Tactical One, all that he heard were other firefighters on the radio, cutting each other out, nonstop. He didn't hear any directions from any of the Chiefs during the entire emergency. He looked at his watch.

9:45.

Tommy acknowledged the direction for the NYPD people, but he didn't care what they were doing. Tommy was "old school." It would be a cold day in hell before he took orders from any cop. The Fire Department had a long, running battle with the NYPD over who was more capable to handle certain emergencies at several major incidents over the years. Some of those arguments made the newspapers. The question was never really answered with definitive lines of jurisdiction during any emergency situation. The cops leaving just now answered the decades-old dilemma. This incident was clearly a Fire Department Operation, from the beginning, anyway. Most of the NYPD was responsible for the ground-level evacuation and clearing street routes for the fire apparatus needed on the scene. There were also Port

Authority Police and some NYPD personnel inside both towers, but most of the first responders were from the Fire Department.

After Tommy passed the cops going down, he and other rescuers ran into a cluster of people from the Carstan Company, a small insurance firm that specialized in insuring tug boats and barges all over the world. There were over a dozen employees, mostly men, with two young women who were trying their best not to stumble anymore. The entire group had tears streaming down their faces. They had no time to be upset. They had wasted valuable minutes when a 911 operator followed protocol and told them to remain at their location and await evacuation assistance from first responders. Most 911 operators gave those instructions to civilians in both towers, following the procedure for large building evacuations. After the second plane hit, several floors above their office, the Carstan people finally left their work area on the 68th floor of the North Tower and began the long descent. They ran into quite a few detours due to malfunctioning elevators and smoke-filled stairways. The firefighters ran into the Carstan group between the 51st and 52nd floors. The rescuers knew the stairs that the civilians were currently using would not have enough air a few floors below them.

Tommy Bowen took the initiative to find another staircase on the 51st floor. He trekked across the center of the office with his ninety pounds of equipment on his back and rerouted the chain of people down a less smoky staircase. He held the door open and looked out of a nearby window while the group, assisted by a dozen firefighters, ran through a cubicle-lined office next to the staircase. He glanced at his watch.

9:59.

Tommy was staring out a window at the flames shooting out of the building next door. He tried to ignore the two people who jumped while he watched the billowing smoke pour out of the bottom of the gaping hole that climbed almost ten stories from the 77th floor. He saw a large puff of smoke shoot through flames. He was mesmerized for a few seconds. He had already temporarily forgotten what he'd witnessed when he first arrived at the Towers; the civilians jumping, the firefighter who was struck... As he was looking at the opposite Tower, reluctantly remembering his first horrors of the day, he began to see another unravel before his eyes. The scene looked to him as if it were being played in slow motion. As he stared into the inferno, the building across from him began to move...slowly...downward. He watched in awe as the WTC #2 South Tower collapsed right in front of him. He pressed his face against the window and looked downward in disbelief.

The building where he was standing shook violently as the crash next door reverberated against the windows and steel of the remaining tower. It sounded like a freight train. He grabbed onto a desk to steady himself. The massacre, witnessed by Tommy Bowen, the remaining firefighters and some civilians attempting to get to the staircase in the lone tower, was nearly crippling. They stood for about thirty seconds before the rescuers realized the same fate was now surely ahead of them. The firefighters quickly snapped out of their brief shock and continued to direct civilians into the stairwell, a bit more hurriedly than just two minutes ago.

As they descended, Tommy thought about the other temporary headquarters that was set up at the base of the South Tower to direct personnel and responding trucks and ladders for that building. It was now demolished.

Now I know why the cops were moving so quick...fuckin' radios!

Tommy also knew that the Fire Department radio transmissions that were few and garbled initially would be replaced by even more silence. Most of the antennas, relays and originators of any emergency directions for firefighters were now buried beneath 110 floors of concrete, dust and jet fuel.

Tommy's group of firefighters continued to do their job efficiently even after they had witnessed from a few feet away, an occurrence that would have left a typical human paralyzed with fear. Tommy's stomach turned as he went back to his business of moving people along at the top of the stairway. He knew, as did the other firefighters, there were quite a few men from the battalions and trucks who went down in the South Tower; not just men, a lot of friends, too. He didn't think about it too long, though. He couldn't afford to. He looked at his watch again.

10:13.

Tommy and his crew's original objective was to get as many civilians out of the building as possible. It was part of their training. It was who they were and what they did. Except this time, they too were part of that same objective. He knew he wouldn't be making a fourth trip.

They continued a quick pace down the stairs. Every one of them, firefighters and civilians, had their hearts in their throats. A few gagged from the dry mouth that people sometimes experienced in times of great distress coupled with unexpected strenuous exercise. There were periodic pockets of civilians and firefighters that the group passed on their way down. They were resting and catching their breath. They had no idea about the collapse of the South Tower. Tommy and the other firefighters told them about the collapse and suggested they get moving as fast as they could. Some listened and joined their group. Others remained or lagged way behind. On the 12th floor heading down, one of the Carstan people, Anna Donati, a twenty-seven year old secretary with dark hair and darker eyes, twisted her ankle and was unable to walk anymore. The group of civilians passed her quickly and left her on the stairs, following the lead firefighters in front of them. Tommy Bowen was the sole firefighter following up the rear. He looked at what little air he had left on his gauge. He periodically used it in pockets of smoke throughout the building. He dropped his tank and other equipment from his back and grabbed the 120 pound girl like a sack of potatoes, threw her over his left shoulder, and kept going at nearly the same rate of speed. Tommy heard one last clear transmission. It sounded like it came from a bull horn in the stairwell, rather than the radio.

"ALL NYFD; GET THE FUCK OUT!"

As he and the girl rounded the 2nd floor stairwell, they had lost some ground and were one flight of stairs behind the rest of the group. Firefighters continued to guide the small pack in front at a good pace. By the time Tommy approached the lobby area, he heard the beginning rumblings of the freight train again, except this time it wasn't from the building next door. Tommy could see the group in front of him make it to the West Street exit doors. Tommy and Anna were running for that nearest exit. He noticed a straggler to his immediate right who'd stumbled out of an elevator in front of him. The man from the elevator, a fifty-year-old manager with a receding hairline, glasses and a gray suit, fell in front of them and banged his head on a marble flower box near the exit. He was hardly moving. The freight train was loud and coming closer. Tommy put Anna on the floor and looked directly into her eyes.

"RUN!" he screamed.

Anna quickly forgot why she was so scared. Tommy Bowen's look and bark were scarier. She ran, albeit limping badly, straight for the West Street exit. Her life depended on this last mad dash and she received that message loud and clear from the exhausted firefighter. Tommy grabbed the older man by his upper arm as he lay on the floor and began dragging the short, heavy set man towards the exit. The freight train was deafening. He could see the walls crack before him and some debris coming down. Windows shattered everywhere and it was raining glass and metal. His helmet was struck by a chunk that felt like a cinder block just skimming his head. He looked forward towards the exit as he pulled the man by his forearm, dragging him on his butt, twelve feet from the glass doors. He could see a few of the last people running at full speed just outside the exit door. They were about a quarter of a block away. Anna Donati was one of them.

"COME ON!" He yelled to himself.

Ten feet.

Five.

He continued to drag the middle-aged, unconscious manager on the floor. Tommy's thoughts were singularly about getting this last person out to safety.

Last one. I won't be coming in again. There's nothing to come back into.

He didn't think about his wife and two boys as most would believe would happen to a man at a time like this. He was still doing his job. Moreover, his own arrogance was stronger than any emotion he could ever muster, even in the face of death. The rubble came up from behind him like a wave on the ocean and heaved him through the glass doors, head first. He was still holding onto the older man when he went through the windows.

Thirty-five minutes later, Tommy Bowen picked his head up slowly as lay face down in the debris. He had no idea how long he'd been out. His head pounded. He was buried up to his chest in broken concrete and glass. It was pitch black for the first five minutes. His eyes and lungs were caked with dust and fine pieces of gravel. He threw up and coughed violently. He reached around in the dark for his mask. It wasn't there. Neither was his helmet. The darkness finally gave way to a glimmer of light and dust. He brushed his eyes several times before he could finally see. He looked down and noticed his torso was lightly pinned between a 'Y" section of a steel beam. When he looked up he realized that he was in a small crevice and a beam of sunlight pierced through the dust from a two foot hole about twenty feet above. Tommy couldn't stop blinking. His eyes burned. His whole body felt pummeled. As the dust settled, he regained more feeling in his legs and arms. He felt that his legs moved freely underneath the 'Y' beam. One of them felt as if a baseball bat had been recently used on it. As he was attempting to move other parts of his body and regain some strength, he noticed the manager was still holding onto his right arm from underneath the rubble. Tommy remembered that he was dragging the civilian toward the exit doors prior to the collapse. The firefighter was weak. Tommy took a deep breath and lamely pulled up on the manager's arm with no luck. He rested a while. After a minute his strength began to slowly come back. He then proceeded to pull the 50 year-old from under the rubble...he thought he felt one more squeeze from the manager. Tommy closed his eyes and pulled with all his might.

He made it!

Tommy opened his eyes and observed all that was left of the unconscious, middle aged father of three, who he was pulling to safety minutes ago; his arm from just above the elbow down to the hand, and nothing attached to it. It was still clutching Tommy's forearm. Tommy hung his head down. As the tears began, he realized that they weren't just caused by the dirt and dust.